CAUGHT WITH THE PERFECT CATCH

It was clear to the world that Kit Moresby was the perfect choice to rid Alyson of the burden of young widowhood. He was handsome, wealthy, charming, and adoringly devoted to her.

She could clearly see the warmth of his feelings as he bent over her hand—yet all she could think of was to find a way to gently extract her hand from his firm, eager hold and make a graceful escape from the room in the inn where they found themselves alone.

She never heard the footsteps at the door when it opened as Damon, Lord St. Albans stepped into the room. His dark eyes took in the situation at once, before Alyson could break free of Kit's hold.

Alyson saw no surprise in Damon's gaze. She had only confirmed his suspicions of her virtue and motives.

She could see another thing clearly as well. She had lost her last chance of changing his mind and finding a love so long lost. . . .

THE EARL'S RETURN

by

Emma Lange

A SIGNET BOOK

SIGNET
Published by the Penguin Group
Penguin Books USA Inc., 375 Hudson Street,
New York, New York 10014, U.S.A.
Penguin Books Ltd, 27 Wrights Lane,
London W8 5TZ, England
Penguin Books Australia Ltd, Ringwood,
Victoria, Australia
Penguin Books Canada Ltd, 10 Alcorn Avenue,
Toronto, Ontario, Canada M4V 3B2
Penguin Books (N.Z.) Ltd, 182-190 Wairau Road,
Auckland 10, New Zealand

Penguin Books Ltd, Registered Offices:
Harmondsworth, Middlesex, England

First published by Signet,
an imprint of New American Library,
a division of Penguin Books USA Inc.

First Printing, April, 1993
10 9 8 7 6 5 4 3 2 1

 REGISTERED TRADEMARK—MARCA REGISTRADA

Printed in the United States of America

Prologue

August, 1806

An unnatural stillness enveloped the house. Nothing disturbed it, not the trilling of a bird, not the rustling of a servant, not even a breeze stirring the air. To the girl waiting in her room it seemed that even time had stopped.

The high collar she had to wear chafed her neck, and the cuffs of her long sleeves clung damply to her wrists.

Abruptly she rose. There was water in a pitcher on the washstand. She did not reach it. Thinking she heard a sound in the hallway, she froze suddenly, water forgotten and knees trembling, only to collapse upon a stool more often used as a footrest, when no one came.

Oddly, given the intensity with which she listened, she failed to hear the maid's approach, when the girl did come. Perhaps her footsteps were muffled by the carpet, but the first Alyson knew of her coming was a hesitant knock at the door.

She shot to her feet. "Yes?" Her voice emerged too small to hear. "Yes?" she tried again.

The girl, Maddie, peeked around the door. "Mr. Haydon wishes you to go to his study, Miss Allie."

Alyson nodded, her throat too dry for speech.

Always she approached her stepfather's study with a sick feeling in the pit of her stomach. That day was no exception, only the knot seemed larger, tighter, more unbearable than ever before. She could taste bile in her mouth as she lifted her hand to knock.

Her stepfather's response rang out sharply. He was a spare man of middle height. Alyson had never realized before that he was not, really, very tall. He held himself with such authority he seemed larger than he was.

But for once, Mr. Haydon was overshadowed by another. Much younger, this man stood a head above Alyson's stepfather. He'd broader shoulders, too, and long muscled legs. It was his eyes, though, that commanded attention. So dark as to be black, they seemed to leap with the force of his personality.

And, that day, they were alive with anger. Alyson felt something shrivel inside her. Instantly she jerked her gaze from the younger man's dark, glittering one. Her hands clenched tightly at waist level, she fastened her attention upon Mr. Haydon.

"Mr. Ashford asks for your hand in marriage, Alyson," he intoned in the cadence of a judge announcing a sentence of death. "What is your decision?"

She opened her mouth, but could force no word by her dry lips.

"Well?" The word cracked through the thick silence lying like a pall over the room.

Unconsciously she licked her lips, her eyes never wavering from her stepfather's. "I . . . I cannot marry you, Mr. Ashford."

"Speak up, Alyson!" her stepfather commanded. "We cannot hear you well. And tell us what else you have decided."

"I . . ." Her voice caught in her throat.

"Alyson."

She knew that quiet, deadly tone too well. Fear loosened her tongue. "I . . . I am to marry Edward, the Viscount Ainsley," she said swiftly. And before she could control herself she was looking at Damon Ashford.

"There, sir." she heard Mr. Haydon say.

But Damon did not seem to hear the older man. He stared at Alyson, his eyes dark as night and his mouth tight with fury. The words *I am sorry* died on her lips unspoken. She had hoped he would understand. But he did not, as his words and his farewell proved.

"I see," he said, his low voice taut as vibrating steel. "Your stepfather said you had decided to accept Ned, but I did not believe him. I thought you neither mercenary nor faithless, Miss Haydon, but it seems I was wrong. May I wish you joy of the title that has bedazzled you."

She did not move when he mocked her with a bow. She could not even move when he strode by her, blind now to one as low as she.

Only when he slammed the door behind him, did Alyson whirl about. Suddenly she'd energy to spare. But Mr. Haydon had anticipated her reaction. Even as Alyson thought to dash for the door and Damon, never mind the consequences, her stepfather reached the exit before her.

His hand upon the door, he thrust his livid face down to hers. "You have not yet controlled your lust for this upstart, Alyson! You have need of the rod, it seems. After I have punished you, you will remain in your room three days praying to God to help you overcome the perilous harlot's streak I have discovered in you, and when you emerge you will go nowhere without either myself or Simms in attendance. Nor will you look cast down!" he demanded, his voice shaking now with fierceness. "I act only for the good of your immortal soul! Never will you see that vile seducer again!"

Chapter 1

January, 1812

"Do describe him, Lady St. Albans! You're the only one of us has met him. Even Lady Bardstow does not know the new earl, and she is his aunt."

"But I am not really the earl's aunt, Mrs. Rundel," Lady Bardstow corrected almost apologetically. "I am only his cousin, just as I was Edward's. It was Alyson started her husband addressing me as his aunt out of courtesy."

"La! I did forget!" the squire's wife admitted with a self-admonishing shake of her head. "Still, whatever your relation to the new master of Whitcombe Hall, Lady Bardstow, my point is that you have never met him. Oh! I do wish we had not been away the summer he visited Whitcombe. We enjoyed Tunbridge Wells, but to have missed meeting the new earl!"

"Of course, he was not Damon, Lord St. Albans then," observed Lady Bardstow. "He was only Mr. Damon Ashford, come to pay his respects to his ailing uncle before he left for the army. Though he was next in line— after dear Edward—to the title, no . . . No one guessed then he would return to Whitcombe one day as the earl."

"We would know his looks, however!" responded Amy, at sixteen Mrs. Rundel's youngest daughter.

"And I'd have formed an estimation of his character," Mrs. Rundel added as a sensible mother ought. "Is he a man of good character, do you believe, Lady St. Albans?"

"I beg your pardon, ma'am?" Alyson, the achingly young Dowager countess of St. Albans glanced up from the piece of embroidery she held. "I, ah, attended to a missed stitch." She smiled penitently and prayed that the flush heating her high, sculpted cheeks would be attributed to embarrassment at failing to follow the conversation.

Alyson's prayer was answered generally if not exactly. Mrs. Rundel attributed her hostess's flushed cheeks to another equally erroneous cause.

"My dear child!" the portly woman exclaimed, flinging the proper formalities to the wind without a second thought, for she had known Alyson since she was a young girl first come to live under her stepfather's harsh eye. "You ought to scold me for my thoughtlessness, not bear it stoically! In my eagerness to know everything about our new neighbor, I never gave a moment's thought to how wretched it must be for you to hear another besides your good Ned referred to as the Earl of St. Albans."

Alyson did feel wretched, and to hear the title Lord St. Albans applied to someone other than her late husband was one reason why she felt so wretched. But it was, in truth, the least reason, and she could not allow Mrs. Rundel to plague herself with unwarranted guilt.

"You must not fret, Mrs. Rundel. Perhaps it is not so easy to hear another besides Ned referred to as Lord St. Albans, but I needs must become accustomed to it soon. I shall be living in, ah, close quarters with the new earl for a time, after all. Did you ask what manner of man he is, ma'am? Ah, well, he was younger then, of course, but Lord St. Albans seemed a fine man."

Until he believed himself betrayed. Then he demonstrated a wicked temper and hideously unfair judgment. Alyson felt a wild sob rise in her throat. Heaven help her! He would arrive at any moment. Already it was two o'clock.

Let it snow! Please, dear God, let it snow. Heavy, gray clouds had hung overhead for three days, but they had let fall only a fine drizzle, not nearly enough to keep him away.

Glancing back from the window, she realized Harriet Rundel was looking at her expectantly. "Ma'am?" the girl said.

"I am sorry, Harriet." Alyson forced herself to smile again. "My mind remained upon your mother's question. What did you ask?"

Harriet flushed. "Nothing important, my lady, I assure you! I was only wondering, as it has been almost a year since you put on your mourning dress, if you look forward to giving it up soon?"

Alyson knew it was a measure of the state of her nerves that the simple question made her want to laugh hysterically. Her widow's weeds were the least of her worries. Or perhaps they were not so small a consideration. They would stand as a constant reminder to Damon of the choice she had made.

Oh, Ned! Why did you desert me?

At once Alyson shook herself mentally. Maudlin self-pity would attain her nothing. She'd guests. Miss Rundel deserved an answer to her question, and Lady Bardstow was addressing her.

". . . Of one thing I am most certain: Ned would not have wanted you to wear black one instant beyond the expected time. He'd have wanted you to get on with your life, my dear Allie. You are too young and too lovely for such dreariness!"

Alyson smiled despite her agitation. The sentiment was certainly Lady Bardstow's, whether or not it would have been Ned's. "I shall keep your assessment of Ned's opinion in mind, I assure you, Aunt Edie."

"Well, if you do not, I shall be happy to remind you," Lady Bardstow retorted with most uncharacteristic stoutness.

Alyson's smile deepened. "I shall rely upon it."

"At least you've the consolation that you do not look a fright in black, Lady St. Albans!" Harriet Rundel spoke up eagerly.

Mrs. Rundel's brow lifted as she gazed at her daughter in some reproof. "What a thing to say, Harry!"

"But Mama!" Harriet protested quite sincerely. "I meant no disrespect! I should look quite dreadful in mourning dress. Black turns my complexion sallow. But Lady St. Albans looks . . ." she glanced uncertainly at Alyson for a moment, then burst out with, ". . . heavenly!"

"Heavenly!" Mrs. Rundel groaned and rolled her eyes to the ceiling, causing Harriet to blush painfully.

Alyson chuckled and almost embraced Harriet as well as Mrs. Rundel. Five minutes had elapsed since she had thought of Damon. For the last week, since she had been notified by his solicitor of the specific day he would come, she had not been free of dread for so many minutes at once.

"I am complimented," Alyson assured Harriet. "And I thank you. I've enough vanity not to wish to look the crone I feel. But let us forget my mourning clothes and speak of you, my dear. Tell me of Tom Brady, with whom, so I understand, you stood up twice at the last Assembly in Aylesbury."

"But he is ancient history, Lady St. Albans!" The crowing revelation did not come from Harriet, an earnest, well-behaved young woman, but from Amy, two years younger and quite different in character. "Now Harriet is full of Kit Moresby whom she chanced to meet out riding this morning."

Harriet shot an uncharacteristically lethal look toward Amy, but before she could wipe her sister's gleeful grin from her face, Lady Edith expressed interest in the latter part of Amy's remark. "The Moresbys have returned then?"

She looked to Mrs. Rundel, who nodded sagely. "Indeed they have. I did not believe they would go directly to Mrs. Moresby's sister as they usually do at this time. Dreary though Buckinghamshire is in winter, I suspect even Mr. Moresby longs for a little peace after the excitement Claudia has caused with her latest rejection of a suitor."

"The Duke of Rutland was a most eligible *parti*," responded Lady Bardstow, who kept up a correspondence with several friends in town whom she had known in better days.

Mrs. Rundel nodded once again. "It is what comes of spoiling a child," she declared roundly. "One does not want to be too harsh, of course. But Mr. Moresby dotes upon Claudia so, allowing her her head in every matter. . . ."

A renewed surge of panic scattered Alyson's thoughts, and Mrs. Rundel's voice became nothing more than a buzzing drone in her ears. She, too, had rejected a suitor. One day she had sworn to love him forever, and the next she had told him she would wed another.

It seemed significant in an ominous way that Damon would return in winter. When the sun could be seen, it rose only briefly to shed a thin, meager light upon a world that stretched stark and bare and gray all about Whitcombe. Gone was the warm, lush world of their youth. She felt older by a lifetime. She had had a child. By another man.

"How old is St. Albans, do you think?"

Alyson held her tongue. There was no reason she should know he was precisely twenty-nine years and four months.

"He cannot be quite thirty yet," Lady Bardstow mused. "But I imagine he will be older than his years, he has led men so long and so capably. Wellesley admires him prodigiously, you know. That is why the earl has been so long in coming to take up his inheritance here at Whitcombe. Wellesley simply would not give him leave to go."

And he had stopped for a time in London. Lady Bardstow knew that but did not, apparently, see any need to mention the new earl's month-long sojourn in town. He had spent Christmas there with his friends rather than at Whitcombe with his family. But then, why should he rush home, when he had declared one member, fully one third of the little family awaiting him, to be a shallow, faithless fortune seeker?

A movement across the room caught Alyson's wandering attention. Percival, a white cat of great majesty, rose from his seat to stretch. Briefly he eyed the tea tray. He liked tea time excessively. Crumbs invariably fell to the floor, as he had discovered the day he had strolled into the Hall with magnificent unconcern for the inconsequential fact that the ancient house was not his. Sniffing about, he had come upon Alyson at tea with Lady Bardstow and realized on the instant that the generous lady with the little cakes was precisely the mistress he ought to have.

Percy was not interested in food that day, however. With a flick of his tail, he leapt soundlessly to the floor and made his unhurried way directly to the concealing shadows beneath an Adam chest in the corner.

Someone approached. Percival always took himself to that secret recess to survey new entrants.

Alyson's heart began to thunder so the pounding disoriented her. She no longer heard the other ladies speaking, was not even aware they existed, as she stared at the door.

It opened slowly, prolonging her suspense. When she saw the housekeeper, Mrs. Hobbes, she clenched her hand, pricking it inadvertently upon the needle she held.

"My lord is here, Lady St. Albans!" Mrs. Hobbes's face was flushed, and her words more rapidly spoken than usual. "He came by horse. 'Twas why we missed seein' him until he was halfway up the drive. We were expectin' a carriage. He'll be in the door in a moment, no more."

There was a general stirring in the drawing room. Alyson vaguely heard "He's come!" and "I wonder if he will be handsome," from one side, while on another, Mrs. Rundel cried fretfully, "Do you suppose he will be put out that we are here? We never should have come!"

Alyson knew she ought to say something assuring, but she could not think what.

"Alyson?"

Lady Bardstow smiled gently when she got Alyson's attention. "If you do not mind, I will wait here, while you go to the door."

"Of course," Alyson said, for she knew Lady Bardstow was suffering a bout of arthritis, but she felt, still, as if she were in a dream. "Do you await us here," she said and was surprised her voice sounded steady. "I shall return with the earl in a moment."

As she proceeded from the room she moved stiffly, as if she had to remind each leg to move and each foot to lift. Her arms hung straight at her sides, and she had to think to unclench her fingers. Alyson knew she must look pale. She felt drained of all vitality but could not think how to revive herself.

When she entered the hall, her eyes flew to the great oak door that was the front portal to the house.

It stood closed, but she could hear sounds without, and she had to resist an urge to wipe her palms on her skirts.

Then the door was flung wide. And she drew up short. Had Alyson been capable of absorbing details, she'd have noticed the footmen upon the steps, each resplendent in the midnight blue and gold livery of the Ashfords, but the footmen were a blue blur to her. A single tall, broad-shouldered figure eclipsed everyone and everything else in her line of vision.

He was striding up the stairs quickly, greeting each footman with only a brief nod, for, too late, the drizzle had turned to ice. Alyson had time only to gain an impression of hair as black as a raven's wing, an athletic stride, and a decided authority of manner before, seeming all of a sudden, Damon Ashford, the seventh Earl of St. Albans, stepped over the threshold of the home that had been hers, but was now his.

He found Alyson instantly. Though he came to take possession of one of the oldest, most venerable seats in the country, Damon spared not a glance for his inheritance. As if he had known precisely where she would be, he stepped into the hall and penetrated the shadows edging the pool of gray winter's light filtering through the mullioned windows above the door.

Their eyes locked, though for how long Alyson could not have said, but when Hobbes came forward to take his new master's caped coat, and Damon released her, Alyson felt herself sag.

Only mentally of course. Thanks to Mr. Haydon she'd learned control of her body. A slip in her stepfather's presence had meant the birch rod, and thanks to her rigid training she also managed to swallow the keening cry of despair that welled inside her.

But she could not force her mind to work. Mr. Haydon had not required her to speak, or if he had done, he had supplied the words she must say. Now, her slender figure unnaturally still and erect, Alyson stared, helpless to think beyond what she had learned, what she had lain awake night after night dreading to learn: he despised her still.

You do not understand! she wanted to cry. Just as you did not six years ago, when you seared me with a look of such contempt, I dream of it still!

In another moment her silence would have created amazement among the footmen who had followed Damon into the hall. Though not one trespassed so much as to dart a glance at either the new earl or the painfully young widow come to greet him, they all listened for the exchange to come.

Chapter 2

Alyson never spoke the expected words of welcome, but just as Damon gave his great coat into his butler's keeping, a child's cry rang out, drawing everyone's attention to the top of Whitcombe Hall's justly famed carved staircase.

"Rowena! Stop!"

Alyson turned sharply at the sound of her own child's high voice, but still, as she looked upward, even as she watched a mildly chaotic episode unfold, Damon's tall form never left the periphery of her vision.

But then Alyson knew the enormous black wolfhound that lunged into view at the top of the stairs. The dog paused there briefly, glancing back, perhaps to consider the pleas—more than commands—that had been shouted at her.

The mastiff's answer was to bark loudly enough to waken her Irish forebears, and to plunge, tail wagging furiously, down the stairs.

"Roe! Come here! Roe!"

The dog bounded across to Alyson just as a girl of five or so appeared at the top of the stairs. When the child saw the hall below her was not at all empty, she clapped her hand over her mouth and wailed miserably, "Mama! Oh, Mama! I did not mean to let Roe out!"

Her daughter's embarrassment pierced through Alyson's mental paralysis, or perhaps it was the time she'd been allowed, after she discovered the worst had indeed come to pass, that restored her composure to her.

"Do not worry yourself now, Annie," she called in a

voice that was entirely natural, low and calm. "The earl
has arrived. Come down and meet him. Sit, Roe." Alyson
looked sternly at the mastiff that could easily have snapped
her wrist in two with no more than a playful bite. "And
quiet yourself."

When the dog sat still but for her rhythmically thumping
tail, Alyson turned to see that her daughter, having reached
the bottom step, had stopped to dart a shy, uncertain glance
at the man they had been expecting. Alyson's expression
softened, and she held out her hand. Annie flew to her instantly.

"Make your curtsy to the Lord St. Albans, please, and
welcome him to the Hall."

Damon met the child's eyes, eyes that, unsettlingly,
more resembled his than her mother's, but he had only a
moment to remark how dark they were before Annie's
chin dropped abruptly. She did not, in her shyness, forget
her mother's admonition, however. She bobbed a curtsy
just as she had practiced. "Welcome to Whitcombe Hall,
my lord."

Damon's welcome had come at last in a whisper.

"I am pleased to present my daughter, Lady Anne, to
you, my lord." Alyson spoke her first words in six years to
Damon as she placed her hands upon Annie's shoulders in
a gesture that conveyed pride but, unmistakably, protec-
tiveness as well.

Damon returned Alyson's regard only briefly. The single, cool look was unreadable, and she tightened her hold
upon Annie. The gesture was unnecessary. As she found in
the next moment, Damon did not extend to her child the
disdain in which he held her.

He did not smile broadly. He was as uncertain of Annie
as she was of him, but neither was his expression un-
friendly. "Lady Anne." Damon inclined his dark head formally. "I am pleased to make your acquaintance."

Reassured by her mother's touch, as well as Damon's
stock, expected phrase, Annie peeked up at the new earl.
He seemed vastly tall. She had thought him grim-featured
when she glimpsed him from the top of the stairs. She

changed her opinion. He did not frighten her now. He did disconcert her still, however. She was too young to know quite why she could not look at him long.

But when she looked away, she felt her gaze pulled back, as if the earl were a magnet. His eyes were very black, she found before she saw him smile slightly. His smile made her giddy. She giggled and ducked her head again.

Her head down, Annie caught sight of Rowena sitting patiently by her mother's side. Immediately she flung up her little head and eyed the earl anxiously. "You will not turn Roe and me and Mama out, will you, my lord, because I did not keep Roe in my room? Nanny Burgess said you might not like dogs."

"And Roe is very much a dog," Damon observed dryly, flicking a glance from Annie to Roe. Sitting, the dog was as tall as Annie standing.

"She is an Irish wolfhound," Annie supplied helpfully. "Squire Rundel gave her to Mama and me."

Alyson's stomach clenched. Annie would have done better to claim the dog as her own alone.

"We could keep her in the stables, my lord," Alyson offered quietly before Damon could decree the dog must go altogether.

"I had a dog when I was a child," Damon replied, addressing Annie. "I liked him very much, as I recall, and so would not deny you your dog, Lady Anne, but I will ask that when company comes, you keep her either locked in your room or on a lead. Rowena might scare an unsuspecting visitor to death."

Annie's elfin face lit. "Mrs. Brady screamed when Roe bounded up to her," she recounted rather proudly.

"But Mrs. Brady fears all animals," Alyson added. She may as well not have spoken. Damon continued to confine his attention to Annie. "Have we an agreement?"

When he held out his hand, Annie giggled shyly again. But after a moment, she slipped her hand into his. "Yes, my lord."

Alyson let out a breath she had not realized she held.

"To live up to your agreement, my love, you are obliged to return Roe to the nursery now. Mrs. Rundel and her daughters are here."

Annie looked suddenly woebegone. "Nanny will fuss at me!"

"No doubt," Alyson agreed mildly. "You will listen to her respectfully, poppet, but afterward you may tell her of your agreement with the earl. And you may tell her as well there is no reason for you to come to the Queen's salon as you have met Lord St. Albans already."

"You will come to read to me before dinner, Mama?"

"Of course. Now get along with you. And you, as well, Roe."

The dog stood but destroyed the illusion of obedience she gave when she paused to salute Alyson's hand with a large, wet, unsolicited lick, before she trotted off quite docilely behind Annie.

"Thank you, my lord."

Damon watched Annie and the dog a moment before he flicked his gaze back to Alyson. He neither acknowledged her thanks nor remarked on the episode. "Did you say there are visitors?"

She stiffened. "Yes," she said, matching his cool, stranger's tone. "The squire's wife, Mrs. Rundel, and her two daughters await with your cousin, Lady Edith Bardstow, in the Queen's salon."

"Let us not keep them waiting any longer then." Alyson turned on her heel without another word.

In complete silence Alyson preceded Damon to the Queen's salon, so dubbed when Queen Anne had visited the house at the beginning of the previous century and pronounced the room, "handsomer than a Queen could desire." It was no great distance they walked, but Alyson had to struggle to keep her pace even. She wanted to run, to escape from the black eyes she could feel boring holes in her back.

The footman who leapt to open the salon door reminded Alyson of the interested audience within. She had never denied meeting Damon, but no one had the least inkling that she had fallen head over heels in love with him and had only been separated from him by force.

Taking a deep breath, she pinned a pleasant smile upon her face. "We came as quickly as we could, ladies," she said, leading the way to the group arranged about the fire. "Rowena delayed us a bit. She thought to make her greetings to the earl as soon as she could."

"That dog!" Mrs. Rundel cried, as mortified as if Rowena were her child. "I tried to dissuade the squire from introducing that great beast into your house, Alyson . . . merciful me, my wits are to let today! I cannot seem to remember you have been Lady St. Albans nearly six years."

"You are eager to meet the earl," Alyson said, so calm now she was among friends, she did not even flinch at the mention of six years. "May I present Damon Ashford, the Earl of St. Albans? Lord St. Albans, Mrs. Rundel and her two daughters, Miss Harriet Rundel and Miss Amy Rundel. With the squire, they live at Littlefield Manor."

Alyson had not considered at all what effect Damon would have on her neighbors. There had not been room in her thoughts for such details, but had she, she'd not have known what to expect. Much could change in six years.

Still, she was not surprised that his entrance into the room was enough to cause the ladies to straighten in their chairs. He was an earl, after all, and tall and handsome and elegantly dressed to boot. But when his smile flashed, white and strong in a face bronzed by the Spanish sun, she noted the charge that rippled through the room, and knew it to be remarkable.

Accustomed, or immune, to his effect upon women, Damon greeted the squire's ladies with an easy charm that caused Mrs. Rundel to turn a rosy pink, Harriet to stammer her greetings, and Amy to giggle breathlessly and flush like her mother had done.

"And here is Lady Bardstow, your cousin, my lord." Alyson continued struggling to keep a sudden, bewildering bite from her voice. "As you must know Lady Bardstow has made her home at Whitcombe Hall for some time."

If Damon was surprised to learn of Lady Bardstow's existence, he hid it gracefully. "I am delighted to meet you, cousin." Damon lifted Lady Bardstow's thin, birdlike hand to his lips. "I look forward to hearing your stories of the Hall in bygone days."

"I should be very happy to tell you the stories I have heard, my lord, but I do not know the Hall half so well as Alyson. Though she would make me seem a fixture here, I have made Whitcombe my home only two years."

Damon had not known of Lady Bardstow's existence before Alyson had mentioned her in the Hall, but he did not need to know her well to guess why her smile did not quite reach her eyes.

With some relief Alyson watched him gently pat the elderly woman's thin hand. "Two years is a long while to me, Lady Edith. I am delighted you are here to help me establish myself."

He needed her or said he did. Lady Bardstow clutched Damon's long-fingered hand gratefully. "You are too kind, my lord. I shall be honored to do all I can to help you settle in."

With Lady Bardstow's future safely disposed, at least for the moment, Alyson slipped into a chair on the edge of the cozy group. She did not need to be in the center. With Mrs. Rundel on hand, she suspected she would have little need to enter the conversation at all beyond asking Damon how much cream and sugar he desired in his tea.

She did not serve him his cup herself. She gave Harriet the honor, and when Mrs. Rundel mentioned that she and Damon had met before, Alyson left it to Damon to reply. He brushed off their previous acquaintance.

"Yes, Lady Alyson rode by when I fished once. I hope there are still trout in the stream that runs through the beeches? Can you assure me, Mrs. Rundel?"

"Yes indeed, I can," Mrs. Rundel replied. "As can Lady St. Albans. Your dear husband fished there many a time, did he not, my dear?"

Calmly, her eyes never straying from Mrs. Rundel's motherly face, Alyson said, "Yes, there are still many trout in the stream, though I doubt they are biting now. Do you not think it is colder this winter than last?"

And obligingly Mrs. Rundel was off on a discussion of the weather, after which Lady Bardstow inquired about Damon's journey from London. He did now know what had prompted him to ride his horse in such foul weather. "I suppose I needed the exercise," he said offhandedly, before explaining that a carriage followed with his baggage.

His hair still curled slightly over his collar. Alyson looked away to study the toe of her shoe before, carefully, she shot Damon another look from under long lashes that half hid her eyes. She need not have worried. He kept his attention from her.

In the flesh he seemed different than she remembered, though, oddly, in most details he was precisely the same. His hair was still thick black as a raven's wing, and his cleanly fashioned masculine features were as appealing as ever. His nose was still straight, his jaw square, his mouth . . . She dropped her eyes to the fragile, gold rim of her cup.

She would not think of anything for a moment. Nothing at all. His mouth, of course, was the same. He had not been wounded in the fighting on the Peninsula.

At the thought she flicked her gaze to him again. No. There was no scar. And he was tall as he used to be, long-legged and broad-shouldered.

Her memories had blurred, that was all. Mechanically sipping her tea, Alyson covertly glanced Damon's way again. *No*, she saw, her memories had not blurred. They were merely pale reproductions. She had not animated them with his magnetism. How could she have forgotten it? She had recognized it even when she was only a green girl, unaccustomed to men. Almost upon their first meeting she had thought to herself that when his fellows formed teams at school, he'd have been the first chosen.

Still, she decided, studying Damon more closely as he replied to something Mrs. Rundel said, there were changes. Though his eyes were still black as night, distinct lines radiated out from the corners of them now, and new lines, albeit faint ones, bracketed his mouth as well.

She watched him several moments, unable now to pull her gaze away. He really had changed, subtly perhaps, but distinctly.

He'd an even more authoritative manner. That was not surprising. He was older, had been a commander in battle, had faced death. But there was something else, something that eluded her. It came to her suddenly, when Mrs. Rundel said something amusing, and he smiled. He was harder now. He smiled still, but not nearly so openly. Before his smile had been ready, even a little cocky, perhaps. And it had lit his eyes. Not now, though. No, not once in the half hour he had been at Whitcombe, had liquid lights danced in his black eyes.

" . . . but I fear I have only shown off my ignorance. You must help me, Lady St. Albans. You, and your dear husband of course, are the ones who discussed the fighting on the Peninsula with the squire."

For a split second Alyson's eyes met Damon's before he forced her gaze to Mrs. Rundel. "Lord St. Alban's understanding of that subject would shame us all, I am sure," she said, relieved to hear her voice was steady, for the one interchange, brief though it was, had jangled her nerves again. Those forceful black eyes had regarded her with all the warmth of steel. "Do you not agree though, Mrs. Rundel, that the squire will be delighted to have an authority on Wellesley within reach?"

Once more Mrs. Rundel caught the conversational gambit and ran. By the time she had done telling Damon how highly the squire thought of Sir Arthur Wellesley, it was time for her to take her daughters home, and time for Alyson to excuse herself to go to the nursery to read to Annie. The privilege of showing Damon to his room, she yielded to Lady Bardstow.

Chapter 3

Late that night, long after she had presided over a dinner of which she had been able to eat almost nothing, Alyson sat before the fire in her room, Percy in her lap and Rowena at her feet. But, though she stroked the mastiff's back with her foot, she was scarcely aware of the animals.

Old memories she had resisted for years crowded in upon her. Where she had not been able earlier to recall precisely how Damon had looked at twenty and three, she could see him, now that she was alone, in minute detail.

She could see the day she had met him as well. It was June in her mind's eye, and her stepfather was away, settling some affairs to do with his own father.

Without Mr. Haydon, Alyson, and indeed everyone at Alton House, breathed more freely.

She wished to ride quite alone for once, and when she went to the stables for her regular midafternoon ride, the head groom granted her wish. "You'll stay on Mr. Haydon's property, Missy?" Jim Higgins asked, with an informality Mr. Haydon would have reprimanded severely had he heard it.

"Yes, Jim! I've nowhere else to go. I only want to be free a little."

He nodded. Like most who were acquainted with Mr. Haydon and his stepdaughter, he'd a deep, if hidden, sympathy for Alyson. "Away with you then, Missy. With Simms gone, too, no one will be the wiser."

Simms acted as Mr. Haydon's bailiff. By a stroke of

luck, he, too, had been called away by a family emergency. She had been made so happy by the misfortune of others, Alyson felt almost guilty. But only almost. Simms was as righteous and unbending as his master.

Alyson meandered far afield on that gloriously solitary ride and eventually let her mount take her down among the beeches that grew by the stream dividing her stepfather's estate from their neighbor's, the Earl of St. Albans. When she caught sight of a man, a stranger, fishing on Mr. Haydon's bank, she pulled up her mare more abruptly.

She ought to have departed at once and reported him, but he turned before she did. He was younger than she expected, and though he was carelessly dressed, Alyson saw he was no rough poacher. His mud-spattered boots were of expensive leather, his shirt of fine lawn, and the coat he had flung down upon the ground was a gentleman's.

She had no sooner registered the quality of his clothes, than she discovered something else, something that sent a thrill not untinged with alarm through her. He was more attractive than any man she had ever seen, with hair so black it gleamed like polished ebony in the sun.

When he smiled at her, having determined she was no angry game warden or irate land owner, Alyson's breath caught in her throat. "I hope you have not come to reprimand me for fishing on your side of the stream, Miss. . .?"

Only seventeen, Alyson had not much experience with young men, much less white, flashing male smiles. Her voice sounded high and breathless when she said, "Miss, ah, Haydon, sir," and she blushed to the roots of her hair.

Damon detected her blush, of course. He could not have missed it, but if his grin deepened slightly, and it did, he did not tease her. "Miss Haydon." He inclined his dark head with innate grace. "I am Damon Ashford. I've come to Whitcombe to pay my respects to my uncle before I go into the army."

Alyson understood what he did not say. It was common knowledge in the neighborhood that the old earl was in failing health.

"Is your uncle resting comfortably?" she asked in a voice that was a trifle softer than normal.

Unexpectedly Damon chuckled. The sound was infectious and made Alyson want to laugh, too. She did smile.

"My uncle would be the first to tell you that nothing about him is comfortable, most particularly not his temper." He shrugged then, his eyes still laughing. "I hope I will be half so crusty at his age. But my uncle, as he would be the first to admit, is a poor subject for conversation when the fish are biting. Can you assure me that no one will object greatly, if I fish on your bank? My uncle's side is too steep at this pool."

Because her stepfather and his bailiff were away, Alyson could report with perfect honesty, "Oh, no. No one will mind in the least."

"That is . . ." Damon's voice trailed off as he turned in swift response to a tug on his line.

Still safely mounted on her mare, Alyson watched him land a fat trout. She had not noticed the string he'd tied around a sapling. When he hauled it up, she saw he had caught two other fish.

Very probably, had Damon pressed Alyson to stay, she'd have taken fright. But he made no entreaties, only held up his fish with a grin, then set about tying a new fly on his line.

It was when he flicked the line into the pool, that Alyson spied his other pole. It lay on the bank unused.

Mr. Haydon was far away. Her gentle mother was enjoying the nap Mr. Haydon frowned upon, and Jim Higgins's words came back to her. *No one will be the wiser.*

On a sudden, rash impulse, Alyson slid from her mount. The day was warm, even hot, but among the beeches along the stream, the air was pleasant, and that was one reason why Alyson wanted to stay—the least reason, of course, but it made a good opener.

"It is so pleasant here," she said hesitantly as she

made to approach Damon. "The sun is very hot today. Is
anyone using that pole?"

The moment she had uttered the question, Alyson
wanted to sink into the ground. She could not imagine
how she had become, suddenly, so brazen. Blushing
hotly again, she even half turned back toward her mount.

But Damon sounded as if he thought it perfectly reasonable for her to ask to fish with him. "I would be delighted for you to use my extra pole, Miss Haydon. I'll
have that many more fish for Monsieur Fornet, my
uncle's chef. Do you know how to tie a lure?"

The practical question caused her to frown anxiously.
"Actually I have never fished before," Alyson admitted
in a rush.

She thought she saw a light dance suddenly in her new
companion's eyes, but before she could be certain or decide the significance of it, if it was indeed there, Damon
was bending to fetch her the other pole.

"I shall be delighted to teach you, then," Damon said,
as he straightened.

"It will not be too much trouble to you?" Alyson
searched his expression. His eyes were twinkling. She
had not realized how dark they were until now, when she
looked closely and detected what looked almost like liquid lights gleaming in them.

"Teaching you will be a pleasure, actually. I have
missed my younger brother and cousins, whom I used to
tutor on every subject imaginable. Without them I have
not once felt old and knowledgeable."

He grinned lazily. She smiled. "We will suit then," she
said softly. "I have always wanted to have an older
brother or a sister."

The gleam in his black eyes changed subtly, but
Alyson had not the time to wonder at the change. Damon
handed her the pole. Feeling as if she were taking a mo-
mentous step, she extended her hand to receive it. In-
evitably his fingers brushed hers. Startled, she lifted her
eyes to his. But Damon was not even looking at her. He
was adjusting her line, for she did not need as much as

he, being smaller. Feeling foolish, for her hand seemed to tingle where he had touched it, Alyson bit her lip and told herself to act like a reasonable young lady, for heaven's sake.

Without prearrangement, Alyson met Damon at the same spot the next day, then the next, and the next.

She confided in no one, afraid that somehow word might get back to her mother. Mild by nature and deeply attached to her only child, Mrs. Haydon might, in different circumstances, have been delighted to hear of her daughter's new friend, but even she would require that Alyson meet him in a drawing room with proper supervision. And mindful of Mr. Haydon, she would not allow Alyson even that much until her husband had first met and approved the young man.

Every time Alyson smiled innocently at Jim Higgins and rode off to meet Damon, she felt a little wicked, but she did not feel so sinful she stopped going to the stream. The only wrong she committed, she reasoned, was that of meeting a young man without the benefit of a chaperon. Even Mr. Haydon could not have objected to her fishing, and that was all she and Damon did when they were together.

And talk, of course, though at first Alyson did not find it easy to converse with Damon. Indeed early on she found it difficult even to look directly at him. She had only to catch an impression of his height, or his strong, lean build, or his cleanly chiseled features to become appallingly bashful, and meeting his dancing black eyes with anything more than quick, uncertain looks was completely out of the question for the first few days.

Gradually though, she grew easier in Damon's company. He treated her differently from the few other young men Mr. Haydon had allowed her to meet. They had embarrassed or disconcerted her, stammering when they spoke, or if they spoke easily, speaking so flatteringly, she could not credit a word they said. Worse still, one or two had smiled oddly, almost hungrily, upon her, frightening her.

Damon spoke to her as if she were nothing out of the ordinary, or he teased her lightheartedly, particularly about her fishing. But he never mentioned her looks and certainly made no forward remarks, nor ever looked at her as if he meant to devour her.

When she did begin to converse more readily, Alyson drew her subject matter from her friends and neighbors around Whitcombe. Sarah Wolverton, her best friend, had recently married Mr. Philip Davenport, the vicar in the village, and she confided to Damon that she envied Sarah her freedom. As Philip was the gentlest of men, Sarah could, or so it seemed to Alyson, do as she pleased.

Alyson never explained precisely why she envied Sarah so. The one subject she avoided was her own family. Beyond saying that she had been seven when her widowed mother married Mr. Haydon, Alyson did not speak of her stepfather.

She did not wish to speak of him for many reasons, but in the main she did not, because even to think glancingly of Mr. Haydon—and how he might react if he discovered she had met a young man in secret—was to cast a shadow of fear over days that seemed sweet and golden and full of promise, days when Alyson was more lighthearted than she had ever been in her life.

William Haydon was not an evil man. Alyson had seen him give a cottager whose home had burned a generous sum of money. But he was an exceedingly righteous man who believed himself to be, as head of the family, appointed by God to guard those in his care from the evil in themselves. His temper, his rages, he considered an instrument of God, and he made no effort to control himself. On the contrary, if he were offended, then God was as well, and woe be to the sinner.

He firmly subscribed to the adage, "spare the rod, spoil the child," and still took a birch rod or his hand to his stepdaughter when he believed she had trespassed grievously. But Damon did not need to know that.

Alyson would have been embarrassed to tell him because he seemed so removed from such harshness.

Mr. Haydon thrust as far to the back of her mind as possible, Alyson took full advantage of the world, so different from her isolated one, that Damon presented to her. Peppering him with questions about his life, she learned that though he and his younger brother, Nick, had been orphaned as children, they had been taken in by an aunt and uncle with a large, boisterous family. Alyson delighted in the stories Damon told her of his brother, whom he affectionately described as a little devil, and of his cousins, but she was equally interested in his future. It particularly amazed her that he had been able to choose that future. No one had decided for him that he would go into the army. "You can do anything you want!" she exclaimed more than a little wistfully one day.

In response Damon gave her the teasing grin that, curiously, Alyson found more appealing every time she saw it. "You will soon do anything you want, I imagine, for you will marry and wind your husband around your little finger. Or does Mr. Haydon keep a stout stick handy to beat off all the young men who must come calling at Alton House?"

Reminded of the birch rod Mr. Haydon did have and how harshly he applied it, Alyson's expression darkened momentarily. But her face was averted from Damon, and when she looked up at him, her expression was merely pensive.

"Mr. Haydon does not allow young men to call at Alton House, nor has he said when he will." A plaintive sigh escaped her. "Indeed, he cautions me so against young men, I sometimes think he does not want me to like them."

It was some three weeks after Alyson had met Damon and had grown so comfortable with him, that she gave little thought to how she looked, sitting on a rock, her hat on the ground, her gloriously thick hair unbound and stirring in the breeze, her skirts awry, and her blue-green eyes so bright and clear.

It took her very much aback, therefore, when Damon remarked upon her casualness and supported Mr. Haydon.

"Perhaps your stepfather is a little old-fashioned, but he is right to be concerned for you in relation to young men. You've precious little awareness of your looks, Allie."

As they had been addressing each other casually for some time by then, Alyson did not color up in reaction to the familiarity. She flushed because Damon had deliberately flicked a glance down to her blithely displayed ankles. When he looked up at her again, he regarded her steadily, though there was a familiar light dancing in his eyes. "When I first met you, Allie, I did not have entirely honorable intentions toward you myself."

"Beg pardon!" Alyson gasped, dismayed. She did not understand precisely what dishonorable intentions encompassed, but the phrase conveyed to her unimaginably despicable behavior.

Damon smiled a little, seeing her reaction. "Perhaps nothing so wicked as you are imagining, but your looks did inspire me to consider how I might lure you here often enough to win a kiss, at the least."

Alyson did not know what to say. Damon seemed suddenly a stranger. He returned her wide-eyed regard a moment before asking softly, "Have you never thought of kissing me, Allie?"

Her cheeks flamed, and she could not hold his gaze. She had thought of kissing him! Not when together, so much as later, at home, at night in her bed, she had dreamed of it, and of him holding her, too.

"Those thoughts are quite natural, you know."

Because she could not look at him, Alyson could not say with certainty, but she did not think Damon was laughing at her. He sounded serious. Biting her lip, she slid a sidelong glance at him.

No, he was not smiling. He was watching her, however, and she looked away immediately. "We are both healthy and young, and in your case, at least, surpassingly lovely."

That brought forth a gasp and a consideration of bolting entirely. She did not know what to say! She wanted to talk of fishing poles or life in Kent where he had grown up.

She darted another slanting look at him. He was still waiting for her to meet his eyes, it seemed. She did, quickly, and blurted before she could stop herself, "I am so embarrassed!" Appalled, she hid her face in her hands.

But Damon did not laugh. He came to her, took her hands, and gently tugged them away from her face. When he lightly nudged up her chin, she found him regarding her with such tenderness, she suddenly clung to his hands.

"There is no reason for you to be embarrassed. Your looks are God's doing, after all."

"It's not my looks!" she cried in a strangled voice.

"It is my noticing them that embarrasses you?" he guessed, smiling lopsidedly.

Truly she did not know what it was. "I don't know. I suppose. I . . . I don't know what to say now."

Why had she admitted that! Alyson wanted to die of mortification, but the words had spilled out before she'd realized she meant to say them.

"I think you could say simply, thank you, Damon. I find you pleasing, too."

A grin took her by surprise, unfurling inside her and playing on her lips. When Damon smiled back at her, Alyson realized, in fact, how pleasing she did find him.

"Thank you, Damon," she heard herself saying softly. "I am glad you find me pleasing. I . . . I do find you pleasing, too."

Damon's smile faded even as she watched. "Alyson," he said, a rough edge she had never heard before to his voice. All of a sudden she became entirely aware how attractive he truly was to her. She ran her eyes over him.

He had shed his coat, and his lawn shirt clung to his strong shoulders. She wanted to feel them. "Don't look at me like that, Alyson," he warned in something like a growl. "I want you enough as it is." Her heart began to pound so hard in her chest, she had to concentrate to hear him. He wanted her! What could it mean? "But my desires have gone beyond a mere kiss, sweeting. I want you for my wife, Allie."

Wife! Alyson felt as if she might burst. "Oh, Damon!"

Before she considered what she did, she hurled herself off her rock, and they came together almost with a crash. It felt so right to be folded in Damon's strong arms, Alyson lifted her head to smile brilliantly. He lowered his for a different purpose.

Alyson had no hesitation returning her first kiss. She wanted to kiss him, to prolong the heady, magical, soaring feeling that made her want to spin and laugh all at once.

When they separated, she was almost shaking with the feelings Damon had aroused in her. Nor could she think of anything but him until she rushed into his arms again the next day.

They did little fishing in the week that followed. Sometimes, often, they kissed, and discovered the pleasure their mouths and hands could give. Other times they talked, Damon leaning back against a rock, his arms encircling Alyson while she lay against him.

But still Alyson did not speak of Mr. Haydon. She allowed Damon to fill all her thoughts, instead. Later there would be time to discuss unpleasantness, after Mr. Haydon sent word notifying them of his return.

Chapter 4

But Mr. Haydon sent no warning. He returned unannounced four days later, confident all would be in readiness for him, whenever he chose to return.

Alyson was in her room dressing to ride out to Damon when a maid hurried in to say she must join her mother in the drawing room to make her greetings.

"Now? Mr. Haydon is come now?"

"Yes, Miss Allie. Only a few moments ago, and Simms with him," the young maid said.

Alyson went pale. Clenching her hands together, she tried frantically to still the fearful beating of her heart that she might think what to do. She must send word to Damon somehow, to explain not only why she would not see him that day, but to warn him not to come to Alton House until she found some way to meet him and give him an understanding of Mr. Haydon.

"Miss Allie? Have you taken sick?" Maddie, the maid-servant, regarded Alyson anxiously. "Are you in need of salts, Miss?"

"No, Maddie. I . . ." Alyson's gaze focused. Maddie's sister had once worked at Whitcombe Hall. "Maddie, does your sister still work in the kitchens at the Hall?" When Maddie answered in the affirmative, Alyson grasped the maid's hands in hers. "Would you give a note to your sister to give to the earl's nephew? He is Mr. Ashford. I imagine your sister will know of him.

"All the maids do, Miss," Maddie admitted. "Sal says he's the handsomest bloke she ever saw. But as to takin' a note, I dunno. If Mr. Haydon learns of it, he'll turn me off without reference."

"Of course, Maddie!" Alyson felt the most self-centered of young women. "I asked before I thought."

Turning away, her mind churning, Alyson hurried to exchange her riding dress for an afternoon dress, not the least aware that Maddie watched her, frowning. Like Jim Higgins in the stables Maddie felt a keen sympathy for her master's stepdaughter. She knew Alyson was allowed no gentleman callers at all—had, indeed, been allowed to attend only one social event in the neighborhood, a Boxing Day celebration at Whitcombe Hall, and Maddie knew, as did Jim Higgins, how severely Mr. Haydon punished his stepdaughter when he thought she had trespassed.

"Cor, Miss!" she sighed gustily. "I'll do it for you, take the note, that is. But hurry! I'll be missed soon."

"You will do it! Oh, Maddie!" Alyson caught the girl's hands and squeezed them tightly. "I'll give you my pearl earrings. They are all I have of value."

"Get on with you, Miss Allie," Maddie replied almost gruffly. "And what would I do with pearls? Unless I'm caught. Then I'll come askin' for 'em."

Damon received Alyson's note the next day, and though he was not surprised to learn Alyson's stepfather had returned for he had guessed as much, he was surprised by the second portion of the note in which Alyson begged him not to come to Alton House until she had an opportunity to speak with him privately about Mr. Haydon.

Damon smiled to himself, seeing no more in Alyson's appeal than a sudden case of nerves any young, sheltered girl, who had not been behaving with the utmost propriety, might experience when her guardian returned. He, for his part, was delighted Haydon had returned, for earlier that same day Damon had received his summons from his regiment. The letter came to him late, as it had gone first to his aunt and uncle, and to report on time, Damon realized he must leave Buckinghamshire the

very next day. To his great relief he could now depart
with Alyson's hand officially his.

Alyson knew nothing either of Damon's summons or
his arrival at Alton House. Mr. Haydon taught her still,
lessons centered upon the Bible, and she was in the
schoolroom, copying verses from the book of Amos,
when she heard a door slam hard somewhere below.
Startled, she went to her window, but it looked out over
the back of the house, and she could not see the dark-
haired rider galloping angrily down the drive. She did,
however, shortly afterward hear footsteps outside the
schoolroom. It was Mr. Haydon, she knew. No one else
in the house walked with such force.

Rushing back to her seat, she waited, her stomach
clenched in a knot of foreboding. Somehow she knew
the worst had happened.

Mr. Haydon exploded into the room, flinging open the
door, sending it crashing against the wall. Alyson cried
out, cowering back from the strong hand already raised
against her.

"Harlot!" her stepfather screamed, backhanding her
with such force Alyson's head struck the wall. "You
have met a man in secret!"

"No! I—"

She screamed when, his flaming eyes pinning her to
her seat, Mr. Haydon struck her again, leaving the print
of his hand upon her pale cheek.

"You will not lie! I know what you have done. He admitted trysting with you! How else could he know you
well enough to ask for your hand in marriage? You
wicked girl, you took advantage of my absence and
played tricks on your foolish, weak-willed mother!"

At the mention of her mother Alyson cried out again.
"No! It was not like that!"

For her pains Mr. Haydon struck her again, bringing
tears to her eyes. "Did you lie with him? Is that why he
dared to ask for you in marriage? Are you with child?"

"No!" Alyson shrank back when he lifted his hard
hand again. "No! I am innocent! I swear it."

He loomed over her. "Swear by God that you are pure in body!"

Alyson's cheeks flamed. To discuss such a thing with Mr. Haydon almost made her ill. Almost. In a shaking voice she swore. "I swear by God that I am pure in body."

Mr. Haydon lowered his hand slowly, his eyes still fastened upon Alyson, searching for evidence that she lied. Alyson's face ached, and the back of her head throbbed where he had driven it against the wall, but she forced herself to return his gaze steadily, afraid that if she did not, he would be driven to hurt her again.

"In keeping with my duty as your guardian, I have tried to purge you of the wicked wilfullness that was your father's only legacy to you!" Alyson no longer took angry offense when Mr. Haydon slurred her father. He had done it so often, the disparagements had lost their power to sting. "From the moment you came into my care," he continued, his voice coldly contained now, "I sought to save you from Satan's grasp. I have failed, or you would not have behaved as wantonly as you have this summer. I can only hope your husband will do better with you than I have done. Oh, yes, you will marry," Mr. Haydon said grimly when Alyson gasped with surprise. "You may not be my flesh, Alyson, but you are my child, and I would not be remiss in my duties to you. You will not, however, marry this rake who came asking for you today. He would lead your soul astray. Just look at how he persuaded you to meet him in secret!"

No! No! Alyson wanted to scream. *He persuaded me to nothing. Our meetings simply happened. They were innocent and carefree. We fished!* But she bit back the words. Protests served only to incense Mr. Haydon the more.

But even had she thought a protest of any use, Mr. Haydon's next words so stunned Alyson, she gaped at him.

"I have already accepted an offer of marriage from a far better man. We arranged the match between us last

December. I would have told you of it then, but the gentleman in question persuaded me you were too young to think of such things as a husband and marriage. He wished to wait a little before he paid his addresses. It would seem we both misjudged." Alyson held herself rigid as Mr. Haydon's gaze narrowed. "You ripened early."

Damon! What of Damon! Alyson could scarcely absorb what her stepfather had said. He had already arranged a match for her. "Who . . .?" she could not force more than the one word by her trembling lips.

"A far better man than the presumptuous rogue who dared enter my study today," Mr. Haydon declared icily. "I have given your hand to a man of substance and breeding. You will wed the Viscount Ainsley."

Ainsley! Or as he would soon be—Lord St. Albans, the earl's son and heir. And Damon's cousin. Alyson could only stare. She had spoken to the man only once, last year at his father's annual Boxing Day party.

Alyson's reaction, or the lack of it, caused her stepfather's temper to flare again. "I see you do not react with pleasure! This upstart has seduced you with his good looks and surface charm. But he will pay! As will you, Alyson, for your weakness. I have told him to come again tomorrow. You will meet him then and inform him in person, first that you will not marry him and second that you will marry the viscount. Should you decline to send him on his way, Alyson, I will banish you from my house and keep you from ever seeing or communicating with your mother again. I will not have her or anyone else in my house contaminated by a willful sinner. Think on your choice carefully. I will send your mother to help you."

A gentle rapping at the door moments later announced Mrs. Haydon. "Alyson?" she whispered urgently as she stepped into the room.

"Oh, Mama!" Alyson hurled herself into her mother's arms, sobbing as she had never done before.

Mrs. Haydon gasped, for she was a frail woman, but

too, she had seen the red mark on Alyson's face. "What have you done, Allie?" she moaned into her daughter's dark chestnut hair. "What, oh what?"

"Nothing!" Alyson lifted her head. The sight of her mother's pale, pinched face made fresh tears spring to her eyes. "I swear it, Mama! We did nothing but talk and fish."

"Oh, sweeting! It is not done to meet a young man alone. You are a young lady now. At the very least, he ought to have asked Mr. Haydon's permission to pay his addresses first."

"But Mr. Haydon was not here! And, anyway, he had already decided upon my future for me. Did you know, Mama?"

Mrs. Haydon's eyes, a pale blue, nothing like the striking blue-green of Alyson's, fell. "Yes, Allie, but Mr. Haydon did not wish you to know."

Alyson wanted to tear herself away, to scream and shout and rail that it was her life, her future, had been decided upon. Who had a greater right to know of it?

But even as she stiffened in anger, she heard her mother draw a ragged, trembling breath. Guilt flooded her instantly, dousing her anger. Alyson would not be the only one to pay for her clandestine if innocent meetings with Damon. Mr. Haydon would hold her mother accountable, too.

"Mama! I am so sorry! He has not hurt you?"

"Hush, child!" Mrs. Haydon darted a nervous glance at the door. "Mr. Haydon is my husband and has the right to demand obedience of me. As he has of you. Allie, you cannot refuse the viscount."

"But Mama! I do not know him. I have seen him only half a dozen times in my life and all of those at a distance, save for the Boxing Day entertainment at the Hall last year. He took me in to dinner, but that is all the favor he showed me. How could he want me for his wife?"

The strain on Mrs. Haydon's face faded a little. "Is it so hard to believe a man would fall in love with you upon first meeting? You are surpassingly beautiful, my dearest, if I do say so myself. The viscount remarked upon it, and your grace of manner, too. He thought you'd a rare amount of poise and dignity for one so young." She managed a smile. "And you've a kind nature, Allie. He may not realize fully how good you are, but he must have seen he would get no shrew. He certainly did not leave getting you to chance. He came the very next day to speak to Mr. Haydon, and it was he persuaded Mr. Haydon not to tell you. I think Ainsley wants to woo you, wants you to want to wed him, before he asks for you."

"But, Mama, I was not told, and I fell in love with another man! You would not have me wed Lord Ainsley when I love his cousin, surely?"

"Oh, my darling! You are so young! Girls fall in love with a new young man every day! You will not recall this Mr. Ashford within a year of wedding Lord Ainsley."

"Mama . . .!"

But Mrs. Haydon resisted her daughter's anguish. "Believe me, Alyson, I know whereof I speak! Your father was as handsome as you are beautiful. He swept me off my feet, and as you know I married him against the wishes of my parents. Would that I had heeded them! He shamed me from the first, Allie, spending his money on other women as well as cards. A handsome face is no proof of character.

"And think of your children! Who will provide for them better: the viscount who is heir to an earldom and Whitcombe Hall, or this Mr. Ashford who is off to the army. He will be in the thick of battle soon, Allie. What will happen to you or a child you conceive by him, if he is killed? Mr. Haydon will not take you back. Oh, Alyson!" she cried, catching her daughter to her on a sob. "What would I do without you? You are my only child!"

Now Alyson clasped her mother to her as tightly as Mrs. Haydon had held her moments before. "Hush, Mama, hush," she whispered. "Oh, please, do not cry!"

"I . . . I cannot bear it if you go, Allie!" Mrs. Haydon sobbed pitifully into her daughter's shoulder. "God help me, but I cannot!"

"You'll not be put to the test, Mama." Alyson stroked her mother's thin hair, tears streaming down her own face unchecked. "I'll not leave you."

"Oh, Allie! Do you mean that?" Still sobbing, Mrs. Haydon searched her daughter's tear-stained face.

"Yes, Mama. I could not go and leave you."

And Alyson could not. Loving her mother well, she knew how her mother needed her. She was her mother's only solace, and too, her mother's only friend. Mr. Haydon forbade idle socializing. Mrs. Haydon knew the other ladies in the neighborhood, could call them acquaintances, but she could not name one a real friend.

"Oh, my dear! Oh, my dear!" Mrs. Haydon patted Alyson's face, trying to smile, though the tears continued to well in her eyes. "You'll not regret your choice. I know you will not."

Chapter 5

When she felt tears on her hand, Alyson came to herself with a start. It had been years since she had allowed herself to think of that time, of that summer and of its end. She had made her choice for the best of reasons, and once she married, once she had made her vows, she had not allowed herself to think of Damon again. Dredging up old memories, whether sweet or bitter, would have served no good purpose.

Alyson shivered in the cold room. There was no escaping those memories now, though. They had returned in the flesh.

Rising stiffly, she sought her bed. Percy followed in his own time to curl up by her feet. Alyson noted his familiar, comforting presence and Rowena's even snores coming from the Axminster rug before the fire. She'd have liked to scoop up everything dear and familiar to her at Whitcombe and escape with them that very night.

Damon. He controlled her future, this new, hard Damon whose dark eyes hid his thoughts—but for that one moment, the initial one, when he had cast eyes on her for the first time in six years. Alyson shivered yet again. Dear God, but he had reduced her to a green, raw girl of seventeen with that one scathing, emotion-laden glance.

Oh, yes, she did very much want to fly from Whitcombe. She wanted a fairy godmother, too, and a coach and six, and . . . forgiveness. Alyson's mouth twisted in a grim smile. The most impossible wish of all. He'd not forgive her. She knew that now.

And she had to stay. Alyson pulled her coverlet up to her chin. She had nowhere to go. Mr. Haydon and her mother could not give her refuge. They had died the year before Ned, three years after Annie was born, both of influenza.

She let out a ragged sigh, any bitterness she might harbor going with it. They had acted for what they thought was the best. No one could have guessed what would happen. Mr. Haydon had even left her a generous inheritance. Of course it had gone into Ned's control, and Ned, having never considered that he might suffer a fatal fall from a horse when he was only thirty-six, had not made a will to settle upon his wife the portion of his estate that was free of entail. Without a will everything had gone to Damon.

Alyson did not think Damon would harm Annie in any way. He had not changed that much. She could trust that he would make provision for her and Annie, but it would take some time for him to know what he had inherited and what he could spare to set them up in a dower house. Until then she must live with him.

Perhaps she could talk to him, explain her decision six years ago. Perhaps . . . Alyson drifted off to sleep and fitful, uneasy dreams of Damon.

Alyson awoke groggy and tired from her restless sleep, Damon still on her mind. It was early yet, and she was glad. Before she faced him again, she wanted to have some breakfast, to gather herself, and to steady nerves that seemed as raw as they had when she sought her room the night before.

Later she would remember that a military man's day likely began early, but she was not thinking very clearly that morning. She stepped into the breakfast room with relative confidence, only to have her step suddenly falter.

Damon sat in Ned's place at the head of the table, a London journal in his hand. He looked up, catching her staring dumbly, but at least he gave Alyson the satisfaction of knowing she had taken him as much by surprise as he had taken her. His dark eyes flared with the unexpectedness of finding her come down so early for breakfast.

Damon recovered more quickly than Alyson, though. In the next instant a mocking gleam lit his black eyes.

He knows, she thought, her gaze locked with his. He knows I could not sleep. And he knows why.

She took a step back, prepared to whirl about in full retreat. She did not care what he thought of her. She suspected she was not up to Damon in the best of conditions, and she knew she was not then.

But Hobbes, carrying her pot of chocolate, appeared at the servants' doorway.

"Good morning, my lady," he said pleasantly as he placed her pot at her usual place. It was, of course, by Damon's. "Will there be anything else?"

Courage? Alyson forced a smile and shook her head as she slipped into the chair Hobbes held so helpfully and so compellingly for her. "No, thank you, Hobbes."

The butler's footsteps echoed unnaturally in the stillness of the breakfast room. Alyson had never realized how many steps it took to reach the servants' door. Perhaps she ought to suggest to Damon that he move the table.

She shot Damon a glance from under her lashes. He was engrossed in his journal again.

She could sip her chocolate quickly and leave. The cup was there before her, waiting, filled to the brim. She would spill every drop—she felt that unsteady.

She must do something. The silence rang in her ears, stretching her nerves, making her unbearably aware of Damon so close by her. Her spoon leaped out at her. She lifted it to stir her chocolate but struck the side of her cup clumsily, making a sharp, clattering sound.

It brought Damon's head up. Their eyes locked again, and Alyson, as if from a distance, heard herself blurt, "Did you sleep well, my lord?"

She spoke because she could not bear a return to the

deafening silence, because, in spite of everything, she hoped that if she behaved normally, he might, please God, do so as well.

Almost as soon as she spoke, though, Alyson regretted the impulse. Damon fixed her with a faintly contemptuous look. "Did I sleep well? How shall I answer? Let me see. Perhaps we might consider my day yesterday. I returned then to assume responsibility for an estate I was never trained to administer; for a child, who is not mine; for a cousin, I had never met; and for a woman I had hoped never to see again. Does that answer your question, my lady?"

When Alyson flushed to the roots of her hairline, Damon's mouth curved in a mocking smile. "I did wonder, idly, if you'd outgrown your tendency to blush, dearest Alyson. I see you have not. The curse of fair, creamy skin, I suppose, and undoubtedly a pity. Blushes sit so much better on a young girl than they do upon the cheek of a bereaved widow. Don't you agree?"

"This is unfair!" Alyson cried, her hands clenched together in her lap.

"What is unfair?" Damon shot back curtly. "That you did not marry the right one, after all? Does it sting, my lady," he mocked her with his emphasis on her title, "that you made the wrong choice?"

"Mr. Haydon made the choice!" Alyson protested, her voice low and trembling with emotion. "I did not want Ned or his title."

"I have chosen to accept the addresses of the Viscount Ainsley." Damon mimicked not only Alyson's words, but her voice too, capturing its low, slightly husky timbre exactly.

Alyson felt the heat sear her cheeks again and fought against a feeling of helplessness. She recognized the feeling from her interviews with Mr. Haydon and knew it could paralyze her so that she failed to summon even the simplest defense.

"Mr. Haydon forced me to say those words to you. Why else do you think he was in the room?"

"To prevent me from throttling you to within an inch of your mercenary life?"

For a moment Alyson could not reply. She was caught by the look in Damon's eye. His tone might have been all light, mocking inquiry, but the flame at the back of his beautiful, dark eyes suggested he might still find satisfaction in taking a hand to her.

With a sense of hopelessness Alyson recalled her plan to tell Damon what had happened after his first visit to Alton House. She had had even, she remembered, a vague thought of pleading with him to understand that she had been only seventeen, when the choice between what little family she had and her love of only a month had been put to her.

He would not believe her, though. She could see his dismissal, even before he heard her, in his eyes.

Alyson forced her chin as high as it would go, and if it was not much, still, in her own mind, she gave Damon notice that she would not meekly suffer his doubts and barbs.

"Mr. Haydon remained in the room to be certain that I put an end to any interest you might still have had in me," she informed Damon stiffly.

He laughed, an ugly sound with no charm or joy in it. "The man succeeded there."

Alyson colored miserably again. But she tried to keep her voice level and tried as well to keep any plea from it. "I understand what you think of me—"

"If you do," Damon cut her off, half growling now, "then you must know I have not the slightest desire to exchange meaningless pleasantries with you while we share a cozy breakfast!"

"But we must live together!" Alyson cried. "Can we not make the best of what we cannot alter?"

She thought the point irrefutable. Only a madman could want to live in enmity.

Perhaps Damon was a little mad. "You are as good at that as you are at employing those great aqua eyes of yours, are you not, Lady St. Albans?" Damon sneered.

When Alyson only regarded him blankly, however, he had to clarify his point. "I meant you are obviously good at making the best of things. You certainly seem to have made the best of your—was it forced?—marriage."

Alyson was still. She had hoped he had not registered Mrs. Rundel's references to Alyson's "dear" Ned. A baseless, even craven wish. She could not regret her love for her husband. Still, she wished—

"Tell me," Damon continued, his voice slicing through Alyson's unhappy thoughts. "I really am curious. Did you address him personally as 'dear Ned' or did you only refer to him so sweetly when you were—"

Alyson did not wait for the end of the question. She did not doubt it was only rhetorical. Still, if she conceded the field, and she did, leaving her chocolate entirely untouched, she did not run cravenly. She flung down her napkin and pushed back her chair abruptly before she departed the room with her back as straight and rigid as a board. She walked, too, though she wanted to run, and for the discipline that allowed her that dignity, she did for once send up thanks to Mr. Haydon.

Chapter 6

Alyson glanced in her pier glass, smoothing her black bombazine as she did, then she made a little grimace. The movement had been automatic. Bombazine was too heavy to wrinkle. It did not even move with her when she walked, but had a stiff, tentlike life of its own. She did not like the stuff. Nor did she like black. She felt like a crow in it.

Abruptly she turned away to pick up the kid gloves her maid, Bernie, had laid upon the bed for her. They were black, too, of course. Black was the proper color for her. It proclaimed her bereaved state.

She was a "bereaved widow." Mouth tight, she jerked on the gloves. The phrase made her feel ancient, as he had intended, she did not doubt.

Well, she would not allow him to discompose her so. He had a right to some grievance against her, she did not dispute that. She had not stood firm against Mr. Haydon.

And she had come to care for Ned.

But how could she not have? How could she have kept her heart locked against a man who introduced her with the greatest pride to his friends; who showered her with costly baubles to proclaim his affections; who never tired of telling her how he had fallen in love with her at first sight?

Ned had not knowingly destroyed any possibility of a match between her and Damon. He had asked for her before Damon even came to Buckinghamshire, and had been away in London, enjoying the last of the Season, when Alyson had fallen in love with his cousin. He had known nothing of Mr. Haydon's ultimatum. He had wanted to woo her, not threaten her.

And for pity's sake, she had thought she would spend the rest of her life with him! What was she supposed to have done? Resent Ned for all eternity? Make both herself and him miserable for all their lives?

Damon took her good relations with Ned as proof she had gone willingly to the marriage—or proof that she was shallow and feckless. Well, he was wrong on both counts. She set her delicate jaw. The man could disparage her all he wished. She would not be made to feel the worst of people. Nor would she feel an ancient hag, either.

Abruptly, a mutinous light in her eyes, Alyson returned to her pier glass. She did not find it easy to stare at herself. Mr. Haydon had punished the sin of vanity with particular severity and had never allowed her a glass in her room.

Holding her eyes steady, Alyson noted her dark chestnut hair. Though it was caught in a modest coil at the nape of her neck, one could see it was thick and shone with the high gloss of well-buffed boots. Her figure was slender and lithe still. She was neither too tall nor too short, and other people said her even features were pleasing. Ned had particularly admired her blue-green eyes, calling them luminous. Alyson supposed they were. Certainly they were large enough, and she thought the contrast with her dark, curling lashes not . . . Alyson stared more closely at her eyes. There were lines at the corners! Crow's-feet. Oh, perhaps they were not so deep yet, but there were definitely lines: tiny, etched, and irreversible.

Abruptly she whirled in exasperation from the glass. What was she doing? Why was she going on this way? She was to accompany Damon and Aunt Edie to the Rundels, true. But it was a gathering in honor of the new earl, not her. The attention would be upon him, and the other guests were all people she had known most of her life.

The only new person would be Damon. Chin up, Alyson marched to her door. She already knew his opinion. She could not think why she fretted. The appearance, or absence, of a few lines about her eyes would certainly not change Damon's attitude toward her.

She was certain of that, though she had seen little of him in the last few days. She had gone out of her way to avoid him. Breakfast, for example, she now took in her room. If they met, they did so at dinner when Lady Edith was present to act as a buffer. Alyson had done no more than say a perfunctory greeting, and even then she had seen no reason to meet his dark eyes.

Just as Alyson stepped into the hallway, Annie came running, Rowena trotting behind her.

"Mama! Nanny said I might come down and bid you good night."

"We are well met then, for I was just on my way to the nursery to say good night to you, pet. No, Roe! Ah, well." Alyson sighed when Roe disregarded her command and leaped at her in greeting. "Mercifully your paws are not muddy."

"She was only trying to say she thought you looked pretty." Annie tried to excuse the dog as Alyson shook out her dress.

Her mother chuckled. "I see. I thought she was merely misbehaving, but I shall take your word for it, poppet. Will you give me a farewell embrace, too?"

Annie swarmed up her mother, holding her tightly. "You will come home, Mama?"

The uncertainty in her young voice caught at Alyson. She had lost her father less than a year before. "Of course, my love. I am going no farther than the Rundels' with John driving the carriage. And while I am away, I believe you and Nanny will enjoy a special treat I have left for you in the nursery."

Annie peeped up at her mother, her interest caught. "A treat?"

"A special one," Alyson assured her, only to realize Annie's attention had flown to something behind them.

Or to someone. Only one person in the house could elicit such sudden intensity, and Alyson felt herself stiffen even before Annie's breathless, "Lord St. Albans!" emerged. To mask her reaction, Alyson lowered Annie to the floor.

"Wish Lord St. Albans a good evening now, love. We must go."

Annie did so, a shy little smile curving her mouth as she gazed up at Damon. Alyson wished her child might look a little less awestruck, but she conceded grudgingly that she asked a great deal of one so young.

Black became him. Of course he had hair as black as his evening clothes. Even in low light, it gleamed like a raven's wing. And he did not wear unrelieved black. The elegant fall of white lace at his throat set off his dark coloring. It also, by virtue of being so feminine accentuated the very masculinity of his features. He looked, in fact, unbearably handsome. Aware of a wrenching sensation in the area of her heart, Alyson looked away from Damon at once.

Giving Annie one more kiss on the cheek Alyson sent her off, and Rowena as well. "And what of you Percy?" she addressed the cat sitting in the doorway of her room, observing at a stately remove the goings on in the hall. For answer he turned, tail high and waving just slightly, back into her room. She shut the door behind him.

A quick look from beneath her lashes confirmed what her ears had registered. Damon had not continued on his way. Surprised, she met his eyes. He had not stayed to admire her, that was plain. The gaze he flicked to her skirts conveyed how little he thought of her appearance. He did not remark upon it directly however.

Instead he said, "You ought to develop the backbone to discipline that dog before you are out of bombazine. You'll be a permanent mass of wrinkles if you do not, my lady."

My lady, indeed! He goaded with what was intended to convey respect and courtesy. Just as he goaded her with the assurance that she was, indeed, clad in material as stiff and unappealing as she had very well known it was. Alyson lifted her chin. "Thank you for your concern, my lord, but I like exuberance in an animal. Did you have any other reason for lingering?"

"The only reason, actually." A mocking smile lit his black eyes. "I remained to offer you escort downstairs. Lady Bardstow awaits us, and I expected you would wish to make a united appearance when we descend the stairs together."

The taunting gleam in his eyes intensified as he extended his arm. She did not want to touch him. Alyson told herself she did not, because she resented conceding a victory to him even in so small a matter.

Perhaps that was the cause of her reluctance.

But when she touched Damon, as gingerly as she could, Alyson experienced the most acute awareness of him. It almost was as if her fingertips could feel through the satin of his evening clothes to the warm skin beneath. Her hand trembling ever so sightly, she registered the breadth of his arm, the strength of it, and she recalled with acute clarity how it had felt around her.

No! her mind, or a part of it, screamed at her. How could she allow her thoughts to spin on so? He had lingered in the hall for no reason other than to discomfort her. Lady Bardstow and appearances meant nothing to him. Suddenly all her distress seemed to coalesce into anger.

By heaven she would not let him rout her so easily again. He was not Mr. Haydon, she fumed to herself. He had no real power over her.

A thrill of daring shot through Alyson. Dizzied by such an unaccustomed emotion, she had no idea what she would say, until she actually heard herself say, "How very considerate you are this evening, my lord." She put the same exaggerated emphasis on the "my lord" as he had on "my lady." "I am astounded."

As retorts go, it was nothing to crow about, but Alyson had never put any one in his place in her life. Her heart raced as she awaited Damon's response.

It came, of course. Damon would not cede the last word. "No doubt you are," he said. "But I find I am inordinately fond of Lady Bardstow, and would stoop to almost anything to spare her discomfort."

It was a far more effective thrust than Alyson's had been, but oddly, Damon flung it with so little emphasis it cut not at all. Alyson even glanced up at him in surprise, only to find herself the more mystified. When he could have marked his victory with a mocking look or disdainful smile, he, instead, stared straight ahead, his jaw set at a determined angle almost as if he was exerting every ounce of will not to look at her.

"Thank you, Bernie." Alyson gave her maid a weary smile. It had been a very long evening. "That will be all. I shall do my own hair tonight."

Bernie, who had taken an almost proprietary air with Alyson from the moment she had entered her young mistress's service, said, "Very well, my lady," dutifully enough, but then added, in her direct way, "Shall I fetch you some headache powders from Mrs. Hobbes's supply, my lady? I believe you would benefit from a dose."

"Do I look so haggard?" Alyson asked wryly, thoroughly accustomed to the Scotswoman. "I must say I feel it."

"You do not look haggard at all, my lady, though it is past midnight, and you have not kept such late hours for many months. I simply know you very well. When you fall wearily back against the door to your room the moment you enter, I cannot but imagine you are suffering from the headache."

Alyson did have a headache, and furthermore, she was up to no battle of wills with her stout Scots maid. Very soon Bernie returned with a glass of water made opaque by the dissolved headache powders.

"Now then, you will sleep well and be fine as a new penny in the morning." Bernie watched with satisfaction as Alyson drank the concoction. "It cannot have been an easy thing to go out for your first evening without your dear husband, God rest his soul."

"Yes, Bernie. Thank you. Good night."

Alyson held her head up until she heard the soft click of the door closing behind her maid. Then, at last, she allowed her aching brow to sink forward to rest upon arms she had folded on her dressing table.

It had been the most dreadful, draining evening. From the first, almost, she had wished herself at home in her bed.

Perhaps it was, as Bernie had said, Ned's absence had affected her so badly. Perhaps she ought not to have attended, though she had done so only after discussing the matter thoroughly with Lady Bardstow and Mrs. Rundel. She was in mourning still and had not accepted even dinner invitations, except from Philip and Sarah Davenport. Not only was Sarah her oldest and best friend, but they had children close to Annie's age, and Annie needed company, if Alyson did not.

But Whitcombe was the most important estate in the neighborhood, and its master was the highest-ranking— and most consequential—person in the area. Alyson understood that everyone nearby wished to meet Damon. His practices as the largest landowner in the district would affect them greatly, and already they had waited almost a year to judge him for themselves. To keep them in continued suspense until Ned's family was out of mourning had really been out of the question.

Mrs. Rundel, ever helpful, had offered to hostess a simple gathering at her home, thereby sparing Alyson the necessity of planning an entertainment. Though Alyson knew the squire's wife was delighted with the opportunity to be the first to fete the new earl, she appreciated the offer. Truly, she did not feel up to having the requisite champagne delivered to a house of mourning. And she had agreed when both Mrs. Rundel and Lady Bardstow had given it as their considered opinion that she should be on hand when the new earl made his first bow in the neighborhood.

Lady Bardstow had put it most succinctly. "Your being by Lord St. Albans is so important for the transition, don't you think, my dear?"

The transition. The old presenting the new.

Perhaps that had been the problem with her evening. She had felt old.

One person present had all but said she was close to being beyond her prime. Restless suddenly, Alyson straightened, and began to brush out her long hair with smooth, rapid strokes.

Of course, Damon had entered into that scene, the end of it, actually, though they had avoided each other the entire evening. And by then he had overcome whatever it was had kept him from mocking her with his eyes before they left for the Rundels.

Chapter 7

Alyson thought back to the beginning of the scene. She had gone to speak with Mrs. Brady, the woman Rowena had greeted with such disastrous results, and a small party of elderly ladies had gathered about her, greeting her at length, for many had not seen her since Ned's funeral almost a year before. They were full of compliments for her, and they asked after Annie, of course, but it quickly became clear that the real object of their interest was the new earl. They bombarded her with dozens of questions, all of which she answered readily and easily, having prepared herself in advance for just such a quizzing. She did not look to Damon, however. She had managed, in fact, to have her back to him almost all the evening, and so it came as a surprise, when one of the ladies remarked in a quavery voice, "I must say that it would seem Miss Moresby, particularly, has captured Lord St. Alban's attention.

As if the girl had heard and wished to prove Mrs. Weatherby's point, the little group was treated at that precise moment to the sound of Miss Moresby's full-throated laughter, followed by a coquettish, "I think you are teasing me unmercifully, Lord St. Albans! I may well demand a forfeit."

Damon's response was not lost, either, though his voice was not so high and carrying as Claudia Moresby's. Perhaps it was because the group of ladies had gone very still that they each heard him reply, amusement threading his voice, "Is that a threat, Miss Moresby? Or a promise?"

Alyson never turned. The ladies about her did not notice, however, nor did they note how stiffly she sat. They were far too busy discussing the earl and Miss Moresby, whose dress, a white gauze over a rose satin underslip, they judged to be fresh and extremely becoming. True the neckline was cut off the shoulders, baring a good deal of Miss Moresby's bosom, but the ladies, tittering among themselves, agreed a girl would have to use particularly enticing bait to capture a man like the new Earl of St. Albans.

Feeling older and drabber by the moment, and unaccountably spiteful about Miss Moresby, who had never been called a beauty by anyone, Alyson cast about for some excuse to leave. Her mind seemed unable to function, however, and she had to hear the ladies count Miss Moresby's vitality as a mark in her favor, as well as her figure. It was full, as Alyson knew without having to hear the ladies say so.

They had begun on Damon, tittering far more and far more appreciatively, when Alyson was rescued. Her gallant was Claudia Moresby's brother, Kit Moresby, an attractive young man whom Alyson knew far better than his sister, for soon after his family moved into the neighborhood—it was their father had bought Mr. Haydon's estate—young Moresby had been sent down from Oxford. Bored, he had come to the Hall very soon, and after discovering he had in common with Ned a love of fast horses and fighting cocks, had taken to visiting nearly every day.

Alyson smiled at him with the greatest pleasure. For one thing, he looked young, and she was pleased to remind herself he was her age. For another, he gave her the perfect excuse to escape the older ladies' wildly flattering commentary on Damon.

Mr. Moresby was also the most amiable of young men, and as Alyson sipped the punch he procured for her, she was reminded why she had always enjoyed his company, for he regaled her with a half dozen amusingly recounted *on-dits* making the rounds in town just then.

As she knew the people, she could appreciate Mr. Moresby's apt descriptions, and as he was not the least cruel, she could listen without wincing.

They were laughing over the predicament into which an aging rake had got himself, when Miss Moresby's ringing voice interrupted them. "I see you and Kit are enjoying yourselves, Lady St. Albans. May I join you?"

The younger girl did not wait for an invitation, but immediately commandeered a chair by Alyson, who could not have been more surprised. Miss Moresby had never sought her out before.

Alyson had not long to wonder why she did then, however, for even as Mr. Moresby was greeting his sister with something less than unbridled enthusiasm, she said baldly to Alyson, "You have had quite a change at the Hall, have you not? It must be a difficult adjustment for you, Lady St. Albans. Indeed, I wonder you have stayed on."

Staring, not quite able to credit such ill-mannered bluntness, Alyson could summon no more adequate response than a faint, "Do you, Miss Moresby?"

"Indeed, I do," Miss Moresby replied with all the cool confidence lacking from Alyson's reply. "For myself, I could not stay under the same roof as my husband's successor. Just think how difficult you will find it, when the earl takes a wife, as doubtless he will soon do."

Miss Moresby might as well have said, "I intend to have him and want you gone," Alyson thought, her usually mild temper flaring as the girl's nerve, and that alone she told herself, put her teeth on edge.

If she had not had much practice in verbal sparring, Alyson learned that day she was not without a desire to learn. Keeping her voice as low and pleasant as Miss Moresby's was, to her mind, sharp and grating, she said with false pleasantness, "You are terribly kind to concern yourself with my feelings, Miss Moresby. However, I assure you, you have no cause for worry. If the earl chooses a wife as gracious as he is, I may stay on at Whitcombe Hall for years."

But Miss Moresby was too single-minded to register Alyson's subtle barb, or if she did, to allow it to silence her.

Her unremarkable brown eyes fairly snapping with impatience, she exclaimed, "But surely you plan to remarry, Lady St. Albans? You are not that old, after all!"

She had to wait a moment for Alyson's reply. Alyson had first to control a desire to snap that she was nearly the same age as Miss Moresby, herself.

At twenty-three, Alyson was, in fact, only four years the elder. Four years, a husband, and a child older—not to mention a lost love.

"I am still in mourning, Miss Moresby," Alyson said, perhaps more sharply than she had intended and certainly more swiftly. "It is not yet the time for me to make future plans, as I am certain you must understand."

Miss Moresby looked as if she did not understand at all and intended to dispute the sentiment, but Kit Moresby spoke up.

"Surely you don't mean to extol the state of marriage, Claudia!" he exclaimed, exasperated. "I'd have thought you would avoid the subject like the plague, given your own recent decision against marriage."

Miss Moresby, not the least put out of countenance, laughed loudly. "Oh, I did not shrink from the state of marriage in and of itself, Kit, only from that particular, prospective groom. The Duke of Rutland and I did not suit. And nothing, nothing on earth, could ever persuade me to marry where I did not wish to marry."

"Now, there's the truth, as I should know!"

It was Mr. Moresby, father to Kit and Claudia. He was a corpulent man, whom Alyson had always found overbearing and pompous. She gave him only a tepid smile when he greeted her, and even that faded as she looked beyond Mr. Moresby to see he had not come alone.

For the first time that evening Alyson looked directly into Damon's eyes. They gleamed with such a mocking light, she felt her cheeks heat to her horror.

He briefly flicked his gaze over Alyson's warm

cheeks before he looked to Miss Moresby and added insult to injury. "I could not help overhearing you, Miss Moresby, and I must say I admire such evidence of a strong will," he said, and Alyson wondered how it could be that she alone detected the derisive edge in his voice.

Mr. Moresby the elder certainly did not. He wagged his large head proudly. "As do I, St. Albans, as do I! I would never fault my Puss for her good, strong will, indeed I would not! Great ladies are never feckless."

"I quite agree," murmured Damon softly as with seeming idleness he turned his gaze to lance Alyson again.

Alyson laid her brush upon her dressing table. Had that scene been the only thing that set her so on edge? Surely not. If she had not known precisely how forward and even obnoxious Miss Moresby could be, she had never thought her a pleasant person, and as for Damon . . . she had known too well his opinion of her.

Weary now, for Mrs. Hobbes's powders had begun to do their work, she slipped out of her dressing gown and crawled into her bed. When Percy leaped up beside her, she began to stroke him absently.

Had it been the feeling that she belonged among the dowagers that had undone her? She was a dowager, after all. Or the glowing comments upon Damon that had come at her from all sides, all night from everyone? The gentlemen had been in equal parts impressed to have a hero of the Peninsula in their midst and relieved to see the earl would make a strong, vigorous landowner, while the ladies . . . their reaction had been predictable.

She did not know what it had been, precisely, but she did know she wanted to leave Whitcombe. It was simply an impossible situation. She gave a desperate little laugh. Miss Moresby had been more accurate than she could know, when she had said she thought it would be difficult to live with her husband's successor.

Unaware, Alyson knotted the bedsheet in her hand. It was clear the girl had fixed her sights on Damon. And he did not seem a reluctant target. Yes, yes, she must escape Whitcombe as soon as possible. She would speak to Damon tomorrow.

When Alyson had taken herself off to her room upon returning from the Rundels, she had caught Lady Bardstow somewhat by surprise, for it had been the custom, when Ned lived, for she and Alyson and Ned to gather in the drawing room after they returned from an entertainment to discuss the evening over, according to the tastes of each, a glass of ratafia, sherry, or brandy.

Lady Bardstow did not change her habits easily, and no sooner had Hobbes divested her of her thick cape, than she began to walk toward the drawing room, only to stop in confusion when she heard Alyson murmur some excuse to escape the black eyes that had continued to mock her every time she met them.

Though Damon knew nothing of the routine that Lady Bardstow had unthinkingly begun to follow, he could see easily enough the uncertainty playing on her face. Making a swift guess, he asked if she had been making for the drawing room. "If you had in mind a final glass of refreshment, I should like to join you. I do not think," he added with perfect truth, "I could sleep quite yet."

Lady Bardstow's anxious expression smoothed instantly. "Oh! In that case, yes. I should very much like a little glass of ratafia, Lord St. Albans."

"Lord St. Albans," he echoed wryly, taking her thin arm in his. "It sounds so very formal, and sometimes I even forget it is I who am being addressed. Could you not bring yourself to call me simply Damon, my lady?"

She brightened up at him. "I am honored that you should ask, Damon, if you will return the favor and address me as Edie as Alyson does."

"But I thought she addressed you as Aunt Edie," Damon observed, allowing her to precede him into the drawing room.

"She does," Lady Bardstow admitted, giving Damon a twinkling, if shy, smile that took him not a little by surprise. "But any lady, even one of my advanced years, could only regret being addressed as aunt by quite the most attractive gentleman it has been her pleasure to meet in a good, long while."

Damon's grin flashed suddenly, very bright and very, very appealing. "I see you are a consummate flatterer, Edie. I cannot but be delighted. Ah look, I see Hobbes had a fire lit for us. It must have been your custom to come here after an evening out?"

"Yes," Lady Bardstow said. "There will be decanters and glasses on the side table there."

"And Percy in the best chair," Damon added dryly. Lady Bardstow followed his gaze and saw the cat was ensconced in the chair closest to the fire. "Shoo him off and take it," Damon directed as he crossed to the side table. "This house is overrun with animals that have been treated more like humans than animals."

"Rowena is large enough to be considered two dogs," Lady Bardstow said, taking Damon's remarks more seriously than he had intended. "And I suppose Alyson does treat both animals rather well, but she was not allowed pets when she was a child, you see. She'd a most hard, unpleasant stepfather, I understand, though from others, not her, for she never speaks much of him. Now then, Percy, may I sit with you?"

If Damon considered inquiring further into what Lady Bardstow knew of Mr. Haydon, he did not then, for she was preoccupied with slipping slowly and carefully into Percy's chair. Despite her care she disturbed the cat. It lifted its leonine head, regarded her intently a long moment, then evidently finding her wanting, leaped to the floor to yawn massively.

"I am sorry, Percy," Lady Bardstow called softly, but the cat remained aloof, responding with no more than a dismissive twitch of its plumed tail as it padded from the room.

"I do believe you are quite as bad as his mistress, Edie," Damon chided his cousin, Mr. Haydon forgotten. She looked slightly shamed. "Perhaps. But I've considerable affinity with Percy. You see, we are both strays given a home by Alyson." She smiled as she took the glass Damon handed to her, but he could see her smile was a trifle strained.

"Surely you were not quite a stray," he said quietly, taking a chair across from hers.

"Perhaps not quite, but very nearly. When Lord Randolph, my husband, died, I was left penniless. The old earl's sister, Lady Agatha heard of it, and offered me a position as companion to her. Did you know her?"

Damon nodded. "Just. I met her once."

"Well, then you may not have formed an opinion of her character, but suffice it to say that when she and I visited Ned and Alyson here at Whitcombe once, Alyson took pity on my situation, and asked if I would consider becoming companion to her. She manufactured a reason, saying she needed an advisor, if she were to become a proper countess, but it was the merest nonsense. From the day she married Nedd, she acted her new role as if she had been born to it."

"I don't doubt it," Damon murmured, studying the brandy in his glass as he swirled it about.

Lady Bardstow did not notice the irony edging his tone. She stared into the distance, a slight smile curving her lips. "I shall never forget," she went on almost to herself, "the expression on Agatha's face, when I told her I would be leaving her employ. She thought she had obtained a slave for life, you see. I am beholden to Alyson for many things, but that, I believe, most of all."

"I understand," Damon said simply and meant it. Alyson's kindness to Edith he counted as a small but sure mark in her favor. "And as we are somewhat close to the subject, I should like to take this opportunity to have you understand that I expect you to continue to consider the Hall your home, Edie. After all, I am new to the role of earl and am in quite as dire a need of an advisor as Lady St. Albans ever was."

"Oh! I did not mean . . ." Lady Bardstow turned quite pink as her voice trailed off.

"I did not think you did," Damon assured her, charming her once more with his strong smile. "I spoke because it was high time I did."

"You are certain? I mean not only that you wish an elderly retainer creeping about, but that there are . . . I mean that you are able to, ah, well . . . to take on the responsibility.

"You are not a grave drain, I think," Damon answered lightly enough, but the look in his eye was not so lighthearted, as he asked, after a moment, "Is it common knowledge Ned was strapped for funds the last year or so?"

Lady Bardstow shook her head swiftly. "Not at all. Alyson has no notion, I am certain. I only guessed. Having seen them before, I recognized the signs that something was amiss. You needn't worry overmuch about Alyson's response, however. She is really quite strong. She will take your news in stride."

"Hmmm," Damon replied and turned the conversation into other channels before Lady Edith could mark the neutrality of his reply.

Chapter 8

Alyson took luncheon with Annie in the nursery the next day, something she had done regularly since the one disastrous breakfast with Damon, though that noon time she went less on Damon's account, than because she had need of Annie's high spirits after the affair at the Rundels.

Annie did not disappoint her mother. No sooner did Alyson enter the nursery and greet Nanny Burgess than Annie skipped forward with the surprise Alyson had left for her the night before, a picture book on South America.

"Just look, Mama! There are all sorts of pictures. The men have long hair! See! It is black as . . ." she paused searching for a comparison and then brightened dramatically when she had it, " . . . Lord St. Alban's!"

By dint of the greatest effort, Alyson kept her smile on her face. She had not gone to Damon's study to demand he tell her when he would settle a sum on her and Annie as she had intended. Her courage had failed her.

Not caring to be reminded of her cowardice, she thrust Damon from her mind in time to hear Annie say, " . . . and one animal eats ants!" She made such a disgusted face that Alyson forgot her unpleasant thoughts and laughed out loud. "It is true, Mama!" the child insisted. "But the birds are not so odd. They are beautiful, though Nanny says the book does not do them justice. She has seen one, you see. I wish I could."

"Well, though I haven't a parrot on hand to show

you," Alyson said, "I imagine we can find a book in the library with a good picture of one."

"Will you help me to look for it?" Annie squirmed excitedly in her seat. "We could trace the picture and then color it!"

"A delightful idea," her mother replied, and after they had fully enjoyed their luncheon, they repaired to the library, where they soon discovered several splendid pictures of bright green parrots.

Chattering as she traced one, Annie recounted everything she had learned about parrots that morning, including the astonishing fact that the birds could be taught to speak. When she wondered aloud what a bird would say, Alyson, having cut out her tracing, held her parrot up to her face and repeated several times in what she thought to be a parrot's voice, "Pretty girls color me. Pretty girls color me."

Annie shrieked with laughter, which only encouraged Alyson to continue her play, for Annie had laughed too little since her father's death.

Damon heard Annie's giggles from the hallway, and looked in on impulse to see what amused her so. The smile just playing on his mouth faded abruptly, though. He had thought Annie with her nurse.

But it was upon Alyson his eyes fastened. She looked almost a girl of seventeen from the back, she was so slender. She was not so girlish seen from the front. He had noted that almost the instant he had clapped his eyes on her that first day. Time and a child had done their work. Very well. She was far more womanly after six years; her breasts were fuller and her hips softer, rounder, more seductive.

Her hair had not changed, though. Six years had not dimmed its burnished beauty a whit. Even in that modest style, a neat coil at the nape of her neck, it looked luxuriant and thick and rich. He might have told her that before they left for the Rundels. The thought had occurred to him, but he had not. For the sake of his sanity, Damon had determined, when he knew he would see her again, to hold Alyson as far from him as possible. And by God, he would.

When she squawked some silly chant and Annie giggled again, Damon finally took in that Alyson was teasing with her daughter. Something tightened in his chest, but he fought that, too. She was as silly as she was shallow. And beautiful, he admitted.

His jaw set, he recalled the unpleasant financial news with which he must acquaint her. He had known the magnitude of the problem for some little while, but had delayed speaking to her. He did not care to think on why particularly. To keep from it, he decided the time was come and stepped into the library.

Holding her parrot before her face and squawking like a banshee, Alyson could see little and hear less. She was, therefore, completely unprepared when Annie cried suddenly, "Lord St. Albans! Lord St. Albans! Look at Mama, isn't she funny?"

Instantly Alyson whipped the brightly colored piece of paper from her face. Damon was indeed there, looking very tall and dark and unsettlingly handsome.

Unaware that she did, Alyson lifted her chin. His black eyes were upon her, and if she could not read them precisely, she could see he had not found her play amusing. Likely he thought it silly.

But for Annie he did have a smile. "Did you want a parrot so much that you turned your mother into one, Lady Anne?" he teased.

"No!" Annie giggled, shy with him as usual, but delighted, too. "Mama is only pretending! But I should like to have a parrot, though Nanny says they are messy. I have made a drawing of one, my lord. Would you like it?"

When Annie held out her messily executed drawing, Damon took it with every evidence of pleasure. "I shall prize my parrot highly, Lady Anne," he said, smiling winningly enough that Alyson had to bite her lip to defend herself against the insidiously warm glow stealing over her.

Her battle did not last long. Damon doused the glow

for her in the next moment. "I am afraid, Lady Anne, that I have not come merely to bid you good day. I've some matters I must discuss with your mother. Would I ask too much, if I asked you to finish your next drawing in the nursery?"

Alyson did not betray her sudden tension to Annie. She spoke quite calmly, though her heart had skipped a beat. "Take these tracings, poppet, and finish them with Nanny."

"But she will not pretend to be a parrot!" Annie objected sorrowfully.

"You may entertain her then, and show her how it is done."

Annie did not argue further. Her mother had risen and was holding out their papers. "Will you come to the nursery for tea?" she asked Alyson, not wanting to give up her mother entirely.

Alyson nodded. "Yes, poppet, I shall. Oh, here is a pencil we dropped."

Annie added it to the load she carried then smiled quickly at Damon. "Good-bye, Lord St. Albans."

"Good-bye, Lady Anne."

As Annie hurried away, Rowena, sensing the prospect of exercise, heaved herself up from the place she had taken by the fire. Damon arched an eyebrow as he watched the mastiff trot off after the child. "Should Lady Anne acquire a parrot," he murmured dryly, "you will own quite a menagerie: an oversized dog, an overtalkative bird, and an overweening cat."

Alyson colored and said defensively, "I did not know Percival was in the habit of visiting the rooms you frequent."

Damon did not lower his eyebrow when he turned to look at her. "You do not know your pet well, then. I have to boot that cat out of my study at least once a day."

"You ought to have said something. I shall confine him to my room," Alyson said, heat entering her voice as she thought of him kicking her cat. She wondered if he would do such a thing out of spite. "You've no fear of cats?" she asked, as another possibility occurred to her. Mr. Haydon had been deathly afraid of felines.

Damon was not. "No, only a liking for my chair to myself, and my papers arranged as I left them."

"I see," Alyson said stiffening at his tone. "As I said, I shall endeavor to keep him confined. It should not be too difficult, as we shall not be here much longer."

She regarded him inquiringly, her delicately arched eyebrows lifted in question. But, though she knew he understood her question—indeed, she believed he had shooed Annie away that they might speak of finances— he made her no answer, only gave her a long, impenetrable look that tightened the knot of tension in her stomach.

She felt so uncertain with him and at the worst disadvantage. She was the lamb to his lion. Damon stood so much taller, Alyson was obliged to arch her neck to look at him, and his broad shoulders proclaimed his greater strength. There was no trace of paunch or fat upon him, either. On the contrary, he was hard and lean, for which she imagined, he could thank his military life.

"Shall we be seated?"

It was more command than question. Alyson stared at him and shook her head. "I prefer to stand," she said tautly.

Damon did not insist they make a pretense of conviviality. He nodded curtly. "As you wish." But he did not get on with whatever he wished to discuss, either. To Alyson's surprise, he strode restlessly away to the window.

Snow was falling, but Alyson did not think Damon had taken himself off to admire the sight. She clenched her hands together tightly, increasingly unsettled about what was to come.

"Did you discuss financial affairs with your husband?" Damon did not address the question to Alyson but to the swirling snow outside.

She shook her head, then realized he could not see her gesture. "No."

She thought she heard him mutter, "A pity," but could not be sure. He was too distant. Abruptly, just as Alyson thought she might scream with impatience and demand that he get on with it, whatever it was, Damon turned to face her.

"I've some unpleasant news, the upshot of which is that you will not soon be leaving to set up your own establishment."

"But I cannot stay here," Alyson said in a tone of someone stating the obvious.

"You will have to."

"What do you mean?"

"I mean I haven't the resources to keep up two establishments," Damon snapped. Even to his own ears, he sounded short and impatient.

Alyson stared, too shocked to form a response. She could only think he was trying to play a trick on her, but she could not imagine what it was.

"You needn't look as if you think I am trying to persecute you, somehow."

Heat stung Alyson's face. She had not imagined he could read her so easily. Damon flicked his gaze to her warm cheeks, and arched a mocking look at her.

"I am telling you the truth," he said. "Evidently your husband did not confide his business dealings to you, but the fact is he invested in some risky undertakings on the 'Change and lost a staggering sum."

"Ned?"

It was a fatuous query, and Damon gave it the response it deserved. "Who else was your husband? Sit down, damn it, before you faint!"

Alyson had never fainted in her life as far as she knew, but he snapped the command with such force, she sank into the chair behind her. Ned had lost a great deal on the 'Change. She could not believe it.

"But he never said anything."

"You know better than I the nature of your relations with your husband," Damon growled. "Perhaps he didn't trust your reaction to bad news."

Alyson paled, and her eyes went unnaturally wide. For all she knew, Damon was correct. Anything might be true, if it was true, as it seemed to be, that Ned had done so unexpected a thing as to speculate unwisely. Too distraught to begin to formulate a response, she sat silent and very still and straight in her chair, looking, in all, as if she might shatter at any moment.

"That was unfair."

Alyson's eyes swerved to Damon, betraying her surprise at his curt admission. He held her gaze a moment, but only a brief moment before he shrugged and turned away to kick at the fire.

He had been unfair, but he would be damned before he told her what he truly believed: that if few men cared to confess failure, none would care to make such a confession to a woman who looked like her. Even then, faint with dismay, she was achingly beautiful.

As he stared into the fire, he saw her perfectly. Her nose was straight, but for the end, where it tipped slightly; her mouth soft and generously made; her cheeks were high, her chin gently rounded, and her skin was as smooth and supple as a babe's. But it was her eyes that made her beauty extraordinary. Framed by arched brows darker than her richly dark chestnut hair, they were a crystalline blue-green, bright and clear as gems.

Devil it! Damon jerked his attention to the fire he had kicked into a roaring blaze. Damn the woman. And damn Ned.

Abruptly he turned back to Alyson, a flat look in his black eyes. "I don't know why your husband said nothing. He may well have thought he would come about before he need do so. And he might well have done, had he lived. The point now is that I haven't the funds to set you up in a dower establishment somewhere."

Alyson had recovered from her shock to the extent that she could speak, but she felt as if she were on the edge of tears and she spoke, as a result, very carefully and slowly. "I cannot stay here. You must see that. Annie and I can live well enough in a cottage somewhere."

"The widow of the sixth Earl of St. Albans and his daughter in a cottage?" Damon gave her a withering look. "If you do not know what is due Lady Anne, I do. And anyway it doesn't matter if you could abide living in a hovel. I cannot afford just now to divert to you funds that might generate the capital that was lost."

"But how long will it be before you recover that capital and I may leave?" she cried, her hold on her emotions slipping.

Damon shrugged. "I cannot be sure. Much depends on my investments. Perhaps a year, perhaps two."

Two years! Alyson bit her lip, struggling to maintain her composure. Two years. It seemed a life sentence.

"I do not care for this any more than you," she heard Damon say from what seemed a great distance. Alyson came close to laughing aloud. She had never heard a more unnecessary statement. "I hope that after a little, within the year possibly, I shall have the wherewithal to open one of the closed wings of the house for your exclusive use. You may treat it as a separate home."

Alyson nodded dully. It occurred to her she ought to thank him for his consideration, but she did not. She thought he was suiting himself more than her. He would want her out of his way, and not simply because he despised her. He had to be thinking of taking a wife and setting up a nursery. She thought of Miss Moresby. Living under the same roof, even if in a separate wing, from that cat—Alyson mentally apologized to Percival for her unintended slur upon him—would be unbearable.

She would have to do something. After all, the thought came to her suddenly, she was free to do whatever she chose. Damon had no power over her but the power of his purse. She could set up herself and Annie anywhere she pleased, if she could find the means. He could not keep her at the Hall as Mr. Haydon had kept her at Alton House. Alyson felt a surge of strength. She

would just have to think. It might take time. But she
would do it.

She looked up, for once undaunted by Damon. "If you
have nothing more to say, my lord, I'll not keep you
from your considerable duties longer."

The sudden energy animating Alyson's face took
Damon very much by surprise. He studied her, wondering what had caused the change. A moment ago she had
appeared so dazed and disoriented he'd had to fight to
keep from taking her in his arms. He had overcome the
impulse to comfort her, but it indicated how dramatically
she had been affected by his news. Now the color had
returned to her cheeks, and there was an eager gleam in
her eye.

A hard, mocking edge to his voice, he said, "It would
seem that as usual, you are prepared to make the best of
a bad situation."

But, at least for that moment, Alyson was insulated
from Damon's taunts. She was going to make her own
way in the world. And she was going to be free of him.

"Yes," she said rising, her eyes steadily upon his. "I
plan to do just that, my lord. And because as you have
noted, I have had a great deal of practice, I fully expect
to succeed."

Alyson departed the room, an unmistakable flounce to
her step, and too buoyed up to care that Damon was
glaring after her. Actually she imagined he was glaring
and would have been shocked to learn he was not, at
first, glaring at all.

As Alyson flounced off, Damon's gaze was drawn
down to the part of her that flounced the most. Actually
her rounded bottom swayed only slightly, but when a
faint though unmistakable groan escaped from between
his teeth, he did glare—and cursed her under his breath
for being a witch.

Chapter 9

Reality soon tempered Alyson's buoyant mood. A widow with a child and few talents did not easily discover an independent means of support, but she did not give up hope. Indeed, her determination to leave the Hall as soon as possible was strengthened several days later, for she had another encounter with Claudia Moresby.

She had gone to the music room to play upon the pianoforte, which she did as often as she could. In Mr. Haydon's house, music had provided a means of escape from the cold isolation that had been her life. At the Hall she played for pleasure.

That day, however, Alyson did not leave the music room as reluctantly as she sometimes did. It was the first sunny day they had had since Christmas, and she had promised that Annie might go with her to take baskets of food to the families of some of the laborers on the estate.

Mentally ticking off the items she had asked Mrs. Hobbes to pack, Alyson entered the long gallery without the least awareness that it was occupied.

The gallery stretched the length of the middle and oldest wing of the house. In summer it afforded a delightful view of the formal gardens just below, and of the rolling, seeming limitless park beyond, but in winter few cared to linger in the drafty room.

Indeed, when Alyson heard people speaking, she thought, for just a fraction of a second, that she must be hearing voices. Then she recognized Claudia Moresby's unmistakable ring, and glancing up, she saw Damon was crossing to the windows, Miss Moresby hanging on his arm.

They were alone.

A sudden, painful throb in her chest took Alyson by surprise, and worse, held her feet still. Though she could easily have slipped away unseen, she stood staring at the pair advancing upon the bank of windows.

Miss Moresby had wound her arm through Damon's and leaned in to talk to him. Alyson could not take her eyes from the sight. She thought he must feel the girl's breasts, and then she flushed hotly, mortified that she should notice such a thing. And mortified, too, that she felt a stab of fury—at least she thought it was fury she felt.

Certainly it was not envy. No, though what Claudia Moresby lacked in height she made up for in lushness. Beside Damon's lean, masculine frame, she looked exceedingly feminine. And if not beautiful, exactly, then very smart and attractive in a stylish sky blue afternoon dress of the finest merino wool set off by a Norwich shawl of exceptional beauty. Her coiffure, too, was excessively fashionable, a riot of very pretty curls nicely highlighted at the windows.

Miss Moresby did not seem to have noticed the windows that were the principal focus of the room, however. She had stopped to inspect a wing chair. "It does not seem this room has been attended to in an age," Alyson heard her declare with a dismissive sniff. "Just look, St. Albans, these chairs are so dusty, we cannot sit in them."

"I fear the servants venture here infrequently in winter," Damon replied, smiling down into Miss Moresby's upturned face. "And it would seem we had best take our cue from them, if you are not to catch your death of cold, Miss Moresby. These old windows allow as much cold air into the room as light."

He sounded very solicitous. He even patted Miss Moresby's soft, white hand. Alyson tore her gaze away. A lump had formed in her throat, and now she thought she could not get away quickly enough.

From over her shoulder Alyson heard Miss Moresby

say, delightedly, "You are too kind to worry for me, St. Albans, but I shall survive a little longer! I haven't had the time to admire the view these drafty windows afford. Why, I can see for miles! Is it all Whitcombe land?"

And preoccupied with listening to Miss Moresby greedily—at least to Alyson's mind—take stock of all Damon had to offer, Alyson very nearly ran into the remainder of the party. Damon had not walked off alone with the heiress. He had merely gone ahead. Miss Moresby had come to Whitcombe with her mother and her brother. Alyson wondered who had contrived for them, in company with Lady Edith, to fall behind the earl and the heiress. Had it been the heiress and her mother? Or Damon?

"Why there you are, my dear!" Lady Edith exclaimed when Alyson appeared in the doorway of the long gallery. "We sent in search of you, when the Moresbys arrived, but set off on a tour of the house before you could be found."

"I hope our unannounced visit does not inconvenience you, Lady St. Albans." Mrs. Moresby, a vague, amicable woman more like her son than her daughter, sighed apologetically. "The children insisted upon taking advantage of this break in our weather."

Kit Moresby smiled amiably. "Poor Mama! She suffers having two energetic children, but such a nice day after so many dreary ones did make us feel convivial. You do not mind, I hope, my lady?"

"Of course not." Alyson managed a quite pleasant smile. "I am pleased to see you."

"Have you encountered Damon and Miss Moresby?" Lady Bardstow asked. "We expected to meet them in the long gallery."

Alyson summoned her vaguest look. "They might be there, actually, though I did not see them. Just as I stepped through the doorway, I thought of something I had forgotten in the music room."

"May I escort you back for it?" Kit asked, his endearing solicitousness only requiring Alyson to lie again.

She shook her head. "No, though I thank you, sir. It is nothing important."

"Then, I hope you intend to join us," he continued, extending his arm. "When Claudia could not wait to have a tour of the house, we started without you, but the result is that we have missed you."

"Missed me?"

It was Miss Moresby. She and Damon had not lingered long by the drafty windows.

"Not you, sister dear," Mr. Moresby said with brotherly directness. "But Lady St. Albans."

Alyson turned to greet Miss Moresby only to find the girl was raking her with a swift, calculating glance. She did nothing to hide the conclusion she reached. When she lifted her eyes to Alyson, they betrayed a sly and galling pleasure. "Lady St. Albans." She smiled with false pleasure. "I can see you were not expecting company, and if we are interrupting you in some errand, pray continue with it. St. Albans has been entertaining us most admirably with a grand tour of Whitcombe."

As Miss Moresby turned a flattering and in all, intimate smile up to Damon, Alyson firmly put aside the niggling, unworthy regret she felt for having chosen a dress that was not only, as it had to be, a somber black, but in deference to the laborer's families she would soon visit, of the plainest wool as well.

Kit Moresby helped to restore her humor, negating his sister's summary dismissal of Alyson by pleading for her company. "I beg you will not leave us to our own devices, my lady!" he cried with boyish earnestness. "I think we are on our way down to tea now, are we not?"

He looked to Damon, unconsciously deferring to the person in charge.

"We are," Damon replied. Something in his tone caused Alyson to glance sharply at him, but she could not catch the expression in his eyes. He stood in the doorway, his large body blocking the light, and he gave her little time anyway, for he looked to Mrs. Moresby then. "Shall we descend to warmer climes, ma'am?" He courteously extended his other arm to her and swept off at once, leaving Mr. Moresby to follow with Lady Edith and Alyson.

To Alyson's shame, Mr. Moresby and Lady Bardstow were obliged to carry the conversation. Alyson would think she was paying Mr. Moresby the attention he deserved, only to find after a few moments that she had little notion what he had just said. Instead she knew how often Claudia Moresby leaned into Damon to give him a coy smile, and she knew to a nicety when Damon returned the girl an amused look she, not surprisingly, took as encouragement.

Nor could Alyson seem to keep herself from comparing Mr. Moresby to Damon, which was most unfair, as Kit was younger by several years, possessed a very different, far more amenable nature, and was built on much more slender lines.

He'd also a penchant for sartorial flights of fancy and that day wore shirt points so high, he had to turn his entire body merely to address one or the other of his companions. Of course Damon would not get himself up so absurdly, but if following the fashion fads was Mr. Moresby's only fault, Alyson thought him far ahead of the man who at least outwardly overshadowed him.

When at last they arrived in the Queen's salon, Claudia Moresby called out in a voice Alyson thought would have been better suited to the headmistress of a girl's school, "Lady St. Albans! We have just been speaking of Whitcombe's woods. We were admiring them from the long gallery, you see, but I told St. Albans that since your husband's death, there have been rumors circulating about a new laxness at Whitcombe toward poachers. Our gameskeeper at Alton Towers says you have had all the mantraps removed. Surely you do not condone poaching, Lady St. Albans? It is stealing according to the law, you know."

Alyson's mind went blank a moment, but not because she lacked an answer to Miss Moresby's accusation, or denunciation, however one preferred to characterize the

girl's ringing remarks. Alyson could not speak, because
she was struck dumb with shame. Thus far, she had
thought only of what Damon's coming would mean to
her, and Annie and Aunt Edie. No further. She had not
given a thought to the poor, local men merely trying to
feed their families in the dead of winter.

She did not dare to look at Damon, to judge his reaction to Claudia's remarks. She feared he would see how
important the matter was to her and act in opposition just
to spite her.

No, she was being unfair, Alyson conceded. Most
landowners believed as the Moresbys did. She had persuaded only the squire to her point of view. Even Ned,
when she had pleaded with him to remove the mantraps
that could break a man's leg in two, had held firm, saying the game in Whitcombe's woods was too important
to him to throw it open to all comers.

Making Miss Moresby wait until she had seated herself, Alyson glanced up to see there was once again a sly
gleam in the girl's eye, as if she not only knew very well
she had discomfitted Alyson but was pleased to have
done so.

Alyson calmed herself, reining in a temper Miss
Moresby seemed to have a positive genius for sparking.
There was far more at stake here than setting an unpleas-
ant girl in her place.

"I do not condone stealing at all, Miss Moresby,"
Alyson said quietly, even pleasantly. "I quite understand
that we could live in a state of chaos if any man could
make off with another's goods. I do, however, believe
strongly in justice. And I do not consider justice to be
the taking of a man's leg in return for a single rabbit,
however plump. As I should be a hypocrite, if I did not
act on my views, I did, indeed, have the mantraps removed. As to the poaching in Whitcombe's woods, it
may well be worse this year, but I would say that if so, it
is because we'd a wet fall and more crops rotted in the
fields than were harvested. As a result the local men had
little to sell at market and less to store away against the

bleak winter. In truth I cannot say I begrudge them a rabbit or two to keep their families from starvation. We, certainly, are not going hungry at the Hall."

"Indeed, we are not!" Alyson turned with no little surprise to Lady Bardstow. The elderly lady's throat worked rather nervously, but still she held her chin high as she came to Alyson's defense. "We had quite a nice pheasant last night that came from our own woods. And I do not believe I have heard our keeper, Michaels, complain of the lack of game."

"Of course you have not," Miss Moresby replied, softening her scoffing tone only little, in respect for Lady Bardstow's years. "He must know that no one in the county, but Lady St. Albans, would keep him on at his age. I doubt the old gray beard disturbs himself many nights to intercept poachers."

Michaels! For a half second, Alyson wanted to do physical harm to the pampered, well-fed, arrogant young woman who so casually denounced an old man who had never harmed her in any way.

Ice seeming to run in her veins, Alyson dismissed Miss Moresby and turned urgently to Damon. Hands curled into fists beneath her skirts, she met his black, piercing regard without flinching. "Michaels has been a gameskeeper at Whitcombe all his life, my lord, and knows the woods here better than any man alive. He is most, most capable. If there has been laxness, it has been at my orders. We have not needed much in the way of game this past year, while the need in the neighborhood, as I said, has been great."

Alyson held her breath. She could not read Damon's expression, could not tell what lay behind the penetrating look he gave her, could not tell what effect her speech had had, though she tried desperately.

The moment did not last long. Alyson's eyes remained fastened upon Damon's only a second, perhaps even less. Claudia Moresby spoke, addressing Damon and demanding his attention.

"What regimen will prevail now that you are the master of Whitcombe, St. Albans? Will you be lenient toward thieves?"

Despite Miss Moresby's insistent tone, Damon only slowly released his hold upon Alyson. When he did look to Miss Moresby, his expression changed. Quite gone were both the taut jaw and the piercing look in his dark eyes. Seeming even slightly abstracted, he shrugged his broad shoulders. "Having spent most of my adult life in the army, Miss Moresby, I know very little of the finer points of gamekeeping. I intend to learn, however. When I do, I can assure you, I shall make my views known."

He sounded every inch the earl. Alyson's hopes for a humane regimen at Whitcombe faded. She would not argue with Damon, though. She doubted she could persuade him to any point.

Miss Moresby, predictably, displayed more confidence in her persuasive abilities. "I advise you to speak to my father, St. Albans," she said. "We've game aplenty at Alton Towers!"

And mantraps to equal the game, Alyson thought grimly. Glancing to Damon, she found to her surprise he was watching her again. She wondered if he had read her disgust for the elder Mr. Moresby's attitude toward gamekeeping. But she could not tell from Damon's expression. Nor, when it came to it, was she given the time.

Nanny Burgess entered the room with Annie, only to stop short, when she saw guests were present. "My lady! I did not know you had company or I'd not have brought Lady Anne to you."

"I did not send word to you, Nanny," Alyson said, smiling with obvious fondness upon the plump little woman who attended Annie so very well. "I wished you to bring Annie, because I fully intend to beg the Moresbys' pardon and take her out as I promised." Extending her hand to Annie, Alyson addressed the people she considered Damon's guests. "I do beg you to excuse us. As I cannot know when the sun will return again, I believe I must honor my promise to her."

It was Mrs. Moresby that Alyson looked, and that lady nodded sympathetically. "Of course, Lady St. Albans. I particularly realize how very difficult it is to keep young ones entertained in winter."

"Come, Annie." Alyson led the child forward. "Make your curtsy and we shall go."

"But where do you go, Lady St. Albans?" Mr. Moresby inquired, after Annie had executed a charming, if slightly wobbly curtsy to the group. "Is it an outing for ladies only?"

"We've baskets for some of the laborers' families."

"What a Lady Bountiful you are, Lady St. Albans!" Miss Moresby remarked in an idle tone, though the look in her eyes was sharp as nails. "I imagine the peasants hereabouts must worship you."

"Actually, there is a shrine to me in the village," Alyson quipped so easily that for a moment, Miss Moresby stared, taken aback.

Then Kit burst into laughter, and Alyson fought an impulse to glance at Damon. And lost.

He was not pleased. He regarded her through cold, narrowed eyes.

She looked away at once and found Kit Moresby still smiling at her. "Bravo, my lady! Few people dare tease Claudia so. But what do you say? Would you and Lady Anne care for an escort? I should dearly like to come. I rode my horse over to Whitcombe and am quite independent of Mama and sister."

He looked so charming and amiable and good-hearted. She thought how pleasant it would be to have a companion along. He might even serve to distract her from thinking on Damon's reaction to her teasing of Miss Moresby.

When Annie, reminding Alyson that Kit had always been charming to her daughter, squeezed her hand and said, "Oh, yes, Mama! May Mr. Moresby come with us?" Alyson accepted his escort with a smile.

"If our outing does not sound too dull, we would welcome the company."

"No drive could be dull with two pretty ladies to escort," Kit assured her with a gallant flourish, and so they were off, leaving Miss Moresby behind with Damon, he of the cold, hard looks, whom Alyson swore she did not mean to think of for an entire afternoon.

Chapter 10

"Here we are almost returned to the Hall again, and I have yet to ask after your husband's gamecocks." Kit Moresby looked across Annie's head to smile at Alyson. "Did you sell them, Lady St. Albans? I should think Old Trojan in particular would have fetched you a good price at Aylesbury market."

Alyson was a little late in answering. She had been enjoying the feel of the sun on her face, for though the air was sharp with winter's cold, the sun felt warm and reminded her that spring would come again. Her baskets delivered, she had allowed her mind to drift and listened only absently while Kit teased playfully with Annie.

Or more correctly, Alyson had listened gratefully, and thought to herself that Mr. Moresby, for all his susceptibility to the latest fashion fads, no matter how uncomfortable, was a genuinely kind person. He had not been compelled to escort her and Annie about, yet he had offered to do so, likely thinking they both missed male companionship.

Pleasantly lost in musings that included some less flattering ruminations on Mr. Moresby's sister, Alyson realized a moment late that Kit had addressed her, and Annie made an answer before she did.

"Old Trojan?" the little girl piped. "But he did not go to Aylesbury market, Mr. Moresby. He's in the chicken yard in his very own pen."

Kit turned such a shocked expression upon Alyson, she had to stifle a smile. "He is in the chicken yard?" the young man repeated, evidently beyond words of his own. Then, finding them, he fairly sputtered, "But, he was a champion!"

To a degree Alyson understood Mr. Moresby's dismay, for Ned had shared his passion for the sport. When she had once expressed revulsion at the thought of watching proud animals fight each other to the death to her husband, he had laughed and told her she must not expect a man to share her refined sensibilities. "Gamecocks, like men, are bred to fight," he had said.

Still, she did not share their attitude. "Old Trojan is a retired champion now, Mr. Moresby," Alyson said firmly, though not without a certain sympathy. "And I should say he is a quite happy one. You ought to go and see how proudly he struts around his pen. He is quite the king of the roost."

But Mr. Moresby was no more to be persuaded than she. He did not even seem to have listened, for he asked, cheering visibly at the very thought, "Will Lord St. Albans fight him, do you think?"

Once more that day it was brought home to Alyson how little she had considered the full effects of Damon's becoming master at Whitcombe. "I cannot say, Mr. Moresby," she replied, trying very hard to keep her mouth from tightening. "I have not thought to bring the matter up with him. But tell me, do you go to the Rundels tomorrow?"

She knew he did. Mrs. Rundel had told her the Moresbys, along with a few other young people nearby, were to play cards at Littlefield Manor that evening. She only asked, as it was the first topic she could think of with which to distract Kit from Ned's gamecocks. She did not want him to mention them to Damon, who would, she imagined grimly, either fight them or sell them to someone who would.

In response to her question, Mr. Moresby assumed a slightly aggrieved expression. "To be sure," he said with a sigh, "I am considered one of the young people in our neighborhood."

"There are worse things to be considered," Alyson

said wryly, thinking of herself among the dowagers, though she and Kit were of the same age. "And I should think it would be rather fun," she went on a little wistfully perhaps, "to be a young man who has all the young ladies hereabouts fluttering their lashes at him."

Mr. Moresby laughed, not unpleased. "The young ladies hereabouts do flutter their lashes, I grant, and they blush readily as well, but not one is able to get out more than three words at a time. I would rather converse with a lady who has some conversation."

"Oh?" Alyson smiled. "You sound as if you've a *tendre* for some lady in particular, Mr. Moresby."

Alyson thought the young man meant to name the lady of his interest. He regarded her a moment, but then he smiled his ready smile and said, "Almost you tempt me to tell you my secrets, Lady St. Albans, but I cannot just yet. It is too soon."

"Ah, well, I will not protest. I know love has a schedule of its own." Alyson smiled in understanding, until quite suddenly she realized she was thinking how time had once seemed to stretch forever, not when she had been with Ned, but when she had been by the stream with Damon.

Alyson tensed, furious at herself. She could not prevent Damon taking over her home. By law he was entitled to it, but her thoughts she ought to have been able to guard.

Mr. Moresby did not notice the change in Alyson's mood. He was grinning at Annie, saying, "Perhaps I shall simply wait until you grow up, Lady Annie, and become as beautiful as your mother is. I do believe she will have your dark chestnut hair, don't you, Lady St. Albans?" he asked before Alyson could feel the least awkward about the compliment he had paid her.

Her attention directed to her daughter, Alyson smiled fondly. "I do believe she will." A burnished curl had escaped Annie's hood, and Alyson tucked it back. "Perhaps it will be a shade lighter. It is early to say yet."

"Dark fire is how the squire describes your hair, my lady, did you know?" Mr. Moresby asked.

"The squire fancies himself a country poet," Alyson said with a chuckle. "Dark fire, indeed. Ah, look here we are home safely with your assistance, Mr. Moresby. Will you accept another cup of tea for your pains?"

When Mr. Moresby declined the offer of more tea, Alyson and Annie waved him off from the stable yard. Alyson suspected he meant to go to the village inn, the Green Man, for something more substantial than tea, but whatever his reason she was glad he had elected not to linger. She had another errand she wished to carry out, one she wished to see to alone.

Annie was not so easily waved off as Kit Moresby, however. Having enjoyed her outing enormously, she did not want her mother to go out again without her, a sentiment she voiced most adamantly.

Alyson, however, had good reason to stand firm. "You would not enjoy this visit, pet. I cannot say I much look forward to it myself, but as I must go, I will, and you may stay behind to enjoy some of the petit fours Monsieur Fornet prepared for tea. Yes, I thought that bit of information might make you happier."

"I would rather go with you, though," Annie maintained, swiftly curbing her display of interest in the petit fours she did, in fact, enjoy especially.

"I am delighted you like my company so." Alyson kissed her daughter's brow. "Now off with you."

"Very well, Mama."

Annie turned, shoulders drooping pitifully. Alyson subdued a smile. "Save one for me?" she called out.

Annie kept her waiting only a moment. Then she turned to nod. "Yes. But only one."

Alyson chuckled, then hurried off to the stables calling for the trap again, and the one basket she had had the groom put aside for her. She had not wanted to say anything to Kit Moresby of this particular family she meant to visit.

They were squatters, the very lowest level of rural society, and people Kit Moresby's father despised as a group. More than once Alyson had heard him rail against squatters, denouncing them as thieves and ne'er-do-wells that should be scourged from the earth. Did he know of them, and she could not have put Kit in the equivocal position of withholding information from his father, Alyson feared Mr. Moresby would make haste to Whitcombe to demand that Damon evict them, without the least care that it was winter and the younger children might perish of the cold.

The law supported eviction. Squatters, as their name implied squatted upon land to which they had no claim, for they neither owned it nor paid rent.

The year before, just before he died, Alyson had persuaded Ned to allow the Sirls, the family in question, to occupy a patch of marshy, useless land for a month, until they found a better situation. When Ned died, and she was nominally in charge, she allowed them to stay on, though she explained she could not say what would happen when the new earl arrived.

Alyson had been particularly sympathetic to the Sirls because she knew the wife of the family, for Mrs. Sirls's father had worked for Mr. Haydon. Poor Jeanie. Alyson could not have denied her permission to stay. She looked to have aged at least a decade in the years she had been away from Whitcombe living with the itinerant workman she had married. Five children had come one after the other, but no steady work for Jim, her husband.

Nor had he found permanent employment when they returned to Jeanie's old neighborhood. The squire hired extra laborers as he could, but Mr. Moresby scoffed openly at the notion that it was his duty, given his wealth, to do the same. He'd laborers aplenty, he said, with those that lived upon his estate, and he would not expend so much as a farthing to hire additional people simply to give them work. It was bad for the poor to spoil them so, he said. It gave them to think they could demand anything they wanted.

Jim did have work that week, however. "Squire needs ditchin' done," Jeanie told Alyson.

"How is the baby this week?" Alyson asked as two of the children hauled the laden basket she'd brought them inside the makeshift, dirt-floor hut that was the family's only shelter against the cold.

"Better, m'lady. The medicine ye brought helped her, but now Jack's ill."

None of the children looked healthy. They were all thin as rails and far too pale, but Jack, a child of four, had a racking cough Alyson could hear even before she stepped into the dank gloom where he lay on a pallet that served not only as his bed but his brother's and sisters' as well.

"There is some soup in the basket should help him," Alyson said as she knelt by him and felt his warm forehead. "I'll bring you a posset of Mrs. Hobbes's, Jack. It should help you." To his mother, she said, "I'll bring more of the soup, too, as soon as I can. Have you wood enough?"

"We've some, but with the new earl comin' . . ."

Her voice trailed off, as she looked anxiously at Alyson. But Alyson could give her no reassurance. "I cannot say if Lord St. Albans will allow you to continue to take wood. I thought it best to let him settle in before I spoke to him. I must tell you, though." She hesitated a moment, then shrugged. They must know the truth. "He does not care over much for me, Jeanie. He may not listen to me at all. I must also warn you that I do not know how harshly he will enforce the game laws. In a discussion earlier today, he did not declare himself, only said he would study the issue. I shall get word to you, if he has mantraps set out again, but you would be wise to warn Jim that I may learn of the earl's decision only after he has acted."

Jeanie dropped her gaze, unwilling to admit that her husband did augment his family's pitifully meager food supplies with poached game. " 'Tis hard just now," was all she would say. "With Moresby not hirin' on any outside men, and the new earl not yet sayin' what he'll do, we're both afraid o' what's to come. Poor Jim. He takes it the worst, as the man."

She did not say more, but Alyson made a shrewd guess. "He is drinking again?"

Jeanie bit her lip. " 'Tis the only pleasure he has, ye see. But he leaves us so little."

She shrugged, trying to appear unconcerned, but Alyson saw tears glistening in her worried eyes. "I shall send Duggins, the groom, with another basket and wood, too. I can trust him to say nothing." Alyson clasped the other woman's shoulder tightly. "I wish I could do more."

Jeanie could only shake her head and whisper in a thick voice, "God bless ye, m'lady."

"And you, Jeanie."

Chapter 11

"*Mon dieu!* M'lord!" Monsieur Fornet, the Hall's demonstrative French chef threw up his hands and exclaimed aloud in the two languages at his disposal, when he saw the earl, himself, stride into Whitcombe's cavernous kitchen. In his own tongue he asked anxiously, "*Voulez-vous quelque chose,* m'lord?"

"No, no, I want nothing," Damon answered in English for the benefit of the rest of the staff, who like the voluble chef, had come to a complete, stunned standstill. Wryly Damon remarked to himself how six years before, when he had been only Mr. Ashford, he had visited the kitchen unremarked but for the younger kitchen maids. "I have not had the opportunity to greet you properly since I returned, Fornet. I came to do so and to compliment you on your fare. It is as excellent as I remembered."

"*Eh, bien!*" Monsieur Fornet beamed proudly as he executed a flourishing bow, despite the considerable paunch he had acquired in the course of his profession. "*Vous êtes très gentil,* Lord St. Albans. I thank you very much."

"You are most welcome, monsieur," Damon murmured, swallowing a smile. The portly man might cut a comic figure, but he was a master at preparing food, and Damon had no intention of losing him, never mind that his salary might have kept Alyson and little Lady Anne in a small cottage for a year. Damon thought he deserved one of the few unqualified pleasures that had come with his inheritance.

"Have you any special preferences, my lord?" Monsieur Fornet inquired, all business now.

Damon shook his head. "I have enjoyed everything, thank you, but I will confide that the cakes you served for tea today brought raves from the ladies."

"*Ah, oui! Les petits fours.* They are the favorite of my Lady Alyson. And La Petite. *Mais voilà! Elle est ici!*"

It was indeed Annie, popping through the doorway that led to the stable yard. She pulled up short, though, her eyes widening when she unexpectedly found herself the center of a dozen people's attention.

Monsieur Fornet came at once to her rescue. "*Bonjour*, Lady Annie! You have come for *les gateaux, non? Alors!* What would you? M'lord has come in regards to them, too."

Annie almost thrust upon him, Damon subdued a spurt of curiosity as to the whereabouts of the child's mother, who had not, as he had expected followed behind Lady Anne. "You have come for some cakes?" he asked, his smile strengthening when the little girl peeped shyly at him through her lashes. "I think I can assure you that you will enjoy them."

"Oh, yes!" she agreed, her shyness overcome by her enthusiasm. "Mama said Monsieur Fornet had prepared petit fours, and they are my favorites."

"I see. And will your mama be joining you for a plate of cakes?" Damon asked, seizing the opportunity to satisfy his curiosity as to Alyson's absence.

"No, my lord." Annie's expression underwent a swift and remarkable change. Suddenly her lower lip pouted, her little brow knit sorrowfully, and her eyes conveyed a great deal of misery. "Mama went out again, but she would not take me!"

Damon had so little experience of children. He took one look at the charming little girl's pitiful expression and found himself furious on her behalf, for he believed he understood very well why Alyson had returned Lady Anne home before she had completed all her errands. He did not, however, betray his anger to Annie. She'd only have been distressed by it, he knew and she appeared quite unhappy enough.

Acting on a sympathetic impulse, he grinned conspiratorially at her. "I cannot say I am sorry. Your mother's absence means there will be more cakes for the two of us. I may join you for your treat, I hope?"

"Oh, yes!" A delighted smile transformed Annie's elfin face once again. "I should like that very much, Lord St. Albans."

"Good. Then we are off to the library, if Monsieur Fornet will be so good as to have the petit fours sent there?"

As the chef was nodding, an approving twinkle in his eye, Annie suddenly caught Damon's hand. "But what of Nanny, my lord? She will be expecting me in the nursery."

"I think we may have Hobbes send word to her that I will bring you up in a little." Annie made no move to let go of his hand, and Damon found he rather liked the feel of her trusting hold, as they made their way by the rows of pots and pans hanging from the lofty ceiling.

"I've a matter of etiquette to discuss with you, Lady Anne," Damon said, adjusting his step to her smaller one. "I must confess I find all this 'lording' and 'ladying' rather cumbersome. Do you think you might address me simply as Damon this afternoon? Later, we shall ask your mother permission for you to treat me so informally all the time, but I think she will not mind, if you do so now. And perhaps I could address you as Anne?"

She was vastly pleased by the request, Damon could see when he glanced down at his young companion. "But everyone calls me Annie," she said with a piquant grin. "Anne was my grandmother's name."

"I should be honored to address you as your friends do, Annie. Ah, and here is Rowena, waiting for you at the door. Sit, Roe."

"She minds you!" Annie exclaimed in some awe when

the mastiff promptly sat and cocked her head, as she obediently awaited Damon's next command.

Damon regarded the dog blandly. "Yes, Roe and I have had a little discussion about who is master here at the Hall, and we have come to a mutually agreeable understanding."

Even the scullery maid, a sullen thing who spent her life on her knees, grinned, then exchanged a knowing look with the rest of the kitchen staff. None had had any question who was master at the Hall, but now, after watching the new earl with little Lady Anne, they'd a great many fewer questions as to what manner of man the master was.

"I trust you found no one in dire straits, my lady," Hobbes said, when he met Alyson at the door some while later and helped her with her pelisse and hat.

Alyson sighed, thinking of the family she had just left. "No one is on the point of death, Hobbes, but the times are very hard for some."

"You do what you can, my lady, which is a great deal more than most. If I may say so, that is why Whitcombe is such a prized place to work."

"Thank you, Hobbes." Alyson gave the man who had been at Whitcombe Hall far longer than she a winsome smile. "I am grateful to you for saying I do not merely play at being Lady Bountiful."

The moment she said it, Alyson felt a fool for having allowed Miss Moresby's remark to sting her so that she found it necessary to seek reassurance from her butler.

Still, it gratified her when Hobbes appeared utterly taken aback. "Lady Bountiful, my lady? I am not certain what you mean, but I assure you hungry people do not consider food a matter of play."

"No, of course not, Hobbes. I am weary and spoke foolishly. Is Lady Bardstow taking tea in her rooms, do you know?"

"She is, my lady, and invites you to join her there, if you wish."

Alyson did and spent a pleasant half hour with Lady Bardstow, discussing the elder lady's secret passion: the formal garden. Lady Bardstow wished to plant more roses, and if Alyson listened only absently, she did feel gratitude. For that little time, at least, she thought of nothing more serious than whether Timms, the head gardener, ought to plant red or white roses.

Unfortunately her reprieve could not last forever. No sooner did she leave Lady Bardstow's rooms than the Sirls came to her mind again. Abruptly she turned on her heel. She had thought to go to her rooms, but if she did, her thoughts would only continue to chase themselves about in her head. It was time she bearded the lion and tried to settle at least the Sirls' future.

When she stood before Damon's study door, however, Alyson thought of a thousand reasons to hesitate. Only the appearance of a maid down the hallway prompted her to use the hand she had raised.

Damon's response to her knock did not bode well. "Yes?" he barked impatiently.

As she had found necessary when she stood at Mr. Haydon's study door, Alyson took a deep breath to steady herself before she entered.

Damon was seated behind his desk, just as Mr. Haydon had generally been, but Alyson reacted so differently to the sight of Damon sitting behind his cluttered desk that she was taken by surprise. Her heart leaped almost painfully in her chest.

She flushed then, shaken by her response to the mere sight of him. He was not even looking impeccably turned out, but perhaps, she thought a little desperately, that was why he had affected her so strongly.

His black hair was dishevelled, a thick lock of it waving down onto his high brow, as if he had raked his hand through it repeatedly. His coat he had tossed carelessly onto the arm of a nearby chair, and he had dispensed with his neckcloth as well, she saw. The instant her eyes touched upon the opening at the throat of his shirt, where she could see bare, bronzed skin, she jerked her gaze away.

And met his eyes. If Alyson's self-consciousness did not die instantly, her sympathy for the difficult responsibilities that had been thrust upon him did. There was nothing tired about his black eyes. They gleamed with such a coolly mocking light, she flung up her chin, as if to ward off a blow.

It was as well she stood prepared. He spoke before she could, his tone as derisive as the expression in his eyes.

"Well, well," he drawled, rising with insulting tardiness. "If it is not the merry widow. To what, I wonder, do I owe the pleasure of this unprecedented visit? Have you come to upbraid me for consoling your daughter with sweets?"

"What?" Alyson blinked in surprise.

"Your daughter," Damon repeated, leaning across his desk for emphasis, his weight balanced upon his hands. He had been biding his time, waiting for her return and this meeting. Obligingly she had come to him, and with the evidence of her pleasurable expedition stamped on her face. Her ivory cheeks were tinted with just the hint of color, either from the sun or perhaps from the excitement of flirtation. His anger surged a mark higher. "You remember Lady Anne," he bit out, "the child whose outing you cut short. But of course, what five-year-old, even a charming one, would not make courtship rather awkward? With her between you and Moresby, you'd have found it most difficult, I imagine, to engage in the flirtations at which you excel."

He would twist anything against her! Alyson stared, but it was not fear she felt, as she had when she stood before Mr. Haydon. Without even needing to think on it, she knew Damon would not strike her. Anger flickered to life in her. "I do not know what delusion you are presently entertaining, my lord," she retorted as nastily as he, "but you are quite mistaken——"

"I met Annie in the kitchen alone!" Damon half roared. "She was nearly in tears because her mother had

seen fit to abandon her in favor of entertaining a beau.
Good God, what a thing to do!" His black eyes snapped
with contempt. "Are you so desperate to cast out your
lures to the first eligible man you see that you would disappoint your own daughter? And what a man! A bit
young, isn't he, my lady? But his father is wealthy as
Croesus, I forget!"

The flicker of anger flamed into an anger greater than
Alyson had ever known. Who does he think he is, she
said, nay screamed, to herself, the Sirls quite forgotten.
Who is he to judge me so harshly at every turn? He, who
scorns me for making the best of a situation I did not desire but thought I must live with all my life! He, who did
not precisely waste away after he left Buckinghamshire!
Who is he to say I may not flirt where I will, even if I
did not flirt at all!

The final straw for Alyson came when through the
mist of her anger, she heard Damon say, "But you are intent on enthralling him regardless of the repercussions
your flirtation will have upon others. And there will be
those repercussions, for even I, after only one evening in
company with the two of them, have guessed at Harriet
Rundel's interest in the boy. Did you close your eyes to
it? No, you do not care, do you? You've need of him and
his wealth."

"You are, as always, absolutely correct, my lord!"
Alyson flung at him, so angry white-hot words poured
out of her mouth before she fully knew what she would
say. "It must be the greatest comfort to you that you are
infallible. No! I am not quite right there. You are fallible.
Kit Moresby is not too young for me. He is my age almost exactly, and that is, as you have implied in the past,
quite a ripe one. And as to your point that I have not
considered the consequences to others, should I succeed
in attaching him, I must beg to differ. I have given the
matter considerable thought. And I have decided that
Annie must come first with me. She needs a father,
preferably a wealthy one. Mr. Moresby likes her very
well, and she returns his esteem; therefore I cannot be

overly concerned with Harriet Rundel. She is only seventeen. Seventeen!" Alyson blazed again, that Damon not miss the point. "And at seventeen she is far too young to have the least idea what love is, just as I most assuredly did not at that very same age!"

How satisfying it was to whirl away from Damon's furious expression, to slam the door upon it, and fly up the stairs to her room! Alone, still exercised beyond anything she had ever felt, Alyson caught sight of a silver hairpin box Mr. Haydon had once given her. Seizing it, she hurled it across the room at the wall.

Her missile went astray. It hit a porcelain figurine of her mother's, shattering the pretty milkmaid instantly, and at that, Alyson burst into tears.

Chapter 12

Alyson awoke early the next morning, but as it was Sunday, a day she had no pressing duties, she pulled her warm bedclothes tightly around her and stayed where she was. She'd little desire to rise and face either the day or Damon. She had not seen him since the scene they'd had in his study. She'd plead a headache to escape dinner.

Coward, she called herself that chilly morning. But she castigated herself with little force. The atmosphere at dinner would have been, at the least, grim. She couldn't have eaten, only made a play of pushing her food about on her plate. Far better to have been in her room, where she did not have to make even a pretense of eating. Bernie had scolded her, but Bernie was only a maid, and could be told, albeit gently, to mind her own business.

If only Damon could be dismissed so easily! But of course he could not, and the real reason she had not gone down to dinner was that she had not wanted him to see the evidence of her tears. She did not want him to know he had the power to hurt her.

Dear God, but he did have that power! A sudden image of him accusing her of abandoning Annie for naught but selfish reasons leaped into her mind before she could deflect it. Squeezing her eyes shut she tried to will it away, but the more tightly she closed her eyes, the more vividly she saw his black eyes gleaming with derision and his so very attractive mouth twisted in a sneer.

Alyson tossed relentlessly. She had not dreamed Damon would continue like this. In truth, she realized she had thought little beyond their first meeting. She had worried there would be a clash, had tried to anticipate what Damon would say and how she would respond, but she had not anticipated by half how deep Damon's disdain would be nor how irreversible.

And why had she so badly misjudged? A bitter laugh, if the wretched sound could be called a laugh, escaped Alyson. She had not imagined a person could fall so out of love—so completely out of love! She could still recall the feel of his arms around her, of his mouth whispering deliciously close by her ear that she was his Allie . . . and she had been married all the years between.

She bit her lip against another cry. He had not fallen prey to old feelings. Oh no. Or perhaps he had, but only to the very worst feelings he had toward her.

She drew a shaky breath. It hurt her that. It hurt her very much, more than she cared to admit. She did not want to feel the pain that was like a burning about her heart, did not want to feel the lump in her throat that robbed her of speech, or the aching tightness in her chest that constricted her breath.

She had loved Ned. She had! She had put Damon from her mind and heart when she married. She was no adulteress. She was loyal and true and paid more than lip service to integrity.

Then why did Damon's animosity distress her so? Because she did not like to be at odds with anyone! It was true. She was not one given to emotional dramatics.

And she had loved him once long ago in another world.

She swung herself upright so that she sat on the side of her bed. It was no crime she should wish an old love did not despise her! Why she felt this heaviness she could not know. He had upset her so, she could not think sensibly.

Her mouth quirked, though not with much humor. Dear heaven, she had neither acted nor thought sensibly the day before in his study. It appalled her, shook her, really, to think how . . . wild she had been.

She had never acted so in her life, spitting falsehoods at him in the hopes they might wound.

But he had accused her so falsely! She realized she was cold and shrugged into the dressing robe Bernie had laid out for her the night before.

Mr. Haydon had accused her falsely, too, but since she had left his house, no one had lashed out at her even with words. Certainly Ned had never accused her of anything, much less accused her falsely. She was not accustomed to such unfair treatment, had thought it far behind her. Little wonder she had reacted so . . . passionately. She did not care to be treated so again, could not accept it as she had with Mr. Haydon because he was her guardian, and she feared the pain of his birch rod.

What was she to do, then, until she could find some means to leave? She did not want to carry on again as she had the day before, though the response was justified. She upset herself too greatly.

Nay, he upset her. She must try not to let him affect her so. But she could not be certain she would remain coolly aloof, disregarding whatever he might say to her. She winced. No, she could not be at all certain. She would never have guessed she would explode as she had done the day before.

Well, then, Alyson decided, she must avoid him, just as she had been doing but even more carefully.

Unfortunately, to avoid Damon successfully, Alyson needed his cooperation, and she did not receive it that day. Only a few hours later he walked into the entry hall just as she and Annie descended on their way to church. Alyson nearly missed the next step.

"Hold tight, Mama!" Annie tightened her hold on her mother's slender hand. "I will not let you fall."

"Thank you, poppet. It would seem, I need assistance."

Alyson flicked her glance down to the foot of the stairs. Damon had heard them and was looking up. Immediately she looked away, but she had seen enough. He was not dressed for staying home. The faultless coat of bottle green, the elegantly tied cravat, and the dark kerseymere trousers could only mean he intended to join them in the Ashford family pew.

"Damon! You are coming, too!"

It was a measure of Alyson's distraction that she did not mark how her daughter had addressed him. She did note how he greeted Annie, however. For her daughter, he had a genuinely warm smile.

"I am. I could not miss my first Sunday, after all. What would the neighborhood think of me? Is Aunt Edie close behind you?"

"No, she has the sniffles. She said she would rely upon us to pray for her."

Damon's mouth quirked. "I see," he said, amused. "We had best go, then, if we are to importune on her behalf as well as our own. My lady?"

His expression cooled just as Alyson had readied herself for it to do, when he looked at her. Having determined he would no longer affect her as powerfully as he had done, Alyson refused to acknowledge the heaviness that settled around her heart. Instead, having no sense how her gesture accentuated the graceful slenderness of her neck, she inclined her head and proceeded without a word out the massive oak door Hobbes held for them.

"Oooh, the horses shine so!" Annie squealed upon seeing the four sleek bays before the carriage.

Behind them Damon laughed. From the corner of her eye Alyson saw he had shrugged into a caped greatcoat and clapped an elegant beaver hat on his dark head. Something caught in her chest, and she looked away before she could acknowledge it.

"It is the light reflecting upon their coats, makes the horses seem to shine, but you are right to admire the effect, sweeting," he said to Annie as he strode down the steps to her. "They are exceedingly handsome animals."

Annie spun excitedly about. "Mama! Your hair gleams

like the horses' coats! It is just as dark and with the same
sparkle in it."

Her daughter made her chuckle. "I didn't know that
my hair sparkled," Alyson remarked.

Annie tipped her head, studying the bit of her
mother's hair her rutched bonnet revealed. "It does not
sparkle, exactly. But it glows like the horses' coats."

"Ah, now I understand," Alyson said with a smile as
she glanced to the horses, whose dark brown coats did
seem to gleam with the suggestion of fire. "They have a
touch of red just as I do."

"And my hair will sparkle like yours one day, Mama!
Mr. Moresby said so."

With the mention of Kit, Alyson became once more
acutely aware of Damon, though she kept her gaze
averted from him. "Yes, I think it will, poppet," she said
to Annie.

But Annie's quick mind had already darted off to a
new concern. "Lord St.—" She clapped her hand over
her mouth suddenly and burst into giggles. "Damon, I
mean! Mama!" She rounded upon her mother in the next
instant. "Lord St. Albans said I might call him Damon
yesterday, if you approved. Do you?"

You ought to have called him Papa.

No! Alyson thrust the unbearable, disloyal thought
from her mind, and looked to Damon in her confusion.

He was watching her coolly. "I met Annie in the
kitchens after you dropped her off yesterday. In the
course of enjoying some of Monsieur Fornet's petit fours
together, we decided saying my lord this and my lady
that was tiresome, and agreed that, if you approved, we
ought to try a more informal footing."

After you dropped off Annie. He made it sound as if
she had pushed her child from the trap. But he meant to
be more than civil to Annie. She returned him a level
look not untinged with relief. "Of course, I approve. I
am glad you enjoyed your tea."

Alyson allowed the footman to hand her into the carriage and settled herself while Damon tossed Annie in, then followed himself to sit with the child between them.

"I wish I could drive a coach! It would be such fun to sit so high!" Prattling innocently, Annie confided gleefully to Damon, "Mr. Moresby allowed me to hold the reins of the trap yesterday. Do you think John would allow me to hold the coach reins?"

Alyson looked resolutely out the window and only heard Damon answer, "I do not. Four horses are far more difficult to manage than one, and he has no reason to curry favor with you."

"Curry favor with me?" Annie repeated perplexed.

Alyson understood, of course, and she tensed. If Damon meant to drag Annie into their conflict by disparaging either her or Kit Moresby, she would call to John to return Annie and her to the Hall at once.

"Yes," Damon said. "Just as Percival tried to curry favor with me yesterday during our tea by first rubbing against my leg and purring loudly enough that I am certain they heard him in the village."

"And we gave him a dish of cream!" Annie exclaimed in quick comprehension.

"You gave him the dish of cream," Damon corrected wryly.

"But I did not give Roe a cake," Annie defended herself, a more than slightly righteous note in her voice. "You said that cakes are very bad for dogs."

"As they are. You were right to be firm with Roe. You know better than she."

"Yes," Annie agreed quite complacently. "Roe is only a dog, and I am five."

"A world of difference," Damon observed dryly.

Mr. Moresby and the subject of currying favor forgotten, Alyson felt a smile tease her mouth, but she kept her gaze on the bare trees lining the drive. She'd not have disturbed the interchange between Damon and Annie for anything in the world. He was responsible for Annie now, and it could only be for the best if they were on good terms.

In the brief silence that followed the only sound heard was the carriage wheels crunching over the frozen drive. The steady rhythm lulled Alyson, soothing her so that she relaxed a little, though she sat in a closed carriage with Damon.

Annie had little appreciation for silence, however. After a few moments she looked inquiringly at Damon. He could not but smile even before she spoke. She wore a velvet bonnet of midnight blue that charmingly set off her delicate, elfin face. She owed her face to her mother, Damon acknowledged. Only her eyes were different, for they were brown, like all the Ashford's. And they lacked the shimmering, dangerous depths of Alyson's.

Damon cursed beneath his breath. He liked to have better control of his thoughts. "Yes, Annie?" he said, almost abruptly urging her on to speech.

"I only . . ." she bit her lip, hesitating suddenly. "Well, that is, I only wondered, do you like fighting cocks?"

"Annie!"

Alyson could not catch back her cry before it emerged, and her daughter turned quickly, a penitent look upon her little face. "Yes, Mama?"

Alyson gave her a rueful smile. The fault was hers, not Annie's, for she hadn't thought to ask Annie not to mention the cocks. "Nothing, my sweet. You took me by surprise, that is all."

"I only wanted to know if Damon will fight Old Trojan," she explained earnestly.

"Yes, I rather thought so," Alyson replied. She could feel Damon's gaze on her, and occupied herself with smoothing a lock of hair from Annie's shoulder.

"Is Old Trojan a dark family secret?" Damon asked finally, intrigued despite himself.

"No, no! He is a fighting cock." Annie looked to Damon, her eyes wide with appeal. "Mama does not want him to fight again, though he was a champion, and Mr. Moresby says he would fetch a great deal at Aylesbury market."

Alyson lifted her gaze slowly to Damon. She did not

know what to expect at the mention of Kit Moresby. She saw amusement, unqualified and unalloyed, gleaming in his black eyes.

"Truth from the mouth of babes?" he inquired so lightly.

She nodded, unable to take her eyes from his. "Old Trojan was one of Ned's fighting cocks. I retired him and all his cohorts rather than sell them to someone who would fight them again. I don't care for the sport."

"You won't make them fight again, will you, Damon?"

"It would seem your mother and I agree on something, Annie." Damon addressed Annie, but the faint, ironic smile lifting his mouth was for her, Alyson knew. "I never cared much for the sport, truth to tell, but after fighting myself, I lost even the little taste I once had for watching two chickens savage one another."

Alyson felt almost giddy. They had agreed upon something. And Damon had joked with her. Through Annie, true, but nonetheless, she heard herself chuckle aloud.

"I'd advise you not to speak so of their gamecocks to any of the gentlemen hereabouts. You will lose all standing with them, if you do. But I am certain Old Trojan would crow with pleasure. He seems most content to rest upon his laurels."

"A cock of the walk, is he?"

"Of the pen, perhaps," Alyson amended, as she found herself almost smiling again with Damon.

"He is very pretty," Annie went on, drawing Damon's regard back to her. "His comb is red as a holly berry, and . . ." she went on describing Old Trojan, unaware that her mother, at least, heard not a word she said.

Alyson was thinking how lovely the day seemed to be, though the air was cold enough to catch in her lungs. They were driving through a grove of beeches, the trees for which Buckinghamshire was famous. Huge, their thick trunks gnarled with age, they had always seemed to Alyson to stand like sentinels against the deadening gray of winter, for their light bark gleamed like old ivory even in the thinnest sunlight.

"Oh, look, Damon!" Annie cried, when she realized where her mother looked. "We are in the beeches. They are Mama's favorite trees."

And as quickly as that the day became merely another cold, unforgiving winter's day. Damon knew all about the beeches Alyson loved. It was in the grove of beeches by the stream that they had met, and under their fresh, green canopy that she and Damon had fallen in love. An unimaginable pain welling up in her, Alyson heard the young girl she had once been promising her love that he would take as much delight in the beeches in winter as he did in summer.

"Look, Annie, there is a falcon." To Alyson's own ears, her voice sounded thick and unsteady. Nor did she have the least notion whether the bird flying high in the sky was a falcon. She sought some distraction from the pain the beeches had caused and achieved it as Annie craned to look outside.

Carefully, without moving her head, Alyson cast a sidelong glance at Damon. There was no hint of humor softening his chiseled features now. He stared out his window, his handsome face looking as if it had been carved from stone.

Chapter 13

It was as they returned home from Whitcombe's charming stone church that Alyson realized how she could acquire monies of her own. A taut silence prevailed in the carriage, for Annie had fallen asleep with her head on her mother's lap, and Damon looked broodingly out his side of the carriage. Acutely aware of him and of the silence, Alyson began to chafe at her wedding ring, twirling it about without knowing she did. And then her hands stilled.

Of course! she thought. She could sell the jewels Ned had given her. Apart from their sentimental value, they meant little to her. She liked the pearls well enough, but she had only worn the other pieces to please her husband. Anyway, even had she adored flashing jewels, she'd no place to wear them now. She would not visit London again soon. And she did want her independence.

The very next day she would go to Aylesbury. She knew the jeweler to whom Ned had given his patronage. Excited, Alyson began to count the pieces in her mind: the ruby pin, the necklace of sapphires and diamonds, the diamond bracelet . . . how would she get there? The smooth, rapid flow of her thoughts jerked to a halt. The carriage was Damon's. She might call for it to go to the village or on a visit to one of her neighbor's, but could she commandeer it for a trip to Aylesbury without asking his permission?

Before she could decide what to do, they arrived at the Hall, where Nanny Burgess came bustling down to take Annie in tow. Alyson thought to trail after the pair who were discussing how thoroughly Annie had attended to Mr. Davenport's sermon, when Hobbes announced formally that Monsieur Fornet had prepared a special luncheon for her and Damon. "It being your first Sunday at Whitcombe, my lord," the butler explained.

Alyson's heart sank at the thought, but she went, neither wanting to raise gossip among the servants as to the possibility of a rift between her and the new master, nor, she admitted, desiring to disappoint Monsieur Fornet, of whom she was sincerely fond.

Luncheon went very much as Alyson had expected. Neither she nor Damon spoke. Without Lady Bardstow, they'd no one with whom to speak. She'd ample opportunity, therefore, to resume her silent debate about whether she should ask him for the carriage. Just at the end of the meal, when Damon had finished the meringue at which she'd only picked, she decided she must at least inquire if he intended to use his own carriage.

Damon had tossed down his napkin, when she gathered the courage to speak. "I should like to use the carriage tomorrow, to go into Aylesbury, if you've no objection."

"Aylesbury?" He gave her a cool, assessing look that served to tighten the knot that seemed to have taken up permanent residence in her stomach. "Odd. But I had thought to go into Aylesbury tomorrow. Oh, you needn't fear," he added mockingly, and she knew she had not kept the dismay his announcement had caused from her countenance. "I had thought, if the weather holds, to ride my mount. Tristan and I both need the exercise. But tell me why you wish to traipse off to Aylesbury of a sudden."

Damon leaned back in his chair and eyed her speculatively. Alyson resented his look, his tone, and his question. What did it matter why she wished to go? The point was she did wish to go. But she did not desire to antagonize him, and so she stiffly gave him the first excuse that came into her mind. "I've need of some clothes."

"Clothes?" Damon sounded well pleased in a grim

way by her answer. "I see. The grieving widow has decided to exchange her drab weeds for bold colors the very first moment she can. I confess I am surprised. I'd have thought you must realize how stunning you are in black. You'd all the gentlemen who attended church today, not to mention young Moresby of course, panting after you on the steps."

A full thirty seconds passed before Alyson could trust herself to answer. And then she could barely force the words by her clenched teeth. As usual he had misrepresented everything! Everyone spoke to everyone after church. He had been mobbed.

"Thank you for the gracious compliment, sir." She rose so abruptly, she caused her chair to teeter and almost fall. "I can only reply that as I understand gentlemen thrive on variety, I deem it necessary to trick myself out in the brightest hues Aylesbury has to offer. May you enjoy your day as much as I will."

Alyson swept from the dining room and went directly in search of Hobbes to inform him briskly that she would need the carriage brought around the next morning for a trip into Aylesbury. Before she sought her own rooms, she stopped at Lady Bardstow's to invite the elderly lady on the excursion, and then she went along to the nursery to inform Annie and Nanny Burgess of the treat in store for them.

Even were it to snow a foot overnight, Alyson was determined to go to Aylesbury the next day and buy the brightest dress she could find.

No snow fell at all, and she found shimmering silk of peacock blue. Lady Bardstow's eyes lit up the moment the dressmaker held the material up to Alyson. "What a lovely color!" she exclaimed. "I know it is a little bold for you, Allie, dear, but it quite sets off your vivid beauty."

It was the word *bold* that decided Alyson. Let him make what he wished of peacock blue, then, she thought, ordering an evening dress of it. She did not allow her anger to completely overcome her, though, For herself, she commissioned only two other quite modest dresses. When Lady Bardstow did not express surprise at the meagerness of her purchases, Alyson realized she, too, knew of Ned's unwise investments. They did not speak of Whitcombe's financial difficulties, however, only exchanged a look that said more than words, and then turned their attention to choosing a dress for Lady Bardstow and several for Annie.

Wearied by their morning spent selecting fabrics and patterns and standing for measurements, they repaired afterward to the King's Head Inn, a local institution, reputed to serve the most delicious pastries in all of Buckinghamshire.

They had gone some way across the market square toward the inn when Alyson realized she had left her reticule behind. Nanny Burgess offered to fetch it, but Alyson said she ought to be the one to pay the penalty for her negligence and hurried back to the modiste to find her reticule underneath a chair, where she had deliberately hidden it.

The jeweler's shop stood one shop down from the dressmaker's. After a quick look to be certain no one she knew watched, she ducked inside.

The jeweler, Mr. Luckett, recognized her immediately and came trotting out from behind his counter to bow repeatedly over her hand and tell her both how glad he was to see her and how sorry he had been to hear of her husband's untimely death.

Face-to-face with the eager, kindly man, Alyson found it more difficult to discuss her errand than she had anticipated.

"I . . . I have not come for the happiest of reasons, Mr. Luckett," she managed to get out at last, a flush rising to stain her cheeks. "I'll not be making a purchase today. In fact the reverse. You see, I wish to sell some of my jewelry as I have so little need of it now."

"Oh my dear lady, I am sorry to hear that!"

Mr. Luckett peered up at her through his thick spectacles, looking so sincerely sympathetic that Alyson feared for an awful moment her eyes might fill with tears. Quickly she withdrew a felt pouch from her reticule. "I've several pieces, all, I imagine, familiar to you."

Almost reverently the jeweler arranged the glittering contents of Alyson's pouch upon a velvet mat. "Yes"—he nodded gravely—"I do recognize most, my lady." A well developed sense of discretion decided Mr. Luckett against adding he even remembered the occasions upon which Lord St. Albans had come to select each piece for his young and extremely beautiful wife. "I can either buy the pieces from you today, or you may leave them with me until I can find a buyer for them. The latter course, if you can wait, will be the most lucrative, my lady."

With Annie to think of, Alyson could not act rashly. "I can wait a little, Mr. Luckett, but not indefinitely, if you understand."

His homely face creased with the deepest concern for her, Mr. Luckett inclined his head. "I do understand, my lady. I shall send word to you as quickly as I can."

"Thank you very much, Mr. Luckett."

Alyson fled the shop, feeling the tears pricking the back of her eyes. If only Mr. Luckett had not been quite so sympathetic! He knew how much the baubles had meant to Ned and had thought they must mean as much to her.

Now she felt the worst of wives. Without Mr. Luckett to prick her conscience, she had not recalled how Ned had presented her each piece, a pleased smile playing on his lips as he told her how greatly he liked to adorn her.

Ah, Ned! She bit her lip. He had been so kind to her, so good. Surely he'd not begrudge her the means to become independent.

Not watching what she did, indeed seeing nothing at all beyond the toes of her kid half boots, Alyson did not see the man who halted in her path. Her vision blurred by tears, she'd have walked into him, but he spoke.

"Well, well, my lady. The jeweler's as well as the dressmakers. It has been a busy day."

Damon—being hateful and mocking and derisive and understanding nothing at all. She flung her head up to tell him to take himself from her way.

But having just come from Ned's local solicitor and more bad financial news, Damon was in no mood to listen to anyone on anything, and he spoke first. "You are a fool if you think I'll foot the—"

He broke off so suddenly Alyson blinked and felt the tears shimmering in her eyes. "What the devil?" he said, frowning suddenly.

Perhaps it was the frown, perhaps it was that he spat out something close to an oath rather than an expression of concern, perhaps it was merely the raw state of Alyson's emotions, but whatever the reason, a surge of anger overcame her once again.

"You needn't concern yourself over a bit of dust in my eye, sir. I have overcome worse!" she snapped. "And as to the bill for the jewels, 'tis you are the fool. Of course I did not imagine you would pay for them."

An unholy light blazed to life in Damon's eye, and he grasped her arm before Alyson could think to escape him.

"There is a word for women who use their beauty to cajole baubles from green boys." His glittering black eyes impaled her, holding her in place as surely as did his hard grip upon her arm. "Be careful what you do, Alyson," he warned her in the same low, dangerous tones. "I swear to you, I'll not allow Ned's daughter to be sullied, because you cannot control your appetite for the trappings of wealth."

He left her then, abruptly, a muscle working in his jaw, before she could overcome the sick feeling that seemed to smother all her thoughts and make him some, any reply. Flinging her arm from him, as if even to touch her through her pelisse disgusted him, Damon strode off, leaving Alyson alone there on the public street, her hands clutched tightly before her.

* * *

Alyson made no mention of Damon, when she rejoined her little party at the King's Head Inn. She'd have betrayed herself had she. She could not think of him without clenching her jaw or feeling a wretched tightening in her chest.

She would not think of him therefore, nor of what he had all but called her, she decided, after she entered the private room where Lady Bardstow, Annie, and Nanny Burgess awaited her. She had done nothing but fume since he had left her. Fume and agonize. No and no! She would not think of him, and she certainly would not agonize another moment about his opinion of her. He was not worth the effort.

She did not succeed, really. All the while she was served the luncheon Lady Bardstow had, with Annie's assistance, ordered for them, Alyson had to fight a horrible innervating heaviness.

But she did fight, and she did try to appear eager for what was served, did try to laugh and to draw out the occasion. For one, it was Annie's first luncheon in an inn, a cause for celebration. For another, the more quickly they finished their luncheon, the sooner they would return to Whitcombe and its master.

It was not difficult to linger at the pleasant inn, really. The King's Head was cozy, with low-beamed ceilings, large, roaring fires in all the rooms, and mullioned windows that gave only a blurry, indistinct view of the outside. Savory soup and steaming pastries preceded succulent roast fowl. The wine was good and the apple tarts at the end delicious, and no one thought to ask after the weather.

It had taken a turn for the worse, the ladies discovered when they emerged from the inn, their pleasant luncheon finally finished. Dark, heavy clouds loomed high in the west, and a biting wind had begun to blow.

John, the coachman, expressed surprise as well. He had been enjoying his own luncheon and more than one

tankard of ale, but he gave it as his opinion that they
could outrun the storm, if they left immediately.

Alyson ought to have remembered old John had a rash
streak, and had, in his younger days, won Ned's father
more than one purse, racing the gentleman's coach and
four. John liked a good race, but this one he lost. An icy
rain began to fall only half an hour after they had left
Aylesbury.

Had it snowed, they could have continued, but when
the freezing rain hit the road, it glazed the surface with
ice. Unable to keep their footing, the horses slipped and
the coach began to slide out of control.

John righted it before it overturned, but he jumped
down to consult with Alyson. " 'Tis bad, my lady," he
said, his collar turned up against the sleet. "Worse than I
expected. There's Booker's Inn just ahead. Shall I stop
there?"

"Yes, of course, John," Alyson replied anxiously. "We
can make Booker's you think?"

"Aye, if the lads and I lead the horses. 'Twill take a little time, but we'll arrive safe and sound."

"Will we be all right, Mama?" Annie cried as John
stamped away into the stinging rain.

Alyson made a conscious effort to relax her hands.
She had not realized she had gripped the seat as they
began to slide. And she smiled at her daughter. "Yes,
puss, we shall be very well. John would not let us come
to harm." To Lady Bardstow and Nanny Burgess, she
added, "I could see Booker's in the distance when I
looked out. It is not far at all, and John has the grooms
and the footmen to help him with the horses."

They started smoothly enough, only to slide dangerously again after they'd gone a few yards. "Oh my!"
cried Lady Bardstow. "I have never stopped at Booker's,
but I do not even care if they've clean linen, so long as
we may get down from the carriage."

" 'Tis a clean inn, Booker's," Nanny Burgess spoke up
to say. "I've not stayed there myself, of course, but I

know others that have. They say it is a small inn but a proud one."

"I stopped for luncheon more than once with Ned," Alyson said. "Booker, the host, sets a good table, and I am certain he would use only clean linen. What will you have for your second meal in an inn, poppet?" she asked Annie to distract the child from the frantic shouts of the men outside in the cold.

Lady Bardstow and Nanny also joined in the game, naming what they might have for dinner, and adding the possibilities for breakfast. Annie was still trying to decide between scones for breakfast and muffins, when they turned off the road into the yard of Booker's Inn.

They were not the only people caught by the weather, Alyson saw, when John opened her door for her. Another coach was in the yard, and with pleasure she recognized it as Squire Rundel's.

Chapter 14

When Mr. Booker, the host of the small inn, showed Alyson and her party into the taproom, they found the squire and Harriet seated by the fire, warming their cold hands.

"Well, now, and it's an ill wind that does not blow someone some good, eh, Booker?" The squire rose with a laugh. A ruddy-complexioned man of comfortable girth, he held a glass of Mr. Booker's warm rum punch in one hand while with the other he motioned Lady Bardstow to take his seat. "I can vouch for it being the warmest in the house, Lady Bardstow, and just the thing to thaw your bones! Lady Anne, here is my Harry. You remember her, I hope?" Annie nodded slowly, made a little uncertain by the squarely built, bluff man she knew only a little. "Sit next to her, child, and Nanny will have room by you. While you, Missy"—he turned to address Alyson with a special smile—"shall draw your chair by me, here. Now then, we can all be comfortable as peas in a pod while we take warming drinks and shelter from this sudden storm."

As they awaited the return of Mr. Booker with refreshments, they heard why Harriet and the squire had gone to Aylesbury—she to visit an aunt and he to look at a cock and then everyone, even Nanny and Annie, had something to say about the storm, particularly how quickly it had blown up.

Just as Mr. Booker hurried in with tea and spice cakes for them, they heard another commotion at the door, and two more travelers blew into the room, bringing with them the smell and feel of the stinging cold air.

"Kit Moresby and Tom Brady!" The squire rose to announce the newcomers in a lusty voice. "Just what we need, a gentleman or two to even out our numbers."

The two young men were delighted to find company while they waited out the weather, and there were smiles all around as greetings were exchanged. When Kit Moresby saw Annie, he made a particularly great to-do. "Can it be Lady Anne I spy there near the fire?" He grinned broadly as she giggled. "I vow, my day is quite saved! I needed the sight of a blindingly pretty maid." With a flourish he lifted Annie's little hand to his lips, sending her into another fit of the giggles.

Alyson could not but be pleased that he attended to her daughter, but his efforts caused her uneasiness, too. She traced her unease to Damon and tried to dismiss it. Kit Moresby was not interested in her. Damon had mistaken the matter, as he had mistaken most others. In all the times the young man had come to the Hall, to visit Ned, he had never betrayed an undue interest in her. Granted, just then Tom Brady, who lived near Whitcombe, had been to the Hall, and knew Annie, too, greeted the child with only a smile and soft remark, but he did not know her so well as Mr. Moresby.

Then she heard him saying, " . . . in those dresses you'll be as pretty as your mother," and her heart sank a little. He had remarked upon her beauty in much the same way the day he'd escorted her and Annie to the laborers' homes.

Still she tried to assure herself, such a remark might well mean nothing at all. Other people remarked upon her looks. The squire was forever doing so.

As if he had read Alyson's mind, Squire Rundel turned from some byplay with Lady Bardstow to lift his glass of hot punch to Alyson. "Here's to you, Missy! You are the only girl I know grows lovelier with the years."

"Is that your way of saying that I am aging, Squire?" Alyson teased with a fond smile.

The squire gave a great laugh. "It is not, though I will say aging is the one thing we cannot stop, save by the most drastic remedy. What I did mean to say, as you well know, is that I'm deuced glad to have you to look at while I am stranded by a winter's storm."

"I second that sentiment fervently, Squire!"

It was Kit Moresby. He beamed a smile down upon Alyson as he pulled up a chair on her other side, and Alyson's heart sank considerably further. The Squire's praise was quite a different matter from Mr. Moresby's. Squire Rundel was like a favorite uncle to her. The one gentleman in the neighborhood Mr. Haydon had received regularly, he had prevailed upon Mr. Haydon to allow Mrs. Haydon to bring Alyson to visit him and his wife at the Manor from time to time. Alyson remembered those visits vividly, for there had been dogs to pet, cats to cuddle, geese to chase, and sweet tarts to eat. In short, much of what Mr. Haydon frowned upon as frivolous had been in abundant supply at the squire's house, and Squire Rundel, with his great laugh and merry eyes, had made certain Alyson had a taste of it all.

"You've eyes in your head, lad!" the squire exclaimed then in reply to Mr. Moresby. "O'course, you second my sentiments, but tell me what you and Brady were about in Aylesbury. Not lookin' at a cock, were you?"

Alyson could have kissed the squire for directing Mr. Moresby to a subject other than her. She did not want Damon to be right, and not simply because she wanted to be able to thumb her nose at him. Though she did like the young man, she had no romantic interest in him at all.

As Mr. Moresby explained why he and Tom had traveled to Aylesbury the day before, Alyson glanced surreptitiously at Harriet Rundel. Had Damon gotten that right? Did she feel more than a passing fancy for Mr. Moresby? Perhaps, Alyson thought, she could discreetly direct the young man's attention toward Harriet and away from herself.

Unfortunately Alyson could not discern Harriet Rundel's feelings. As Mr. Moresby made a long story of how he and Mr. Brady had gone to Aylesbury the day before to inspect a gelding they'd heard was for sale, Mr. Brady chimed in from time to time, and Harriet appeared to listen with equal interest to both young men. Perhaps she did seem a little easier with Tom Brady, but she knew him better, for his widowed mother owned only a small estate, and he could not jaunt off to town for half the year as Mr. Moresby did.

If Harriet was pleased with the dinner, where she had two personable young men more or less to herself, Annie was happy merely to be at the table, for it was her first time to be included with the adults. Listening intently to all that was said, trying to follow the conversation, her brown eyes wide and sparkling, she scarcely ate a bite. Looking beyond Annie, Alyson saw Lady Bardstow, too, seemed to be in high spirits, something the elder lady confirmed when they retired to their rooms after dinner. "It was a very nice evening, was it not, Allie? Dinner seemed very like a party, really, with Kit Moresby so amusing and Tom Brady so very personable. There was nothing wrong with enjoying ourselves, do you think, my dear? Given that we are still in mourning, I mean."

Seeing from Lady Bardstow's faint frown that she was, indeed, a little anxious, Alyson shook her head. "Of course not! We may not seek out entertainment while we are in mourning, perhaps, but we certainly may enjoy ourselves with friends chance met at an inn during a winter's storm."

"You are the most reasonable of young women, Allie," Lady Bardstow replied on an affectionate sigh. "You've put the matter so well, I shall sleep the sleep not only of the weary, but of the just as well."

Alyson laughed. "We'll not be able to wake you until noon if you sleep so well."

"I doubt we shall be able to leave before then anyway. "I shall help you with your dress now, if you wish," Lady Bardstow added, after Alyson had helped her into a nightgown provided by Mrs. Booker.

Alyson shook her head. "No, thank you, Aunt Edie. I'll not retire quite yet. I've something I wish to discuss with the squire."

During dinner it had occurred to Alyson that she might speak to the squire about the Sirls. If he had no position for Jim, perhaps she could persuade him to plead their case to Damon, for it was a certainty that Damon would listen to the squire before he would listen to her—on any subject.

To her pleasure she found Squire Rundel sitting alone before the fire when she looked into the taproom. Pleased to share a quiet moment with him, she allowed him to persuade her to take a glass of claret while he enjoyed his hot rum punch, and she did not rush to bring up the Sirls, when Squire Rundel asked after Rowena. "I hope she is well, Missy? She's a fine, fine animal. Did you know, I had her in mind for you the minute I saw her?"

"And I thought you only recollected me when Mrs. Rundel said she would not have a small horse in the house," Alyson retorted.

The squire roared. "She did say those very words! Mrs. Rundel rarely gainsays me, you know, but one look at the mastiff, and she was prepared to leave the Manor. Tell me, how does the new master at the Hall get on with Roe?"

Alyson was grateful Mr. Booker came then. He gave her a reason to look away from the squire, who for all his bluster was a shrewd man.

Her encounter with Damon on the public street in Aylesbury thrust to the furthest reaches of her mind, she replied composedly after a sip of her claret, "I would not say Lord Damon raves about Rowena, Squire, but he tolerates her. He has made the very reasonable rule that she must be confined when guests come."

"Most reasonable," the Squire agreed, his ruddy, good-humored face creasing into a boy's smile. "I recall the effect Roe's attempt at a greeting had upon Mrs. Brady. The poor woman screamed loudly enough to be heard in Aylesbury."

Poor Mrs. Brady, Tom's mother, had indeed screamed with terror when Roe had come bounding from the stable yard, eager as the puppy she was to greet a newcomer. Alyson shook her head ruefully. "Even when Roe collapsed upon the ground, her head between her paws, Mrs. Brady would not quiet."

"I've the strong suspicion, she will take on so again shortly, but with a good deal more reason this time," Squire Rundel said.

"Has Tom bought a stray mastiff?"

The squire chuckled, but when he shook his head, he sobered. "The lad's acquired something far more troublesome than a mere dog. He's gotten himself a debt. Last night in Aylesbury, when the lads met up with friends of young Moresby's one thing led to another, and they ended in deep play. Moresby lost, but he can afford losses. Tom cannot. Mary Brady hasn't five hundred stray pounds."

"Five hundred pounds?" Alyson repeated stunned, for Mary Brady had several children to support.

"Aye." The squire wagged his head unhappily. "And 'tis Moresby's fault, to my way of thinking. He's old enough to realize not everyone was born to his wealth. He ought not to have taken Tom into company that would play so deep. Ah, but here the lads come back now."

When she, too, heard the young men's voices in the hallway, Alyson bit her lip in vexation. Supposing them gone to bed when they were not in the taproom, she'd indulged in idle chat with the squire and neglected the Sirls.

"Well then," the squire greeted the young men as they stamped through the door. "How were your horses?

" 'Tis always wise to see to them yourself when you travel without a groom."

"I'd like you to take a look at mine, if you would Squire," Tom Brady said. "He's favoring one leg, and neither Kit nor I can see why."

The squire nodded good-humoredly and heaved himself up from his chair. "A rare pleasure it was, Missy, to have you to myself. Rest well, and I shall see you off in the morning."

Before Alyson could draw breath, he ambled from the room after Tom Brady, who waved his good night. Taken aback though she was to find herself alone with Mr. Moresby, Alyson did not excuse herself at once. If she had indulged herself at the expense of the Sirls, she would not be so remiss on Mrs. Brady's behalf.

"What an unexpected pleasure!" Mr. Moresby was saying. "I shall call for Booker to bring me a glass of punch and join you!"

"You may call for your punch, Mr. Moresby, but I have nearly finished my claret, as you can see." Rising from her seat, Alyson held up her glass. "Before I go to my bed, however, I've a bone I wish to pick with you."

"Never say I have displeased you, Lady St. Albans!"

The young man appeared so sincerely distressed, Alyson only just kept from wincing. Alas, it began to appear that Damon had been more perceptive than she.

"It is on Tom Brady's behalf that I am concerned, Mr. Moresby," Alyson said levelly. "The squire has told me how much he lost playing with you and your friends in Aylesbury. It is a sum his mother can ill afford."

Mr. Moresby looked startled. "I . . . I didn't think."

"In truth it was Mr. Brady's responsibility to know what he and his family can afford, Mr. Moresby, but in future, if you would be a true friend to him, you might suggest smaller stakes."

"I shall do it, of course," Mr. Moresby said so earnestly that Alyson not only believed him but realized as well he truly had not given thought to the kind of stakes Tom Brady could afford. "Perhaps I can even think how to lose deliberately to him in our next game, for though you have spared me, I can see how wrong I was not to realize Tom's less to lose than I. You will not think the worse of me, I hope, my lady? I would have your good regard!"

Quite suddenly, before Alyson anticipated any such thing, Kit Moresby was bending over her hand, lifting it to his lips, while she tried hastily to think how to say she thought very well of him without leading him to believe she thought too well. She began to murmur something, she could not have said quite what, as she tried to extract her hand from his firm, eager hold.

She never heard the footsteps at the door. Had she, she'd have assumed the squire and Tom Brady had returned. They had not.

The door opened, and Damon stepped, unannounced, unlooked for, and unwanted into the room.

Behind him hurried Mr. Booker, but Damon paid the landlord no heed. He had pulled up short, when he caught sight of Alyson.

Her eyes flown wide, Alyson stared back at him, frozen, until Damon flicked his glance down to the hand Mr. Moresby still held. She had entirely forgotten Mr. Moresby for that half second, and his hold that now felt as hot as a brand.

"So," Damon said, taking in Alyson's other hand as well, the one from which her glass of claret dangled. "You are quite safe, my lady. I worried when I realized at last how bad the roads had become and set out to look for you. But I see you have landed on your feet very nicely. Moresby."

Alyson stepped forward, forcing Mr. Moresby to release her hand. She heard the young man return a stammered greeting to Damon, and she put the blame for Kit's obvious unease where it belonged. Damon may have spoken casually enough, but there was no friendly gleam warming his expression. On the contrary there was a flat look in his black eyes, and his nostrils were flared, as if he'd found the prey he'd scented.

She was the prey, Alyson knew—twice condemned in one day. She would not have Kit suffer for anger really directed at her. Therefore she stepped forward. But she took only the one step. Damon returned his regard to her, as she intended, but she did not intend, when their eyes met that the air between them should seem to crackle.

She stopped where she was. "I am grateful you concerned yourself with our safety, my lord." Her voice sounded stilted, but Alyson could not speak more naturally, as her blue-green gaze clashed almost violently across the space of five feet with his black, so forceful one. "As you say, though, we managed quite nicely. We have been a merry group, in fact, for the squire, Miss Rundel, and Mr. Brady are here as well," she added, and if there was a defensive note in her voice, the light in her eye was defiant.

As she had expected, the information did nothing to change Damon's opinion of what had taken place at Booker's Inn. His mouth lifted ever so slightly, ever so contemptuously, at one corner.

Before he could say anything, however, they heard the front door of the inn slam, and the squire call out to Mr. Booker.

Alyson took advantage of the distraction. "I hear the other gentlemen now and shall leave you both alone to enjoy them, as I find I am weary. Good night, sirs." She turned with careful deliberation to smile at Kit Moresby before she departed the room without another glance at the tall dark man of whom she was far more intensely aware.

Chapter 15

The party stranded at Booker's Inn slept late the next morning, the gentlemen because they had partaken of their host's justly renowned punch until well into the night, and the ladies because they saw no reason to bestir themselves with the roads still treacherous.

When Damon left his room, intent upon breakfast, he heard only two men's voices coming from below, Mr. Booker's and the squire's, and promptly requested a passing maid to bring his coffee to his room.

He had reason for his retreat. The squire was a genuinely good fellow. Damon did not doubt it, but the man too often spoke of Alyson, whenever he got a moment alone with Damon. He had done so the night Damon had been presented to his neighbors at Littlefield Manor, and he had done so again the night before.

"I must tell you. St. Albans, I was deuced glad to hear you'd enough concern for Missy to take to icy roads to look for her!" the squire had exclaimed, not slurring a word, though Damon could tell by the droop of his eyelids, he'd had no little to drink. "I've always been that fond of the girl. She was a lovely thing even as a child, o'course. But true beauty comes from here." Squire Rundel had thumped his chest, and if he got the side of his heart wrong, Damon did not mistake his meaning. "She might well have become a cold and bitter woman. Her stepfather was hard as that on her. I'll not say all I could on Haydon. He'd his good points, but when it came to his dealings with that young girl. . . ." The squire shook his head direly as he took another draft of his punch. "Ah well, 'tis not for me to judge him. Another will. My point is that Missy kept a rare sweetness about her, and a sense of humor, despite the despot and despite the loss of her mother and her husband. It's been hard for her, though. It couldn't be otherwise. Her mother . . . well, there was a close bond there. Too close, perhaps. I thought at times Mrs. Haydon depended on her overmuch. Haydon knew it, too."

He fell silent, frowning at some private thought. Damon found himself sitting very still, as if he waited tensely for the squire's next insight. The realization made him angry, and he stirred abruptly.

The squire roused at once and looked apologetically at Damon. "Strike me down, lad! I'm rambling on about ancient history that's of no interest to you. I'm sure. You'll want to know no more than that your cousin doted on the girl and would be pleased as this delightful punch in my glass to know you've taken her under your wing. You'll forgive an old man half in his cups, I hope?"

Damon pronounced the squire forgiven, but found himself less lenient later, in his room, when he could not force himself to sleep for thinking on what the man had said.

The squire was the second person to call Haydon hard and imply he'd been unreasonably strict with Alyson. Though he had had only two interviews with Alyson's stepfather, Damon accepted the first verdict readily, and as to the second . . . he conceded he believed it as well. Still, he could not credit that Haydon would have dragged her to the altar. Had she held firm, her stepfather would have relented in time.

She had not held firm, either because she was weak willed or because she was avaricious and desired a title and ready wealth, or both. Damon thought that last the case.

She had certainly not resented the life she said had been forced on her, far from it. She had made herself quite cozy with "dear" Ned. Of course he had doted on her.

Damon stalked irritably to the fireplace. The room was cold and his pillow hard as a rock. How was he supposed to sleep? He kicked the fire, glowering at it.

Damn Ned.

Damon kicked the fire again, harder. Actually he had always liked his elder cousin, though he had not known him well due to the difference in their ages. Ned had been as pleasant as could be, amiable, good-natured . . . and a doting husband. She'd thrived under his dotage, too. Damon gave a harsh grunt. Of course she had. Anyone woman would. And grown plump or at least plumper or demanding in manner, or perhaps, imperious with the servants or . . . damn and damn again! Damon swung away from the fire. She hadn't grown plump—at all. And she wasn't arrogant. The only imperious creature in the house, in fact, was the damned cat. She showed everyone—but him, of course—the sweetest of tempers. As to her looks, Damon's mouth tightened. As to her looks, he addressed himself grimly, she is lovelier than when you fell in love with her and thought her the loveliest girl you've ever seen.

And what does that prove? That she is a brighter, hotter fire, and will burn you more painfully even than she did before.

He reminded himself how he had found her so cozily ensconced in the taproom, drink in hand, with the so-wealthy and so-interested pup.

The memory did not serve to settle Damon's thoughts, however. For a moment all he could remember was the impulse he'd had to take Moresby by the throat and fling him from the room before he turned his attention to the pup's lady.

And what would you have done then, Damon asked himself. Suddenly he swore and slammed his hand down so hard on a table by him it swayed dangerously. He went to bed immediately, refusing to think another moment on Alyson or that the first thing that had come to his mind to do to her was seize her to him and plunder her mouth so ruthlessly and completely with his that she would never think of Kit Moresby again.

By the time Damon had finished two cups of coffee, the rest of the party had assembled at breakfast. At least Damon received the impression everyone was present. He did not have time to count heads, for Annie spotted him even before he stepped through the open doorway, and with a cry of surprise jumped from her seat to run into his arms.

"I did not know you had come, Damon!"

"I came late, poppet, to assure myself you were safe."

Over her head Damon met her mother's eyes. Witch. Despite the late hours she had kept and the drink in which she'd indulged, she looked beautiful, her eyes clear, very clear. He could see the defiant light glowing in them from where he stood, holding her daughter's warm, innocent body against his, and battling an ache in his chest that was unlike anything he had ever known.

Then, seemingly an eternity, but likely only a moment later, Damon heard the clear, carrying voice of Claudia Moresby. Surprise as much as anything lifted his gaze to her, and the world seemed to right itself.

He registered the corseted bulk of Miss Moresby's father beside her, and the others as well, all looking at him. He smiled, put Annie down, walked hand in hand with her into the room, and did not again look to the end of the table where the child's mother sat.

Miss Moresby—and she received a particularly engaging smile—made it easy for Damon to look the other way. She addressed him energetically. "I'd never have taken you for a late riser, St. Albans! Father and I have had the time to come all the way from Alton Towers."

Mr. Moresby nodded vigorously to Damon's look of considerable surprise. "Yes, the weather lifted as quickly as it came! 'Tis no spring day by any means, but the roads are clear again. Puss and I came out quick as we could to assure ourselves the boy was all right."

The "boy" flushed. Damon couldn't blame him. Kit was not that young. Still Damon had to fight an overwhelming impulse to catch Alyson's blue-green eyes and smile nastily, the memory of how he had found her closeted with "the boy" suddenly flooding his mind. When Miss Moresby once more routed his demons, Damon could not but return her another brilliant smile.

"The morning was so fine in fact, St. Albans, and our ride so exhilarating that Papa and I thought to repeat our experience tomorrow by getting up a party to course hares at Alton Towers."

Later as they sped smoothly home to the Hall over the roads that had cleared almost miraculously, Lady Edith gave Alyson a curious look. Alyson guessed the cause of it. She had done only one curious thing that morning.

"Are you looking at me so, Aunt Edie, because you recall that I have said more than once how I do not have a vast fondness for chasing small animals to their doom?" she asked wryly.

Lady Bardstow colored faintly. "Well, I did, ah, wonder, my dear. You have been most adamant on the subject in the past."

"I have," Alyson admitted. "And I can assure you I've not changed beyond all recognition. I am going for the exercise involved. I find I am sluggish when I do not get out and about."

Lady Bardstow's brow cleared, and she gave it as her opinion that exercise was as important for a person's spirit, as for the body.

Alyson agreed and they'd a pleasant conversation on the benefits of exercise, during all of which Alyson was berating herself for being the worst of liars, and to a dear friend at that.

She could have walked around Whitcombe's lake for exercise.

She would course hares on the morrow for two reasons, and neither had the least to do with exercise. First, when Kit Moresby had invited her to join the group, she had felt Damon's gaze shift to her. He had not glanced

her way once that morning, but for the moment after
Annie had clambered up into his arms. Alyson did not
much want to think of that moment. When she had
watched Annie run into his strong arms, she'd felt a
yearning so strong as to be painful. It was a brief pain,
though. She'd then looked up and her eyes had locked
with Damon's.

His gaze held none of the tenderness he accorded
Annie. Dark and brooding, it reminded her forcibly of
their two meetings the day before, of the ugly things
he'd said or implied; of the dangerousness of his mood
when he had come upon her with Kit Moresby, and had,
of course, jumped to the wrong conclusion.

So when Kit Moresby had invited her to course hares,
and she had felt Damon's gaze upon her, Alyson had
been seized by the impulse to defy him as blatantly as
she could.

But there had been one more actor, or actress, to
weigh in. Before Alyson could answer, Miss Moresby
spoke up to inquire, skepticism and condescension coloring her voice, "Do you course hares, Lady St. Albans?"

To Alyson her tone had implied she imagined so poor
a sport as Lady St. Albans surely did nothing so vigorous and amusing.

"Not often, Miss Moresby, but I should like to go tomorrow very much," Alyson had heard herself say,
though, as she did, she could scarcely credit her words.
Not only did she not care to chase some poor rabbit to a
bloody death, but she did not want to give Kit Moresby
the wrong signal.

Had she? Alyson felt sickened by the thought. Nay,
that was not quite right. She worried about Kit Moresby
and his possible interest in her, but it was Damon's inter-
pretation of her relations with the young man that made
her ill.

How could he have said such things to her as he had
said on the street in Aylesbury? She had been so tired the
night before at Booker's Inn, she had fallen asleep al-

most instantly. Not so, when she was returned to Whitcombe. Safe in her own bed, she lay wide awake recalling every scathing word he had said and the look in his
eye when he had found her and Kit Moresby in the taproom!

She had been startled to see him. Painfully so, of
course, because of their earlier encounter and of Kit. But
she had remembered Kit late, she was too honest not to
remind herself.

She had remembered everything late when she had
turned around and unprepared saw who filled the doorway! Abruptly Alyson flung out of the bed in which she
had been lying, wide-eyed. But she could not forget that
moment, no matter how quickly she moved. A blasted
thrill had shot through her before she fully took in his
expression and remembered everything. Then the thrill
had turned to anger, but before that . . .

Very well! She pulled on the dressing robe Bernie had
laid out for her. For that one instant, when she had been
taken off her guard, a thrill of pleasure had shot through
her at the sight of him.

Swiftly she jerked a blanket from the bed to wrap
around her legs when she sat down at the piano in the
music room and, bundling it under her arm, fled her
room and her thoughts.

"You may as well abandon that chair, you wretched
witch's familiar." Damon eyed Percival darkly. "As master here, I am not of a mind to discomfit myself for your
sake."

Damon had built a roaring fire in the library, where he
intended to read himself into such a stupor that he would
fall immediately to sleep, when he took himself to his
bed. He had been selecting his book, his back turned to
the door, when Percy, demonstrating his acute sensitivity
for comfortable circumstances, streaked into the
warmest room in the house and made unerringly for the
most comfortable chair in it.

In response to Damon, the cat suddenly lifted its head and looked alertly to the door.

"A clever ploy, old man, but it—"

And then Damon was listening, too. He could not say what disturbed the stillness that usually prevailed in the house at one o'clock in the morning, only knew something did.

Once in the hall, however, he distinguished the notes of the piano. Percy darted ahead of him and reached the music room first, racing inside to the concealing shadows before Damon arrived at the open door.

She had lit a brace of candles. They stood upon the piano, illuminating her, though Damon had not needed a light to identify the only person in the house who would be up after midnight playing the pianoforte.

She sat with her back to him, her dark chestnut hair for once unbound, and cascading in all its heavy, curling glory down her back. In the light of the candle the tumbling mass seemed to shimmer with fire.

He had had no inkling she played well enough to rivet him in a doorway. Or perhaps it was the sight of her hair that riveted him—and the willowy waist, her sashed dressing robe defined infinitely better than her high-waisted dresses.

Whatever the reason, Damon stayed, her music filling the air all around him.

He learned after a little that Alyson had high expectations of herself, for when she made some undetectable error, missed a note perhaps, Damon could not have said, she groaned, stopped, then started again.

Only to stop abruptly a moment later and swerve around. "Who? Ah!" Alyson cried, recognizing Damon though he lounged in the dark, one shoulder propped against the doorway and his arms crossed over his chest.

Her sound of recognition was not a happy one. Damon's mouth lifted sardonically at one corner. "Not pleased to have an audience, my lady?"

He had intruded into her sanctum, and she had to sit still a moment, gathering herself. Then she said distinctly, "Not this audience, my lord. You wish only to criticize me."

How little you know, my lady.

Damon rejected the sentiment the moment it occurred to him. Instead, he said, never taking his eyes from her, "I have reason to criticize you, I believe."

Alyson stiffened. She did not know how he meant the remark. He had found so many reasons to criticize her, nor could she use his expression as a guide. She could not see Damon's face clearly. The flickering light of her candles only revealed the outline of his powerful body in the doorway.

But in the end, she decided, there was really only one issue between them. "You have reason to ask for an explanation of what occurred that summer. I will grant you that a thousand times over. But I would dispute to the end that you've the right to assume that you know what occurred."

She looked very beautiful and not a little brave, facing him, her slender figure erect, her hands resting on either side of her upon the piano bench, and her chin up ever so slightly.

"All right then," Damon said evenly. "What is your explanation?"

Alyson stared a moment, taken by surprise. Unprepared, she fumbled for where to begin, then with an impatient movement of her hand began at the beginning. "Mr. Haydon had already accepted Ned."

"How convenient."

"It's true!" she flared, resenting that he should mock her so quickly. "They arranged the match in December."

"And no one thought to tell you?" Damon retorted caustically, suddenly levering himself away from the door and bearing down upon her that she might see the skepticism on his face as well as hear it in his voice. "Not even your mother?"

"No!" She fought to keep her back straight, though he stood over her, threatening her with his size if nothing else. "Ned and Mr. Haydon believed I was too young to be broached on the subject of marriage."

Black eyes held blue-green eyes for a long moment, and then he said softly, "Perhaps they were right."

Alyson felt herself flush. "I tried to resist their plans. I swear it!" She leaned forward, her hands gripping the edge of the piano bench. "I swear it! But Mr. Haydon . . . was not one to listen. He threatened me with never seeing my mother again, if I wed you."

There was a close bond with her mother. Mrs. Haydon depended on her, and Mr. Haydon knew. So, or nearly, the squire had spoken. But would any man threaten such a thing?

Damon did not know. He knew only what he then said. "If Haydon did threaten such a thing, and even if he meant it, you did not have to accept it."

"I was seventeen!"

"What excuse is that? You said, as I recall, you were prepared to entrust your life to me. And yet you would not trust me to see you over the first obstacle!"

"You did not know Mr. Haydon!"

"It was you I did not know!" he shot back fiercely. "You revealed nothing to me of Haydon, said not one word about this demon of a man, though you made me think you had opened the hidden recesses of your soul to me. Such was the trust you had in me. And at the first test of your faith in me? You took the easy way, and all that is to say nothing of your earnest protestations of love! May I be so bold as to ask what happened to that 'eternal' love when you cozied up to dear, doting Ned and had the marriage of the century?"

Alyson felt that insidious, paralyzing heaviness settle over her again. Ned. Always there would be Ned between them. Ned, whom she had loved. Ned, who was, less than a year after his death, only the gentlest and vaguest of memories.

Alyson bowed her head. She could not expect Damon to understand about Ned. She could not, herself.

"I am sorry," she whispered, though she could not

have said, really, whom she addressed. Damon, perhaps, but it was Ned, she'd been thinking of.

Damon understood nothing but her bowed head, and the whispered words that to him meant her marriage to Ned had become, if it had not started, a love match.

"Sorry?" He gave a biting laugh that lifted her auburn head instantly. "For what? For having the marriage of the century? I cannot imagine why you would regret that. And if it is of me you are thinking my lady, you may spare yourself the effort. I give thanks regularly for having escaped marriage to a woman whose only recommendation is her beauty. Young then, I did not realize the importance of spirit and courage and integrity—"

Before Damon could lash her with another word, Alyson leaped from her seat. His contempt stung and deeply. She clenched her hands against the pain it brought. "I may be as despicable as you say, Damon Ashford, but I wish you to know I think you worse. You say I did you no irreparable damage, nay, you say I did you a favor, and yet you strike out at me like an adder every chance you get! Not only do you attack me in the only place I have to call my home, making my life unbearable here, but you have even accosted me on a public street to imply I am . . . I am a creature I cannot even bring myself to name! Well, bravo, my lord! You have routed me, you have—"

"Enough!"

There was only the one word, but Alyson stopped abruptly. She held her chin up, but her breast heaved with her emotions, her eyes shimmered with tears that burned her eyes, and she had to bite down hard upon her lip to restrain the sobs she could feel welling up in her chest.

She looked taut as a wire to Damon. He thought, for just an instant, to reach for her, but he curled his fingers into fists at once. He'd the frightening impression she might shatter, if he touched her.

"Meow!"

Alyson jumped, startled into crying out, and spun.

"Percy!" The cat had leaped onto the piano bench the better to make known his irritation at the neglect he suffered.

"Meow!" he wailed. He liked his evenings quiet and warm, and this one was neither. He glared at Alyson, who suddenly gave a shaky tremulous laugh. "You are right. It is time for bed."

She scooped him up and turned again. Damon stood between her and the door. She could have scuttled around him. She did not. She met his eyes, albeit reluctantly.

They stood like that a long moment—Alyson with her cat clutched to her breast, regarding Damon steadily, though she knew not what was in her eyes beyond tears. Neither of them said a word, and then Percy squirmed, and Damon stood aside.

Alyson immediately proceeded to the door and could not afterward be certain he really did say softly, just as she went, "Good night, my lady."

Chapter 16

"I cannot wait a moment longer, Allie, love! We have been chatting ever so amiably a good quarter hour, and I still do not know what I really wish to know: how is it to live with the earl?"

The first thing that came to Alyson's mind was the scene she and the earl had enacted in the music room not so many hours before. She did not betray herself, however. Her mind recoiled so quickly from that scene, she might never have thought of it.

She was even able to smile at her oldest and closest friend with whom she rode to the Moresbys to course hares. Philip and Sarah Davenport had stopped for her, as the Hall was on their way. Presumably they had expected to accompany Damon as well, only the earl, Hobbes had informed her when she had come downstairs, had left early for the Moresbys, as he had received an invitation to breakfast there.

"I hate to disappoint you, Sarah, but in truth, I have not seen a great deal of the earl. He's been extremely busy acquainting himself with the workings of the estate, closeting himself for as much as six hours at a time with Ned's steward."

"Six hours?" Sarah echoed, amazed.

But her husband was not so surprised. Philip nodded readily. "I should expect him to see that much of Latimer for some weeks. It cannot be an easy transition for St. Albans, Sal. He was trained for the army, not landowning. I imagine the enormous change that has occurred in his life must even be something of a shock to him, though I must add, he seems the sort of man who will ultimately be successful at anything he undertakes."

Husband and wife were in accord upon that, at least. Sarah rolled her eyes roguishly at Alyson. "He is quite a man isn't he? Merciful heaven," she continued on a sigh, "but he is handsome!"

Philip chuckled. A tall, lanky man of relaxed bearing, he looked more a scholar than the vicar of a parish. "Ought I to worry, Sal?" he inquired, his rather nice amber eyes twinkling. "No," he answered his own question, as they rode into a chaotic scene in the stable yard at the Moresbys. "Or at least not yet. There is not room for you in the crowd about him."

Sarah and Alyson followed the motion of Philip's head, and eventually made out Damon surrounded by a throng of people.

"At the Rundels it was much the same," Sarah observed. "He was mobbed the moment he entered the room. Of course, it's no surprise he's an attraction. Not only is he an earl, but he's a perfect marriage prospect, a heroic fighter, and a nonpareil. Poor boys. I wonder if they've any notion how they suffer in comparison to him."

"Sal!" Philip chided, but ruined any salutary effect he might have had by chuckling again. "Good lord. I hadn't really noticed, but it is rather the eagle among the pigeons, isn't it?"

"Pigeons?" his wife scoffed amiably. "Have you ever heard a poorer comparison, Allie? No pigeon ever looked as bright as Kit Moresby, my dear. Say parrot, rather, and I will commend you."

"You are very hard, Sal, love," Philip protested. "Very hard, indeed, but I will agree with this, that Kit Moresby, for all he's got up in the height of fashion as usual, would give his eyeteeth to look as carelessly elegant as St. Albans."

No sooner had Alyson caught sight of Damon's black hair gleaming blue-black in the welcome sun, than she had looked away and studiously avoided looking that way again. She'd not meet his eyes, not then, with half the neighborhood milling about, watching. She'd no idea what she might betray. The scene in the music room had left her raw, uncertain, and aching for something she did not understand, or did not want to. No, she'd not chance meeting his eyes.

Alyson did not find it easy, however, to keep her attention averted from Damon. With every word Philip and Sarah said, she found it almost an agony not, at the least, to dart a quick glance just across the stable yard.

Her battle showed. Sarah noted both Alyson's silence and the tightness just at the corners of her normally pleasingly curved mouth, but attributed both to another cause. "Allie! You have fallen unusually quiet, while Philip and I rattled on in our usual fashion. Is it very difficult for you to be here?"

For a half second Alyson could not think beyond Damon, but before she betrayed herself with a gape or a blush, she understood. "No, it is not difficult at all," she said glancing around the stable yard where Jim Higgins had once abetted her to a disastrous end. "Alton House, or Towers"—she smiled slightly—"is so different now, I can scarcely recognize even the stables."

"It is what comes of having a great deal of money but a great lack of taste."

Sarah only whispered the remark, but Philip exclaimed, "Sarah!" with real dismay and cast a quick look about to see who might have overheard his outspoken wife.

As they waited in one of the few relatively calm pockets in the yard, no one seemed to be within earshot. Sarah tossed her head. "I am only speaking the truth, Philip," she defended herself, but in a soft hiss. "This Gothic nonsense is . . . is awful!"

Philip rolled his eyes as if pleading with heaven to assist him, but a gurgle of laughter escaped Alyson, spurring on Sarah. "There are turrets on the barns, just look!" Sarah deliberately flung her gaze up to the roof of the barn by them. Another chuckle burst from Alyson.

There was, to the right of the miniature turret that had offended Sarah, a gargoyle. One hand under its exaggerated chin, it posed with its tongue stuck out at the world. Sarah giggled, seeing the direction of Alyson's gaze. "I concur with the gargoyle," she whispered, in the tone of one who is resting her case.

"And what is all this whispering and laughing about? I'll not be left low-spirited, while you and Missy laugh uproariously, Mrs. Davenport."

"Squire!" Sarah exclaimed a trifle guiltily, as the squire and Harriet rode up. "And Harriet. Good morning to you, both. We were, ah . . ."

"The gargoyle," Alyson finished simply with a grin.

The squire, as she had known he would, scowled immediately. "Deuced awful silliness, this Gothic nonsense! Why, you can't even go in those fool towers! And do you know the other day I almost rode into the absurd moat he's built?"

They all laughed uproariously, even Philip, but he was the one reminded them whose taste they, and he, disparaged. "What say you, Squire, that we go to greet our host? We can leave the ladies behind, I think, the crowd's so thick."

"And I hadn't even the opportunity to tell them both how fine they look this cold, bright morning. You do look very fine," Squire Rundel repeated, sweeping both Alyson and Sarah a magnificent bow. "But the vicar's right. Can't neglect our host." He winked broadly. "Nor the stirrup cup they're just bringing out, if my eyes don't mistake me."

In fact the squire need not have moved. Half a dozen lackeys soon made their way through the yard, each with a steaming stirrup cup. Alyson was not so accomplished a horsewoman that she allowed herself to take more than a sip. Harriet followed her example, but Sarah had two.

"To settle my nerves," she said and grinned archly. "You are certain you won't follow suit, Allie? Surely you are suffering a case of nerves, given how rarely you have coursed hares. I declare I was never so surprised in my life as when Kit Moresby stopped at the vicarage to invite Philip and me and told us you meant to come."

As if Sarah had conjured him, Mr. Moresby suddenly emerged from the crowd. "Good morning, Mrs. Davenport, Miss Rundel." His bright smile deepened perceptibly when he turned to greet Alyson. "Lady St. Albans! I am so delighted you really have come this morning."

Alyson returned him a smile she hoped very much he would not find encouraging, and after greeting him, sought to bring Harriet forward. "While my appearance in the stable yard may create amazement, you, Harriet, look entirely at home on horseback. But I think I remember you sitting a horse before you could walk very well. Is that not so?"

If Harriet was not a beautiful girl, she was a most attractive one when she smiled as she did then. "You remember correctly, Lady St. Albans, but I think Papa would have disowned me, had I not taken to riding early."

Tom Brady, mounted on a huge roan, pulled up by Harriet then, and more greetings were exchanged, but it soon became obvious Mr. Brady had come for Harriet, something Alyson did not fail to note.

"Well, Harry!" He grinned when Harriet flushed at the childhood familiarity. "Shall we make a race of it to Lodden stream? Mr. Moresby said it's the way the hounds will be pointed."

Harriet hesitated, perhaps resenting that Tom should treat her almost as a child still.

"You've not gone soft, have you?" Tom teased when she did not answer at once.

She grinned at the challenge. "Very well, then, Lodden stream, Mr. Brady,"—she emphasized the proper address before adding—"but you must give me at least four lengths."

"Four? You're daft if you think I'll do that! Two. That mare of yours may be small, but she's strong as Thor, here."

They finally agreed Tom would spot Harriet three

lengths and moved off toward the elder Mr. Moresby
who would, as host, lead the riders out of the yard.

"You ought to join them, Mr. Moresby," Alyson urged
the young man. "From the looks of him, your bay ought
to give Mr. Brady and Miss Rundel a challenge."

"I don't doubt he would," Kit acknowledged with a
proud smile. "He's a prime goer. I got him at Tattersall's
along with Claudia's mount."

Alyson had let her guard down. Safely at the back of
the crowded yard, distracted by the pack of dogs being
led, yipping and barking to Mr. Moresby, she forgot to
monitor the direction of her gaze. Kit Moresby's mention of his sister sent Alyson's gaze skimming the yard.
She found Miss Moresby also upon a bay only a hand or
so smaller than her brother's. But it was not the horse
kept Alyson's attention. Holding a stirrup cup in both
hands, Miss Moresby was, at the moment Alyson
looked, making a public show of saluting Damon with it.

He acknowledged the tribute with a smile of purely
masculine pleasure. Bold and white and flashing, it
caused something to twist painfully in Alyson's chest.
He had found, it seemed, the woman who was as strong,
determined, and even bold as he desired.

Mr. Moresby had followed the direction of Alyson's
gaze, and mistaking entirely her interest, said, "Claudia's
bay's as fast as mine, though not so large. She and the
earl ought to make a go of it."

From Alyson's other side came the insinuating murmur, "Do you think so?"

Mr. Moresby heard Sarah, but quite misunderstood
her question. "Yes, indeed, Mrs. Davenport. The earl's
chestnut may be powerful, but don't be deceived by the
looks of Claudia's mount. Her gelding is swift."

"But not too swift, I don't imagine," Sarah remarked,
but this time *sotto voce* enough that only Alyson heard.

Alyson only just kept herself from making a biting
comment about forward, overly endowed women.
Though Sarah might very well have agreed with it, she'd
have wondered about Alyson's heat, something about

which Alyson did not care to ponder much, herself, just as she did not care to muse overmuch on her growing dislike for a girl she had scarcely noticed before Damon's return.

She looked away from the pair just as a sudden, re-sounding cheer went up.

"Father has given the signal!" Mr. Moresby ex-claimed, half rising in his stirrups.

Alyson smiled at his excitement. "Off you go, Mr. Moresby. I know you won't care to bring up the rear with Mrs. Davenport and me."

"But you are—"

Alyson did not know precisely what he meant to say, but she suspected she did not want to hear it. Before Mr. Moresby could finish, she said firmly, "We are slow. Please, go or we may be moved to go at a dangerous pace out of consideration for you."

Mr. Moresby looked, torn, to the front of the group. They were already moving out of the yard into a fallow field. He saw his sister apply her riding crop to send her sleek Arabian suddenly forward. The sight decided him. With an excited wave he charged away.

"The boy is interested, Alyson," Sarah said, her voice a teasing singsong.

Alyson made a face. "I fear you are right. I had no idea."

Sarah gave no quarter simply because Alyson was her dearest friend. "Only because you are blind, my dear. He has adored you for ages. Why do you think he came to the Hall so often?"

"To see Ned, of course!"

"Don't get on your high horse. Your husband tolerated the boy because he only admired you from afar, as it might be said."

"I don't want his interest!" Alyson almost wailed.

"No, I didn't imagine you did."

"But what am I to do?"

Sarah gave her a slow, assessing look. "You might

turn your attention to another gentleman. That ought to cool young Moresby's ardor."

"No one else interests me," Alyson retorted, frustration evident in her voice.

"No?" Sarah queried, giving Alyson an odd look. Then she laughed. "I do swear, I cannot understand how we came to be friends. You are most unlike me, Alyson. But, as no other man interests you, I suppose you shall have to continue to deal with Mr. Moresby as you did today, by sending him away at every opportunity."

Alyson made a face, for the suggestion, though most likely the one she would follow, lacked a certain resolution.

"Tell me, Allie, do you still grieve for Edward?"

Alyson regarded her friend in some surprise. "But of course, Sal. It has not been a year."

"But I mean really grieve, Allie. Not mourn. There is a difference, and I had thought . . . well, that though you of course regret your husband's death, that . . ." she hesitated, glancing at Alyson, and immediately retreated. "Don't look like that, Allie! I meant nothing. You know my mouth and how I prattle. You were the very best of wives, love. And he, truly, was the most satisfied of husbands. Of that I do assure you."

"What did you mean about the other, Sal? About me?"

Sarah cast another glance at Alyson's strained expression and sighed. "I meant no criticism. I meant that though you were precisely the wife a circumspect, mild-mannered gentleman like Edward would want, I always thought you less engaged than I'd have liked you to be with your husband. Oh, Allie! I am making a mess of this! Philip is the eloquent one in the family. But between some husbands and wives there is a spark, a charged current, I don't know how else to describe it. It is there between Philip and me, and I wanted that . . . that passion, I suppose, for you, too. You will cheer up? Edward did not notice the lack, I assure you. He was not a passionate man."

"No," Alyson agreed softly. "I suppose that is true.

And I will cheer up." She pinned a smile to her face. "We've hares to course, have we not? Let's be off."

But as she spurred her mount, Alyson could not put aside Sarah's remarks. They rang too true, answered too much, to put neatly aside for a more convenient moment.

And it really was not a convenient moment at all, to be thinking of her relations with Ned, to test ever so tentatively the observation that there had not been passion between them, and to fight against the knowledge that with another there would have been passion—nay, there was that passion between her and the other, though it was anger triggered it.

Alyson galloped headlong with a group of some twenty-five people. As their horses sped, so did hers, and as they took fences and walls, so must she. She ought to have been paying far closer attention as they raced down the slope of a hill to a wall some four feet high. It was not an easy jump, and though Alyson's mare began well enough, she stumbled as she came down on the far side. Unprepared when the mare's head dipped, Alyson sailed into the air and hit the ground with a bone-jarring thud. For some moments she knew nothing, but gradually felt her shoulder come alive with pain.

Chapter 17

Squire Rundel's voice was the first thing Alyson distinguished after the pain. "Here now, Missy! Come on, wake up. Wake up, my girl!"

Responding as much to the urgency in his rough voice as to the commands themselves, Alyson forced her eyes open. The squire's craggy face swam into view. "That's my lovely girl!" He gave her a relieved smile, and Alyson tried to smile back. She managed little more than a grimace, however, and the squire shouted furiously, "Where the devil's Crofton! He wasn't that far ahead. She's in pain!"

Realizing the command had been addressed to an audience, Alyson made an effort to extend her awareness beyond the pain throbbing now in her head as well as her shoulder. Chagrin overwhelmed her when she realized how many horse's legs she could make out. The coursing had been halted on her account it seemed.

When Sarah spoke, Alyson realized her friend held her hand. "There is some blood here on her head, Squire, but none elsewhere that I can see."

"Lady St. Albans! How can I help?"

Alyson knew then she would survive her fall, for she'd the strength to bemoan the degree of concern evident in Kit Moresby's voice. When his face appeared to her, she simply shut her eyes.

"Will she be all right?"

"I believe so," the squire rumbled in reply. "I wish Crofton to have a look at her before we move her, though."

"Here he is!" Alyson heard several voices announce the doctor's arrival. She wanted everyone to go and finally summoned the strength to say so.

"Please, Squire. No one need stay on my account," she whispered.

"Hush now, my girl. We'll wait for the doctor's say, then we'll see who leaves you."

"Here I am, then." Dr. Crofton hurried forward, breathing hard. "Bless me, but the earl kept me to such a pace I've no breath left!"

As Dr. Crofton began to examine her with his large, competent hands, Alyson considered his remark. He had referred to Damon. Damon had not come to see to her. She had marked his absence without realizing she had. But he had gone to fetch help for her.

"How is she, Crofton?"

There was Damon's voice. It was hard and clipped, demanding an answer. She forced her eyes open. He had not cared enough to get down from his horse, and she could not see his face well enough to see his expression.

"She'll live," came Dr. Crofton's gruff reply. "She's dislocated her shoulder, for one, which won't be difficult to treat, but she took quite a bump on the head as well."

"Is there any need for us to stay about longer, Dr. Crofton? Or can you see to Lady St. Albans by yourself?"

Alyson's heart sank briefly, and she allowed her eyelids to flutter closed. How particularly galling to have Claudia Moresby witness her fall from grace. She could not find it in her to fault the girl for the impatience in her voice.

Dr. Crofton did not sound so forebearing. "You may get back after the hares, Miss Moresby, any time you like. As I told his lordship, Lady St. Albans is not at death's door, only in considerable pain, which she is bearing like the brave lady she is. Squire Rundel will give me all the assistance I need, thank you very much."

"And I shall stay." Sarah's voice came from close beside her, and Alyson opened her eyes to smile at her friend, but she ended by wincing, for in the next moment, Kit Moresby was declaring staunchly, "And I shall stay! I can carry her before me."

To Alyson's relief, Sarah correctly interrupted her expression and rising, said firmly, "You are very kind Mr. Moresby, but I am certain Alyson would be more comfortable with the squire as she has known him since she was a child."

"I understand, of course!" Mr. Moresby said so promptly Alyson wanted to pat his hand and tell him he really was a dear young man. Weary suddenly, she closed her eyes and only vaguely heard him add that he meant to accompany Alyson home to assure himself she was returned safely.

She opened her eyes quickly enough when Dr. Crofton lifted her in his arms, however. Biting her lip to keep from crying out, Alyson was jostled almost beyond bearing when the surgeon transferred her to the squire's steady hold.

"There, there, my girl!" The squire soothed her. "You may cry out. We won't think the less of you. And it may save that lip of yours." Through her pain she smiled faintly, and he nodded his large head approvingly. "You're a trouper, right as rain, Missy!"

The gait of the squire's horse was smooth, but not so easy Alyson did not suffer terribly with every step. Still, when she was given the choice to go to Alton Towers or to the Hall, she chose the longer distance, and mercifully, about half of the way there, she lost all awareness.

After Dr. Crofton with a deft, if exceedingly painful movement, returned her shoulder to its proper place, Alyson ended by sleeping most of the day away, thanks mostly to the laudanum the physician gave her.

Sometime in the night she awoke to find a candle burning in the room and Nanny Burgess dozing in a wing chair across from her, a pair of knitting needles dropped in her lap.

The governess came awake with a start, as if she felt

Alyson's gaze. "You are awake at last, my lady," she said, rousing herself. "Would you like some water?"

Alyson nodded only to realize moving her head made her dizzy. Still, a strange, unfamiliar shape close by her bed, prompted her to turn carefully. "What is that?" she gestured with her hand.

Nanny Burgess expelled a sigh. "That is a cot, my lady. I hope you will not disapprove, but Lady Anne was much affected by your fall and would not sleep away from you."

Alyson winced on behalf of her daughter. "I understand, Nanny." Poor Annie. Alyson could not bear to think what had gone through her mind when she had seen her mother brought home from a riding accident. It was how Annie had lost her father, though Ned had been riding much faster around a track he'd laid out, and he had hit his head upon a rock, dying instantly.

Annie was curled in the wing chair, when Alyson awoke the next morning. Nanny had given way to Bernie, who looked most apologetic when the child cried, "Mama!" the moment Alyson opened her eyes.

Alyson managed a smile. Her head still throbbed, but not so violently as it had the day before, and she was not so dizzy. At least she was not dizzy until she tried to lift her head as she held out her arms to Annie.

"Ah, my head." She fell back. "No, no! It is not your fault, Annie. Don't cry. It is my fault for failing to concentrate when I was riding." She brought forth another smile, that if it was wan was also sweet. "Come and give me a kiss on the cheek, Annie. Perhaps it will help me to heal more quickly."

Annie kissed her softly, then eyes filled with tears, asked in a hoarse whisper, "You will not die, Mama, like Papa did? You will not, will you?"

"No, no, love. I am only hurt a little. Feel my goose egg, and you will see."

"Goose egg?" Annie repeated, the absurd term immediately reducing her fears.

"Ouch! Not too hard, please. There, now you can feel it is shaped rather like an egg."

Annie explored the lump more gingerly. "It hurts?"

"Yes, but not unbearably. I shall be up and about in no time, I am sure."

No time was not to be that day or even the next, for Dr. Crofton would not allow Alyson to rise until the swelling had gone down completely. Annie stayed with Alyson almost all of the first day, playing cards with Lady Bardstow, reading with Nanny, and describing her mother's "goose egg" to each newcomer.

The next day hothouse flowers, winter bouquets, and bundles of notes began arriving at the Hall. Annie excitedly accompanied the largest, a holly wreath. "Look! It is as large as I am, Mama!" The child's unnaturally hushed tone caused Alyson to smile. "It comes from the Towers."

Lady Bardstow read the note that Kit Moresby had penned. It conveyed much the same wishes as all the others, though perhaps a little more fervently.

"He brought it himself," Lady Bardstow remarked. "And he asked after you with the greatest concern. He repeated several times how very pale you looked lying in the field. Though he did add," the elder whispered when Annie became distracted by the arrival of a maid with another tribute, "that even such paleness could not dim your beauty."

"Please, Aunt Edie!" Alyson groaned. "I am too weak for such balderdash."

Lady Bardstow giggled with surprising enthusiasm. "Flattery is never balderdash. It is a woman's lifeblood, my dearest. And you needn't fear a thing. Though I may not look strong, I shall keep that dear, and somehow so very young, Mr. Moresby from your door until you are quite up to him."

"You are the one who is dear, Aunt Edie," Alyson whispered as her eyes fell shut.

When she awoke, she was alone, but only for a moment. The door opened slowly and Nanny Burgess peeked in.

When she saw Alyson was awake, the governess allowed Annie to scoot by her. Behind them both came a footman with a tray.

"If you are up to a little broth, Lady Anne and I thought to take our dinner with you, my lady," Nanny explained.

Alyson felt considerably better. The long rest had done her a great deal of good, and she even looked forward, for the first time, to eating.

But Annie could not wait until dinner had been served to divulge the news she was obviously bursting to tell. Even as the footman set up the table she would share with Nanny, she skipped excitedly to her mother's side.

"Damon took me for a ride this afternoon, Mama! At first I was afraid, but just at first."

"You were afraid?" Alyson asked, puzzled.

"Yes," Annie admitted in a small voice. "Damon's horse is very big, and at first I did not want to sit before him."

The child watched her mother carefully, concerned that she would find such fear shameful. Alyson nodded solemnly, however. "I did not understand you meant you rode on his horse, sweeting. Of course you were afraid. You know too well what can happen, if one is not careful upon a horse. But you went, Annie. You overcame your fear, and I am proud of you."

"Damon promised he would not allow harm to come to me," Annie explained ingenuously. "He held me tight and very soon I was not afraid at all. We even cantered!"

She looked so proud and pleased, Alyson felt a surge of gratitude toward Damon. He had not come to see her. She had not really expected that he would. But neither had she expected he would exert himself to allay Annie's understandable fear of horses.

Feeling almost as if she might cry at the kindness he had shown her daughter, Alyson forced her mind to her broth. Her undue reaction was due to her concussion, she knew. Dr. Crofton had warned her she might weep at odd times.

After dinner Alyson was able to play a few hands of cards with Annie and Nanny Burgess, but fell asleep soon after Lady Bardstow came to relieve them. She awoke suddenly sometime later, but had no idea whether she had slept an hour or hours. She looked to see if someone sat with her, thinking to ask the time. No one sat in the wing chair.

"Do you need something?"

At the sound of the low, masculine voice, Alyson jerked her head, startled. "Oh!" She winced, waited for the sudden dizziness to fade, then forced her eyes open again. It was Damon. She blinked, not certain she believed the evidence of her eyes.

"I am sorry I startled you." He came to stand closer to her bed. The light was low in the room, and she could not read much in his expression. "I told Edie I would stay while she went to get herself a book."

"Oh." Alyson closed her eyes against the sight of him. And against the knowledge that he had come to her only out of compassion for another. She wanted to cry. Overwhelmingly, she wanted to cry, and she wanted Damon to sit by her; to hold her hand; to tell her he would keep her safe.

Dear God! Alyson forced her eyes open. What foolishness was this? Dr. Crofton had not said the concussion would alter her reason for the worse.

She found Damon looking gravely down at her, his hands shoved deep into his pockets. "Thank you for looking after Annie," Alyson said. Her voice sounded so small, she cleared her throat. "It was very good of you to realize she would be afraid of horses and to help her to overcome her fear."

"I didn't realize it," Damon admitted quietly. "I thought to entertain her, that's all, but when the groom brought Tristan out, she froze. I only did what anyone would."

He sounded very offhand. Had he resented helping

Annie? Alyson had to fight tears again. "Whatever your reasons, your effect was enormous and much appreciated. I think it possible she'd never have ridden, had you not taken her in hand, and for that I thank you, Damon."

Damon nodded sharply and wheeled about, allowing the fire to draw him. Alyson bit her lip. It was the first time she had slipped and forgotten his title. She had feared he would resent the familiarity as much as he obviously did.

"Are you in a great deal of pain?" he asked, poking about at the fire.

"I am in no pain at all when I lie perfectly still." She tried to chuckle to lighten the atmosphere in the room. Unfortunately the laugh became a little cry, for she tried, at the same time, to adjust her pillow behind her.

Damon was by her before she realized he had moved. "What do you want?" he demanded. "Why did you not tell me you needed something? I am here to help you, damn it!"

For no logical reason his snapishness soothed her and made her want to smile. Truly the concussion had affected her mood, Alyson thought. "Pardon me for neglecting you, my lord." She attempted to make amends lightly. "But I forget how sore my shoulder is; it pains me so little when I lie still. Could you put this pillow behind my head?"

Damon leaned down to adjust the pillow to her liking. Alyson closed her eyes. She could not watch him come so close. But she had forgotten she had other senses. She felt his arm as it went around her shoulders, lifting her. It was strong and firm, and when his chest brushed against her forehead, it too felt strong and warm with life. His scent surrounded her for that moment he all but held her. Masculine and clean, it was the essence of him somehow, and achingly, achingly familiar.

"How do you feel now?"

Lost.

"Fine. Thank you." They might as well have been strangers. Alyson feared again that she might cry.

Damon frowned down at her, as if he did not trust her reply. "Dr Crofton says your lump has gone down considerably since yesterday."

"It ought to have done," Alyson replied somewhat aggrievedly. "He had me keep ice on it for long enough."

Her irritable tone made Damon smile just a little. Alyson felt her heart speed and could not take her eyes from him. "You sound a typical patient."

She couldn't understand why he found that amusing. "I am like anyone else."

He didn't reply, only continued regarding her, though now there was no amusement to be found in his expression. Abruptly, his expression still closed, he said gruffly, "You needn't push yourself to dangerous lengths in order to impress young Moresby, you know. Were you never to lift a finger again, he would remain completely besotted. He has fairly haunted the Hall these last two days."

"Devil take you." Alyson's curse did not match her weary tone. "I ought to have known you came only to cut up at me."

She closed her eyes against the sight of him, so handsome and so close and so very distant.

"Nay." It was the softest stirring of the air, his denial. She might even have thought she dreamed it, but that he touched her. Fleetingly only, he brushed his fingers over her cheek, smoothing back tendrils of her hair that had come loose from the braid in which Bernie had confined it that morning. "I did not mean to cut up at you. I meant only to keep you from ever again frightening us all so badly."

Her entire body felt warm as if Damon's lightest touch were a balm. "I did not go to course hares on Kit Moresby's account," she murmured. Then she opened her eyes to look up into his handsome face, and if Alyson did retain sufficient presence of mind not to say she had gone to course hares on *his* account, she felt the greatest longing to tell him what was, in fact, a large part of the truth. "I wanted to feel young, Damon," she whispered softly. "Do you understand? I wanted to feel energetic and light and gay for once."

And then she burst into tears.

Chapter 18

"Nay, now! Don't cry, Allie. You upset yourself for naught."

For naught! Alyson felt as if she were crying about the whole of her life, but, of course, he did not understand, and that made her cry the harder. She was too upset even to mark his rough tone or the name he called her by.

"For pity's sake, listen to me. I meant no criticism!"

It was the note of desperation that finally penetrated. "I know," she got out, her voice muffled by her hands. She took a deep breath, her face still buried in her hands. Another breath seemed in order, and then another, before Alyson could lower her hands to begin wiping at her tears. She did not want to look at Damon, but he stood there over her, compelling her. She took another breath before she shot him a swift, embarrassed glance. Oddly the fierce frown she confronted seemed to strengthen her. "I am truly sorry," she said more calmly. "I did not mean to turn into a watering pot on your first stint in the sickroom. I had meant to wait until at least your second." She attempted a smile. It was a bit wobbly, and Damon's expression did not lighten. Strangely she did not mind. "Dr. Crofton warned me I might cry without reason. Again, I am sorry you had to—"

Damon cut her off with a low growl. "I shall make you cry in earnest if you say you are sorry again. Do you need this?"

Alyson had been wiping her cheeks with her hands. The handkerchief Damon extended caused her to realize how childish she must look—and how dreadful. Her hair could only be a wild mess, her face wet and splotchy. "Thank you." She accepted the handkerchief, without looking at him again. "You needn't wait with me until Aunt Edie returns. Truly. I shall be fine."

Damon did not reply directly, only gave Alyson an unreadable look before he took himself off to the fire again, leaving her to mop her face in privacy.

"Da . . . my lord?" Alyson recovered her slip so quickly, she hoped Damon had not heard it. She did not wish him to think she meant to presume simply because he had done Aunt Edie a favor and stayed with her. "Can you tell me if Nelly suffered any permanent damage?"

Alyson asked after her mare, and Damon shook his head. "She needed a poultice to her hock, no more. She is ready for you to ride."

"Oh, I am glad." Alyson sighed, her eyes drifting shut for a moment as she murmured half to herself, "I could never have forgiven myself, had I caused her permanent injury."

She looked very small in her canopied bed. And lovely, her face a delicate oval, her skin ivory pale in the candlelight, and the thick, dark braid of her hair lying on her breast.

Damon shoved his hands in his pockets, just as he had done when he first saw her and experienced the same nearly overwhelming desire to take her into his arms and hold her to him. He also had the fiercest need to tell her he loathed hearing her address him by his title in preference to his name.

A strong man, Damon likely would have defeated both impulses, but he'd have been the first to admit that his determination to keep a distance from the bed and the woman in it was abetted by Lady Bardstow's return.

"Have you been crying, Alyson?" the elderly lady exclaimed in dismay after only the briefest glance at her patient. "Surely no one has upset you."

Damon had withstood more than one dressing-down from a superior in the army, but he had never faced a more potent stare than the reproving, disbelieving look his spare, kindly cousin turned on him then. And oddly enough, he felt he merited her disapproval. Though he could not have said precisely what had caused Alyson's tears, he did have the uneasy feeling it had indeed been he, who somehow precipitated them.

He was not obliged to marshal a defense, however, Alyson did that for him. "Lord Damon did not upset me at all, Aunt Edie. I began to cry, because . . . Dr. Crofton said I would." She smiled wearily. "Truly, I cried for no reason. Reprove Damon unfairly, and I shall burst into tears again."

Lady Bardstow's frown smoothed. "A baseless threat as ever I heard. To my knowledge you have never used tears to get your way, dearest, though every woman knows they are the surest means to confounding a gentleman. Am I not right, Damon? You did not know what to do, did you?"

Oh, I knew what to do. My difficulty was to keep from taking her in my arms.

"I gave my lady my handkerchief." Damon replied to Lady Edith, though his gaze had somehow found its way back to Alyson. She looked about to thank him for that little, but he cut her off. "I hope you feel even more the thing tomorrow, Alyson. I shall bid you farewell now and let Edie put you to sleep with her reading."

It was a clever ploy, Damon thought, teasing Lady Bardstow so that he might leave the room on a light note and without another word to Alyson. He did not want to look at her again. He had looked at her enough in her night dress. It was silk and clung like a second skin to her agonizingly full, soft breasts.

Damon did not return to the sickroom after that. Alyson was not surprised. He had come that once on Lady Bardstow's behalf, not really on hers, and what had she done? She had cried like the weak-willed, silly ninny he thought her. Unable to say for certain that she would not do the same again, Alyson decided she was relieved by Damon's absence.

She was not ignorant of his activities while she recovered from her concussion, however. Lady Edith was full of them, as was Annie. If one did not inform her he was riding with Claudia Moresby, or out shooting with Claudia Moresby, or dining with wretched Claudia Moresby, the other was sure to do so. What time he did not spend with his steward, he spent, it seemed to Alyson, with Claudia Moresby. Her impression was confirmed by Lady Bardstow who quietly remarked that if he continued to dance attendance upon Claudia Moresby, she did not doubt there would be a new countess at the Hall within the year.

Alyson did not react visibly to Lady Bardstow's opinion. She was walking across the Queen's salon and continued walking as if the elder lady had said nothing extraordinary. But she did register the opinion. She registered it with such a sharp, biting pain, she wanted to cry out. Instead she kept her feet moving, one before the other, exercising as Dr. Crofton had only that morning said she might do.

Very soon she was well enough to stay up for dinner, and of course she saw Damon then. He was formally polite with her. She was not surprised, she told herself, and of course, his careful formality proved that he had not addressed her by her pet name when she was crying, as for some reason, it had occurred to her he might have done.

She did not want to think how much she wished she had not imagined or dreamed, perhaps, that he had called her Allie. She felt on the edge of a frightening, unknown abyss when she thought of almost anything to do with Damon.

Uncertain as she was, the least thing seemed able to upset. Lady Bardstow meant only to distract Alyson, to lift her spirits, when she mentioned that there was to be an Assembly in Aylesbury some fortnight later. "If you will forgive my impertinence, Allie, I think it is time you entered into company again," the elderly lady remarked, color staining her cheeks ever so slightly. "There is noth-

ing for a young woman as lovely and warm as you to
gain by sitting alone at home. Ned would not expect
more than the year of mourning you have observed so
strictly. He would not feel betrayed, I know it. He is in
heaven and knows what is in your heart."

Alyson managed a nod, no more, and she soon found
reason to excuse herself. In her room, her door locked,
not merely closed, she faced what in Lady Bardstow's
well-intended remark had made her want to cry out a denial.

Could Ned read her heart now? The thought made her
cold, despite the warm fire heating the room. What
would he find? Merciful heaven! She did not want to
think what he might see. In the next breath she chided
herself sharply. She was upsetting herself for naught. In
heaven there could be no pain! But what would he find
in her heart to pain her?

Her room seemed suddenly too small and confining.
She left it to find Annie and Roe and take them for a
slow walk, and when she returned, Alyson wrote a note
to Philip Davenport requesting a small, commemorative
ceremony for Ned on the anniversary of his death three
days hence.

Lady Bardstow approved. Damon only inclined his
head and said, "Of course," when he was told at dinner.
At the service he stood by Lady Bardstow, Sarah by
Alyson and Annie while Philip read prayers and said a
few, comforting words. Annie then placed the holly she
and her mother had gathered earlier in the day upon the
stone that marked her father's place in the family crypt.
She clung to Alyson tightly afterward, tears in her eyes,
but neither she nor Alyson wept.

It was later that night that Alyson cried. Finally, alone
and tired, her defenses worn down, she began to weep at
first softly and then harder and harder, her head buried in
a pillow, her hands clenching the bedclothes.

But it was not Ned's death made her sob with such
wrenching pain. She had shed her tears for his passing
the year before. That cold, lonely night, Alyson cried for

what Ned would have found in her heart, were it possible for him to see into it. What had always been in her heart, though she had denied it.

Sarah had seen, though. Not fully, of course. Sarah did not know why Alyson's love for Ned had been in the end little more than a mixture of fondness, affection, and gratitude.

And she had been grateful to him! She had not known how different her life could be from that which she had lived under Mr. Haydon's roof until Ned had surrounded her with love and ease.

Dear God, for that alone she had owed him all her heart! Truly, she had meant to withhold nothing. Yet she had. She had withheld the kernel of herself.

Ned had not known! Sarah said he had been satisfied. And he had doted on her. Surely he would not have made over her so, had he known.

But she knew and had known, all the while, only had not admitted to herself what she knew—that though she had sworn before God to love Ned alone, she had continued in the most secret recesses of heart to love another.

Not once had she ached for Ned to take her in his arms, as she had longed that night in her room for Damon's merest touch. Not once. But Damon would never love her as she loved him. It was her punishment, surely, for not loving Ned as she ought to have done.

Forgive me, Ned! I tried! I did my best. I gave you a child. I'd have given you others.

Alyson shook she wept so hard. She wept for Ned, who had deserved a love as strong as his had been, and she wept for Damon, too. At least she wept for the young man, whom she had failed so completely on that one wretched day.

She could not seem to stop weeping. Perhaps she would spend the remainder of her life crying, she thought, but the absurd notion did not seem at all absurd. She wanted to sleep, to forget, and she thought of the laudanum she had not taken for several days. She could have a touch of it. Mrs. Hobbes had put the bottle in her

medicine cabinet in her office. Alyson had her own set
of keys.

She wanted that oblivion. True she would feel fuzzy
the next day, but that consequence mattered little to
Alyson as she seized her robe and thrust on her slippers.
She did not want to think any more. She was so tired.
She wanted to sleep.

It was past twelve as she hurried down the stairs. The
house was dark and cold, but still she walked quietly as
she approached Damon's study. No, he was not there.
She hurried around the corner and screamed.

"It's me, Alyson!"

And it was Damon who stood in the hall, a single candle in his hand.

She shrank from the revealing light. He would think
her unbalanced, he saw her so often in tears. Alyson
nearly laughed at the thought. She *felt* unbalanced.

"What do you here?" he asked, holding his candle
higher. She could see the frown marring his attractive
face as easily he could see the tears streaming down
hers. "You are upset." Then after a pause, he added simply, "Of course."

Of course! He never knew the half of anything. He
had no idea why she cried. Alyson did not realize the
tears had begun to slip down her cheeks again, until
Damon said in a hoarse voice. "Don't cry. Dear God,
don't cry. I've no handkerchief for you this time."

And then he reached out to wipe the tears with his
hand.

Alyson reacted as if his touch were fire. She leaped
back, pleading almost, "No, no! Don't touch me."

And then she burst again into tears because she
wanted so much for him to catch her up in his arms even
on that night, the anniversary of Ned's death.

A muscle flicked in Damon's jaw. She did not want
his touch, because it was for her husband she yearned.
Of course she would cry today. Damn, and he had pur-
posely avoided the house after the ceremony and the luncheon at the Davenports.

"I shall summon a maid to you," he said far more gruffly than he had intended. "Why you did not call one to you, I cannot imagine. Is it warm milk you wanted?"

"No." She fought for breath and calm. His tone helped. Had he been the least sympathetic, she'd have cried the more.

"Port, then?"

"No. I had not thought of port. I came to take some laudanum."

"Laudanum?"

The disapproval in his voice brought her head up. "Yes," she said almost defiantly. "Dr. Crofton left some for me."

"He left it should you have physical pain, Alyson." His so handsome face was set in stern, implacable lines. "You cannot go down that path, taking laudanum every time you grieve for Ned."

What do you care? Alyson wanted to demand but realized in time how self-pitying the question would sound.

"Play for yourself instead."

Alyson stared at him so uncomprehendingly, Damon's expression softened. "On the piano. When you could not sleep before, that is what you did."

A lullaby for Ned?

Tears pricked Alyson's eyes, though whether in response to her fanciful thought or at Damon's softened manner, she could not have said.

Her throat thick again, she could only nod.

"Good then," he said quietly. "Come along, I shall make up a fire for you."

She was too weary suddenly to protest his company. She did not even protest, when he took her hand in his. It felt large and warm and comforting, covering hers.

In the music room she sat at the piano while he built a fire, and she played. She chose a piece by Handel that had been a favorite of Ned's. After a little, absorbed by her music, she forgot Damon's presence, or at least she was not disturbed by it. At the last she played as well as she was able a requiem by Bach.

When the last note died away, she knew that she would be able to sleep. She knew, too, that Damon was still there. When she turned, she looked directly at him.

And saw he was asleep, his head bent at an uncomfortable angle. He looked very young, somehow, and handsome, of course, and very dear.

She woke him with a gentle touch and smiled. "Thank you for staying with me."

He smiled too, sleepily. "Your music was soothing."

It might have been a question. "Yes. It was," she answered. "Thank you."

Chapter 19

"Well met, Lady St. Albans!"

Alyson could not say the same, and when she drew up her trap, her response to Kit Moresby's greeting was lukewarm.

He did not notice, the force of his smile seeming to compensate for the lack in hers. "I was just on my way to look in on you at the Hall, but I see you are recovered enough to visit your laborers' families again. Will you make me a happy man and allow me to escort you?"

Alyson had to stifle a groan. The young man had visited the Hall every day since he had discovered she could receive visitors. He had brought her gifts, too— hothouse flowers from Aylesbury, a book of poems, a book of music for the piano, all thoughtful, all unwanted. Sarah had given it as her opinion that Alyson must speak straightforwardly. "Moresby's *tendre* deepens daily, Allie! You must do something, and he is too besotted for hints."

Alyson agreed. "Rather than escort me in the trap, Mr. Moresby, I should like to ask you to walk with me a little. Will you? We can find some privacy among the beeches, I think."

An invitation to walk with Alyson ought to have put Mr. Moresby in alt, but he was not a fool. Her tone made him look at her a long moment before he nodded acceptance of her offer.

They walked a little way in silence while Alyson tried to think how best to say what she had decided she must say. At last she smiled ruefully. "I am not very good at this, I fear, Mr. Moresby. I don't know how to put what I wish to say delicately, and so, I will simply be direct and say that I sense you have some regard for me. No, please! You needn't say anything. This is so awkward, and I only speak because I have the greatest respect and affection for you. You see, I . . . I cannot return your regard, Mr. Moresby."

She tried to soften her rejection with a smile, but still the young man looked so stunned, Alyson almost felt his pain. "Never? I know that you loved your husband very much, Lady St. Albans, but I had thought that in time, when you had recovered . . . "

Alyson shook her head slightly. "I am so sorry, Mr. Moresby. This has nought to do with Ned."

"I see," he said, suddenly stiff and not a little pale. "I will not embarrass you by pressing my case then. May I assist you back to your trap?"

"Yes, thank you, Mr. Moresby."

The spare answer required all the control that Alyson could summon. She wanted to let forth a torrent of sympathy: to assure him that he was a delightful gentleman; that there were hundreds of young ladies who would give their eyeteeth for his interest; that he deserved a young lady who returned his regard in equal measure, but Alyson held her tongue. She knew better than most that the last thing the young man wanted from her was sympathy.

Still, when he handed her up onto the seat of her trap, she could not restrain herself entirely. "Thank you, Mr. Moresby, for the assistance, but far more I thank you for your sensitivity. I shall never forget how gracefully you have listened to my awkward words."

He smiled a little at that, and once more Alyson had to restrain herself. He'd have particularly resented, she knew, having his blond hair ruffled.

"You did not speak awkwardly at all, my lady. You could not, I think, for you are the essence of grace. I'll say no more, I swear it, but if you are ever in need, I hope you will not hesitate to call upon me for assistance. And now farewell."

He kissed her gloved hand briefly, and then without another look backward, mounted his horse and departed.

Alyson watched him until he was out of sight. He had taken his disappointment gallantly, surprising her. She flicked her reins rather sharply, as she thought to herself that Cupid deserved to be called to task for shooting his little arrows without a care for the human hearts he wounded.

Damon spurred his stallion forward with a vicious oath. He had not intended to play the spy. He had, in fact, avoided as much as possible this section of the estate by the stream where the beeches grew in groves. He had come that day only to inspect some ditching work done earlier in the week.

She did not avoid it, though. Oh, no, not she. Had she taken Ned for walks in the beech groves, too? Undoubtedly she had. She evidently enjoyed taking whoever was her current lover there.

Damon's mouth twisted in an ugly sneer. She had made a fool of him yet again, damned if she had not! He had begun to think he might have done her an injustice when he dismissed her "coziness" with Ned as no more than a facade she had deliberately adopted to keep her husband tied around her little finger. But her distress upon the anniversary of Ned's death had been too genuine to dismiss so easily. She had seemed truly grief-stricken.

Bah! Damon scowled. She had likely been crying over the pain in her shoulder. He had wanted only to believe she had truly loved another man. And was not that the devil of a wish?

But it was why he had fallen in love with her. She had seemed so genuine: seemed a young woman who had within her the capacity to really love. Granted her beauty had attracted him at first. She'd a full mouth he had wished to kiss and teach to kiss back—and cheeks he

liked to watch go pink, skin he wanted to touch, and
eyes . . . but soft lips, soft skin, and captivating eyes, by
themselves, would never have prompted him to pledge
his heart to her. He had done that because she had
seemed so different from the women he'd found so easy
to have in town. They, enjoyable as they might have
been, had seemed capable of little more than flirtation or
lust.

He wanted more from his wife. Alyson had fooled
him twice, six years ago and now. It had been only a little over a week since the night he had found her weeping
in the hall over Ned, he had thought.

Damon leaped the ditch he had meant to inspect,
heeding little but the thundering of his horse's hooves.
He would not think of her. He would not.

Yet, he did—as relentlessly as he rode. He called her
foul names in his mind. And some not foul, but perhaps
more damning. She could be only the shallowest of
women, vaporish, easily swayed, and, of course, mercenary. Kit Moresby was wealthy as Croesus, or his father
was, which amounted to the same thing. He was a silly
boy, too, but they suited there. Damned if they did not!

Did she like the wooing, too—the kisses to the hand?
He had seen Kit's farewell. Damon glared ahead, seeing
not the ground he covered, but Alyson's lovely face.
What had they done away from the road, when they had
been hidden by the trees? It had been a year since she
had had a man.

Such a sick feeling rose in him, Damon could scarcely
think. That he knew he was being absurd, only made
him the more ill. It was too cold for her to couple on the
ground. But perhaps it was the need for a man's caress
that attracted her to Moresby as much as the desire for
wealth?

God! Why had he ever come back to Whitcombe? He
could have given the estate into the hands of an overseer.
It was done often enough. He could have stayed in the
army, been dubbed "the fighting Earl" or some such
nonsense.

He knew why he had come back, of course, and the answer only darkened Damon's mood the more. When he reached the road, he turned away from the Hall. He knew he could not sit quietly behind a desk.

A sharp bend caused him to slow his reckless pace a little, which saved him a nasty spill. Had he not slowed, he'd not have the control to swerve and miss the trap that had been abandoned in the middle of the road.

With a ripple of alarm that infuriated him, Damon recognized the trap as Alyson's and realized she was nowhere to be seen. Examining the woods a second time, he thought he saw something move. Before he could question his own interest, he had swung down from his stallion and was striding toward the movement.

An outburst, unintelligible at that distance, but definitely querulous, spurred his step. Then there was a cry that was unmistakably Alyson's, and he began to run.

The scene Damon burst upon took him so by surprise, he stopped abruptly. Alyson was indeed having difficulty with a man, but it was the man who lay upon the ground, and it was she who bent over him.

Damon did not recognize the fellow, who was none too clean, ill-shaved, and raggedly dressed.

"Ho! Ho! Missus oh, oh!"

The man seemed to be singing, as he lay upon his back in the woods in wintertime.

Alyson was not amused by his antics. "Will you not at least try to stand, Jim?" Damon heard her say with unmistakable exasperation. "You will freeze to death lying on the ground. Oh, will you not listen!"

She shook the man's shoulder impatiently. Damon took a step forward, and she looked up swiftly, wariness on her face. It took Damon a little off stride that when Alyson recognized him, her expression cleared dramatically.

"Damon! Will you help me, please?"

"What seems to be the difficulty?" he asked, though now he approached, he could smell the ale of which the man on the ground reeked. "And who is he?"

"Jim Sirls." She confessed the name a trifle reluctantly, Damon thought. "He is, ah, incapacitated, as you can see. If we leave him, I fear he will freeze to death."

"From the looks of him, the world wouldn't be any much the worse for his absence."

Damon flicked his eyes from the drunkard to Alyson, and recalled as he did so, where and with whom he had seen her only a few minutes before.

Alyson stiffened. Damon had regarded her almost as if he found her loathsome. Did he think her foul because she helped Jim?

"If you don't care to help me, you need only say so, my lord," she bit out, and dismissing Damon, returned her attention to Jim Sirls, who lay muttering incoherently, his eyes now closed fast.

Displeased with men in general at that moment, Alyson shook Jim hard enough that he'd have had to be dead not to respond.

"Eh, whot, whot's tha'?" he shouted, jerking awake.

"Jim, you must get up from here! You are not dressed warmly enough to sleep on the ground."

"Lady St. Albans?" Jim blinked at her in amazement.

"Aye, Jim. You see no ghost. I'll take you home, if you can stand."

"Home." Suddenly his face creased, and he began to cry unashamedly. "Whot's to home, then?" he moaned. "The little 'uns cryin' all the time 'cause there's naught to eat, that's what. And I've no hare or even a bird for 'em!"

"You've no hare, because you got yourself drunk as a lord, Jim Sirls. And you had best be thankful I came along to see you stumbling off into the woods. What sort of notion was that, to look for hare when you're blind drunk? You'll get yourself caught in a mantrap!"

"Nay, m'lady. 'Tis not stupid I am," Jim protested. "I don't go into Moresby's woods. The bloody b . . ." Jim hiccuped before he could offend Alyson's ears beyond forgiving.

He did try her patience almost beyond forgiveness,

though. "You are in Moresby's woods!" she snapped.
"You took the wrong turn when you got to the road.
Now come along, before we're faced with one of his
gamekeepers. I've food for you and the children in my
trap."

"Ah, m'lady! 'Tis an angel y'are!"

When Jim began to cry again, Alyson rocked back on
her heels clearly at her limit. "Jim! This is not the time
for tears."

Though he had reason to despise one of the actors in
the little scene before him, Damon could feel himself
about to smile. He made as little apology for having his
humor piqued as he did for standing fascinated.

One did not often have the opportunity to observe a
countess kneeling in a pile of muddy leaves without a
thought for her skirts. And surely it was not every day
that a man could watch a woman of such incandescent
beauty that she could have had London at her feet had
she found a man to take her there, stoop to scold a
worthless, filthy, tattered, sodden poacher without the
least effect.

And did she scold said poacher for his illegal doings?
Not at all. She remonstrated with him only for choosing
the wrong woods, the more dangerous woods, and for
going into them incapacitated.

" 'Tis too good y'are for the likes o' us, Lady Allie.
Too good."

"Jim!"

Damon decided to intervene, though he really did not
know why he did. Certainly it was not that last at-wit's-
end shriek. Or perhaps it was. He had heard the squire
say Moresby's gamekeepers shot before they asked for
explanations.

And, too, he was curious as to who Jim Sirls was precisely.

He stepped forward into Jim's line of vision. "I think
it time you listened to the lady, my man."

"Wot?" Jim jerked upright, staring at the formidable

man who loomed over him. "Who's he?" He looked wildly at Alyson.

"I am the Earl of St. Albans, come to assist Lady St. Albans. Up."

Jim stumbled to his feet. Despite the happy result of Damon's intervention, Alyson felt rather sour about his instant effectiveness.

"Now where?"

Damon addressed Alyson. "To my trap. I'll drive him home."

"I think we shall both see Mr. Sirls home, actually."

"Cor!" Jim swayed unsteadily as his eyes went wide with dismay. "But ye canna come ta home!"

Damon kept his hold on the man, half carrying him through the woods as he looked at Alyson, his brow lifted in question.

She did not explain.

When they came onto the road, Jim tried to protest again. "You canna—"

"Silence, man," Damon barked and promptly heaved Jim Sirls into the back of the trap. He expended little effort. The poacher was no more than skin and bones.

As Alyson climbed onto the seat of her trap and took up the reins, Jim's protests degenerated into moans. "Steady there, Jim," she said turning to him. "Lord St. Albans had to learn where you live sooner or later."

More intrigued than ever, Damon swung up on his horse and followed after Alyson who did not look back to see if he did indeed mean to follow her.

To Damon's surprise they soon turned off the public road onto one of his own farm lanes. After traveling it for a mile or more, they turned abruptly onto an overgrown track he had never noticed. Soon the ground on either side of the track became marshier, and it was necessary for Damon to take care where Tristan stepped. His brow lifted when they came to a tiny clearing in the willows. In the center of it stood a one-room hut.

From it three thin, ragged children and a pale woman emerged. The woman began to smile at Alyson until she saw the horseman following the trap. Then she covered her mouth with her hand as if to hold back a cry of fright.

"It is all right, Jeanie," Alyson called out. "Lord St. Albans helped me, when I saw Jim stagger into Moresby's woods. He has not come to evict you."

Alyson did not dare look at Damon as he rode closer. She knew he must realize the Sirls were squatters, living on his land without any right, but she hoped he would not order them off on the instant.

"This is Jeanie Sirls," she said, presenting Jeanie, while still avoiding Damon's eye. Jeanie dipped a painful, awkward curtsy, ducking her parchment-pale face. "And this is Annie." Alyson indicated the baby Jeanie held, and then named the other four children who stood by their mother staring mutely at Damon.

When she had done, Alyson directed the boys to fetch their father. "He is in the back of the trap. Girls, you fetch the food baskets."

"Ah! Bless you, m'lady."

It was only a whisper, but Damon heard the emotion thickening the woman's voice. As had Alyson evidently, for she leaned down from the trap to touch Jeanie Sirls lightly on the shoulder.

"I am glad to see Jack is better," Damon heard her say, and glancing to the two dirty, scrawny boys struggling to pull their father upright, wondered how any child could look worse than they. "I am sorry I haven't come for a time," she went on. "I took a spill from a horse. Nay, it was nothing," she said when Mrs. Sirls clucked worriedly. "I am fine now."

The boys passed, their father staggering between them, then the girls came, each with a basket so laden they had to half drag them.

"And here is a bundle of clothes," Alyson said, reaching under the seat of her trap for a neatly wrapped package. "Sarah Davenport included some things her boys can no longer wear."

Mrs. Sirls could not speak. Damon saw her bite her lip

against tears and watched her exchange a long look with
Alyson. He suspected he was, in part at least, the subject
of the silent communication, but then Alyson was moving to turn her trap around.

"Until later, Jeanie. Keep well."

"Mrs. Sirls." Damon inclined his head curtly.

"M'lord," the woman said on a hoarse whisper as she
watched him go.

Chapter 20

"I will drive."

For a moment, perhaps two, Alyson hesitated. She did not care for Damon's clipped, commanding tone. She thought he ought to have been at least somewhat accommodating, considering that she had not invited him to join her on the seat of her trap in the first place. He had said, "I will ride with you," in much the same way he had informed her he would drive.

She did relinquish the reins to him, however, and also mastered a desire to tell him he could keep himself company on the way home, if he were only going to be rude. She reminded herself of the Sirls. Any pleas she might make on their behalf would fall on deaf ears, if she made him angry, or perhaps more accurately, angrier.

And finally Alyson yielded because she suspected Damon had not made a request of her at all. Had she not turned over the reins to him, she suspected he would have simply taken them from her. Rather than have her control summarily wrested from her, Alyson preferred to seem to grant Damon the privilege of driving her.

"I would be most grateful," she said, therefore, with the nicest of smiles. "Trying to rouse Jim tired me more than I expected."

Not a shred of sympathy softened Damon's expression. "Which is one of several reasons that going to the aid of that man was among the most lamebrained acts I can imagine a woman in your position committing."

"Was it?" Alyson was no longer smiling. "And what would you have had a woman in my position do, my lord? Allow the husband of a childhood acquaintance—Jeanie did live on Mr. Haydon's estate, you see—to stumble into a mantrap, break his leg, and likely maim himself for life? He has not, you understand, of course, the wherewithal to pay Dr. Crofton for the service of setting his leg. Or perhaps you wish that I had left Jim to freeze to death on the ground, or be shot by one of Moresby's gamekeepers? Either way there would be one less of those miserable poor—"

"Enough." Alyson jerked her chin up at Damon's tone, but he did not seem to care. "You may flash those magnificent eyes at me all you want, but your litany of reasons for saving that worthless man's hide are not worth the breath you waste on him."

Alyson bit her tongue against another angry rejoinder. She would not aid the Sirls this way. Only in a very remote part of her mind did she mark that Damon had said she had magnificent eyes.

"I know that Jim seemed worthless—no, more than that, he was worthless, drunk as he was," she allowed as evenly as possible. "But he is not incapable when he is sober."

"And how often is that? Once a month?"

Alyson studied her hands. "He is often in his cups, I grant, but he does not drink when he has work. Jim's problem is that he hasn't steady work."

"And you are an authority on the subject, of course."

Alyson flinched. Damon's tone was dry enough to sear. "I have known him for over a year," she replied when she thought she could maintain a neutral tone. "In that time he has always been sober when he had work."

"Which means he's drunk most of the time, judging by the looks of his family and that hovel he's built without leave on my land."

"It is useless land!"

"Not to the Sirls."

"I meant that no one else uses it!" Alyson heard the frustration in her voice and made herself take a deep breath. It would do Jeanie no good, if she allowed

Damon to overwhelm her. "Nor did Jim build in the marsh without permission. Ned allowed him to squat there."

"Because you persuaded him."

"Jeanie grew up here! I have known her all her life. What in the name of God did you expect me to do? See her and her children live in a workhouse?"

Alyson jerked her angry gaze from Damon. He was determined to put the worst construction on everything she said, and she . . . she was no match for him. She could not remain calm or like him, cool and cutting. She lost her temper instead, or fumbled inarticulately for words.

And, too, she could not understand entirely why he was being so difficult. Oh, she did understand why he might object to the Sirls. Jim had not made the best of impressions, certainly, but Damon seemed more interested in pricking her than in discussing fairly the relative merits of the Sirls' case. A week before she might have understood, but not after the night when he had met her crying in the hallway. He had been more than kind that night. He had been tender. Since then he had not held her hand again, or built a fire for her. In fact she really had not seen much of him, but there had been a difference when she had. A slight one, granted, but still she did not think she had mistaken the softening in his expression, when their eyes had chanced to meet.

She slanted him a glance from the corner of her eye, and all her body, not to mention her spirits, seemed to sag. He had, it seemed, recovered from his temporary softening. His finely carved mouth, his strong jaw, and his even, aristocratically straight nose, all looked as if they had been dipped in ice.

But not his eyes. Damon turned to her just then, and Alyson saw his beautiful eyes gleamed once more with derision.

She looked away at once, struggling against the sharpest stab of disappointment. Then she cursed herself for the greatest fool in all the world. She knew better than to build castles on sand.

Abruptly, Alyson turned to look directly at Damon, "Are you so set against me that you will not listen to anything I have to say on behalf of the Sirls?" she asked, determined to go to the heart of the matter.

He lifted a dark eyebrow in seeming surprise. "I will listen to anyone who speaks sensibly."

Alyson clenched her hands against a scream of frustration. He had deliberately made his answer as ambivalent as possible merely to goad her, and he had succeeded, as she could see by the mocking light in his eye he very well knew.

She must try to think clearly. She must think of the Sirls' children, all so young and vulnerable.

It was impossible, though, even as she summoned Jeanie's children to her mind, not to be far more aware of Damon beside her on the trap. Even now, frustrated and disappointed as she was, she was acutely aware of him as a man. She could feel the heat of his body, could sense its strength.

She wanted to touch him.

Alyson cursed herself. Staring out at the frozen fields, she also admitted the truth. She wanted to turn toward Damon, to run her hands along his shoulders, to curl her fingers in his dark hair, to kiss just once his mouth. She did so very much.

But she also wanted him to listen to her, and that was, at least remotely, possible.

"Very well," Alyson said, forcing a briskness to her tone. "I shall try to speak as sensibly as possible on the subject of the Sirls. You may ask the squire whether Jim is a good worker. He hires Jim when he can."

"Why is this paragon so poor then?"

Alyson nodded. It was a fair question. She would not resent that it had been barked at her. "There are several reasons. Aside from the obvious ones, that he's no land of his own and the children have come too quickly, he's been the victim of a change in the neighborhood. When

Mr. Moresby bought Alton Towers, he enclosed land Jeanie and Jim were using, called it his own, and evicted them. He also has made it a policy not to hire outside laborers but to use only his own men."

"Mr. Moresby was a fourth son and has made much of his wealth for himself. I should imagine he has good reason for his policy."

Alyson considered her reply carefully. It would not do, she believed, to abuse the man Damon likely considered to be his future father-in-law. "I do not doubt that Mr. Moresby's policy is of financial benefit to himself. But is personal gain the only standard by which we may judge the merits of a particular policy? I think not. One must also measure its benefit to the community in which one resides, and Mr. Moresby's policy harms a great many in our neighborhood. Without the little extra they earn assisting with the ditching, the hedging, and the draining of land that is the work of winter, the poorer people lack the means to buy food for their children."

"You have not mentioned Ned in all of this."

No, she had not. Alyson took a deep breath. "He did hire on additional laborers in the winter. He had roots here and knew his responsibilities, but he did not hire Jim Sirls." When Damon looked at her in sharp surprise, Alyson bit her lip. "Ned did not know him until after Jim had begun to drink. But I believe, truly I do, that if Jim were given a chance, he would reform himself. There are the children to think of and Jeanie."

"Spoken like—"

"No!" Alyson cried, her eyes suddenly flashing, as Damon's slighting, dismissive tone pushed her temper beyond recalling. "I will not allow you to dismiss me with that insufferable phrase, 'spoken like a woman'! Yes, I see those gaunt, pitiful children, not the fifty pounds that might be saved by allowing them to starve to death. But tell me what it is you men gain by saving that fifty pounds? Ned flung his way on the 'Change. A brilliant notion, worthy of the masculine mind! And what of our new standard in the neighborhood, Mr.

Moresby? To what advantageous use has he put his fifty pounds? Why to stuffing his obese face, I'd say! With what he saves this winter, he may add yet another chin to the three he has already. Or perhaps he will perch another gargoyle upon his eaves. There is a magnificent use of fifty pounds, is it not? And what will you do with your fifty pounds, Damon Ashford, Earl of St. Albans? Buy a new waistcoat with which to dazzle the ladies. Or perhaps—"

"Enough!"

"Is it?" Alyson retorted so furious Damon's growl had no affect upon her at all. "It's not half of what I could say to you, but I see I am only wasting my breath. You're determined to be as callous as any of that new breed the squire has labeled the 'self-made apes.' Well, enjoy an undisturbed sleep in your warm, downy bed, my lord! I shall relieve you of the burden of the Sirls' five starving children, just as I intend to relieve you of the burden Annie and I present!"

In the taut, pregnant silence that followed, Alyson's words seemed to ring out over and over. Damon stared straight ahead, his jaw locked too tightly for speech.

It was not a desire to end their argument over the Sirls that silenced him. The subject of their wrangling had been the merest pretext, anyway. He'd no intention of allowing Mrs. Sirls or her children to starve to death.

The Sirls meant nothing to him at that moment, however. He deduced from what Alyson said that she had accepted Moresby—Moresby the dandy, slim as a willow, devoted Kit Moresby. Likely she had accepted him that very day beneath the beeches.

For an awful moment Damon could not breathe. A massive weight seemed to squeeze his chest. She meant to marry someone else. Again.

He wanted that. He fought to recall how much he wanted her out of his house, out of his sight, out of tempting, tantalizing range.

She was within tempting range now, though she sat with her head determinedly averted and her back fairly bristling at him. Hedgehog. He grimaced. Beautiful, seductive hedgehog, more like. Even with only her back to see, there was more than enough to tempt him, from the soft roundness of her bottom upon the seat, to the outline of her slender back. Damon could too well imagine Alyson unclothed, the flare of her hips, the hollow at the curve of her back, the fullness of her breasts. Her hair would be loose and flowing, not tucked out of sight beneath a black bonnet.

He ached to touch her, though he could not have said whether he wished to throttle her or clasp her to him so tightly she would not be able to escape.

She was going to marry Moresby.

A muscle in his jaw tensed. He would not open his mouth to demand the particulars. He feared what he would say, and he had no real need to know when.

He knew why. That was enough. She wanted wealth, though he did grant now, she did not want it all for herself. She'd blistered him strongly enough on that point to convince him she was sincere.

He wondered if Moresby had any inkling how she meant to use at least some of his wealth. Damon smiled sourly to himself. Did young Moresby know of her attitude to the male sex? Had he heard her lambaste his gender with a scathing, "You men?"

Had she even meant to include Kit Moresby in her indictment? It was not possible to say, but Damon was certain she'd had her stepfather in mind. What other men had there been in her life? She, herself, had excepted the squire. That left him and Ned.

So. She and Ned had disagreed about charity in general and the Sirls in particular. Had they argued? Had she fired up at Ned as she had done at him? Had she turned upon Ned a rigid, furious back?

The question arrested Damon. For no logical reason he considered it carefully and somehow could not imagine such a scene, though for reasons to do with Ned, not Alyson.

Ned had been the most amiable and mild-mannered of

men. Once, referring to his interest in cockfighting, a subject that could excite the squire to apoplexy, Ned had said with a half smile, "Ah, well, as to that, it is a way to pass the time, don't you see."

It was impossible to imagine anyone lambasting Ned. No, she had not ever railed at him, bristled at him, or flashed her aqua eyes at him. Damon was sure of it.

Without warning he felt his mood shift for the better. He did not examine why, and anyway it was the briefest of good humors. They had turned into Whitcombe's drive some while before. Now, as they came out of the trees lining it, they could see the Hall and more importantly, a carriage drawn up before it.

The rather garish crimson and gold equipage belonged to the Moresbys. Damon's smile died on the instant. For a half second he wondered wildly whether Kit Moresby had returned to take Alyson away that day.

Mr. Moresby was not among the group alighting from the carriage, however. As he and Alyson went to greet them, Damon recognized Mrs. Moresby and Claudia, but there was another woman as well, and three young children running about seemingly uncontrolled.

The Moresbys' arrival had caught Lady Bardstow on the steps, likely because she had been consulting with Timms about her roses. Seeing Damon and Alyson first, she waved, relief evident on her countenance. "Damon, Alyson, the Moresbys have visitors. This is Mrs. Moresby's sister, Mrs. Edwards, and these are her, ah, children," she said. Her voice scarcely carried above the shrill shrieks of those children.

Mrs. Edwards was Mrs. Moresby's very much younger sister. "How do you do?" She smiled briefly. "Ah, children!" Her effort to address her offspring went for naught. They ran off around the side of the house. She looked with some embarrassment to Alyson and Damon. "On the journey from Devon, where we live, one of the carriages broke a wheel. As there was not room in my carriage for the children's nurse, I am temporarily without her."

And not doing at all well, Alyson thought.

"We are on our way to the village, to show Aunt Renata the few shops we have nearby," Claudia Moresby exclaimed in her declamatory way. She smiled cajolingly at Damon. "Come with us, won't you? I did mention to you the other day that my aunt was coming, and we should be obliged to entertain her. As to the children"—she looked to Alyson now, her expression cooling slightly—"they are eager to meet little Lady Anne, for they care nothing about tame shopping excursions. You will not mind having them, will you, Lady St. Albans? You've such a marvelous nurse as I was just telling my aunt."

Mrs. Moresby, gentler than her daughter, hurried to add, "We do understand, Lady St. Albans, that this might not be a convenient time. Simply say so, and we shall bring the children another day to play with Lady Anne."

At that moment a piercing shriek announced the girl, the youngest of the three at seven or so, as she came running to tattle shrilly on one of her brothers.

While the Moresbys were distracted, the mother chiding ineffectually, Mrs. Moresby shaking her head, and Claudia giving some ignored direction, Damon whispered mockingly in Alyson's ear, "Shame on you for that taut look, my dear. Not only should charity begin at home, as the saying goes, but you will need to accustom yourself to these little darlings."

She could put only one construction on his remark. He meant to marry Claudia and open Whitcombe to the "darlings."

"Not yet I don't," she replied under breath, unwittingly confirming for Damon the conclusion to which he had come regarding her and Claudia's brother.

His smile became as forced as hers then, though in another moment he was hard put not to laugh wickedly. The boys' path had somehow or other crossed Rowena's, and they came flying as fast as their legs could carry them screaming in fear as the great mastiff bounded after them.

Whatever Alyson and Damon's differences were, at that moment they stood united. Neither of them made a move to utter a reassuring word. To the contrary Damon stepped authoritatively forward. "Sit boys!" he commanded in such a way that both sat down upon the steps instantly. "Rowena is not accustomed to rowdiness and can become overexcited." All three children turned fearful eyes to the massive dog who sat with her red tongue hanging from her mouth, her great jaws exposed, and her eyes fastened upon them.

Mrs. Edwards cried, "Oh, my!" in a faint way, and Alyson realized it was just the moment to say, with quite counterfeit sorrow, "I do wish you had sent a note this morning, Mrs. Edwards. Annie is not here, you see. Her nurse took her to the vicarage to play with the Davenport children."

Chapter 21

The alliance Alyson and Damon formed in the face of the young Edwardses lasted briefly. When they met again at dinner, no trace of it remained. Damon greeted Alyson with the coolest of nods, and she returned him a muted good evening.

Had it not been for Lady Bardstow, they might not have spoken further, but they did have Lady Bardstow, and for her sake, they both made the effort to appear natural.

Dinner went smoothly enough until sometime during the meat course, when Lady Bardstow raised a subject that had been briefly alluded to earlier by Mrs. Morseby, as she tried to make idle conversation while her niece and nephews fought one another to be the first into the carriage.

"Allie, dear, I was a little surprised earlier today, with the equivocal reply you gave Mrs. Moresby when she asked if we would be attending the Assembly in Aylesbury next week. I thought you did mean to go."

Alyson had had second thoughts about the Assembly. She did not feel very gay, for one. For another she expected Kit Morseby would attend. The prospect of spending her evening trying to avoid the young man's eye but not too obviously, held very little appeal. And last, and most strongly, she did not want to watch Damon dance attendance upon, or even dance with, Claudia Moresby.

"Do say you have not changed your mind, Allie!" Lady Bardstow exclaimed, when Alyson did not answer at once. "Damon," she called almost anxiously for the earl's authority, "do tell Alyson it is time she went out."

But Damon had reason to resist his cousin's appeal. He knew, or thought he did, that Alyson had little need of a ball. She had gotten herself a new husband without waiting for her year of mourning to be done.

He flicked a cool look at Alyson. "I think Alyson is of an age to decide the matter without benefit of my advice, Edie."

Lady Bardstow looked so taken aback, Alyson immediately regretted being the indirect cause of her dismay. Damon was the direct cause, of course, but Alyson could see he was not the least repentant. He was too busy regarding her with a brooding air she could not understand in the least.

The thought that he might deem it wrong of her to attend the Assembly occurred to her suddenly, and her mood veered sharply. Why should she not go? Aunt Edie would be disappointed if she did not.

"You have both decided me." She made certain to include Damon in her brilliant smile. "I am of an age to decide, as you say, my lord, and likely do need to get out and about as you say, Aunt Edie. I shall go."

"Oh, I am so pleased!" Lady Bardstow's thin face lit up so, Alyson felt guilty for dithering even a little. "I do so want to be festive, and I can think of no better way than to attend an Assembly with companions who are sure to be the most attractive gentleman and lady, respectively, present."

"Did I say you would be attractive, Alyson, my dearest?" Lady Bardstow clapped her hands together in almost childish glee when Alyson made her entrance into the Queen's salon almost a week later. "I fear you may sue me for libel! Look at her, Damon! Is she not the loveliest creature imaginable?"

She was. And with Lady Bardstow looking on Damon could not deny it. "Without a doubt," he said, inclining his dark head as he raked Alyson with a look that took in every detail of her appearance, from the top of her burnished head to the tip of her kid slippers.

Had he thought her beauty could not be served better by a color than it had been by black? How very wrong he had been. The widow's weeds spoke of death and mourning and distress. Not so peacock blue. She was radiant that night, thoroughly, thoroughly alive, and he found it nearly impossible to tear his eyes from her.

Her eyes seemed especially luminous. Was it the vibrant color of the dress set them off? Or was it the prospect of dancing with Moresby?

Damon noted the tension the thought caused him, even as he watched her cross the room to accept a glass of ratafia from Hobbes. The heavy cloth of her mourning clothes had obscured her grace of movement and had masked her figure. Damon found it necessary to take a draught of his claret. This dress was of the thinnest, finest silk. It clung to her, flowing about her hips and slender legs as she walked, outlining them clearly, far, far too clearly.

Which was to say nothing of the décolletage. He had never seen her in real evening dress, that is to say in a dress cut as low as was the fashion. He ought to have expected the effect. He had seen thousands of evening gowns in his life. He found he was not, though, in the least prepared for the ripe fullness of her breasts, for the pearly sheen of her skin, so exposed and so out of reach.

In her room as she looked in her pier glass, Alyson had felt almost indecent. She had not worn an evening dress in over a year and had forgotten how much fashion exposed. A little defiantly, for it was truly the fashion, she glanced to Damon. She found his masculine gaze lingering precisely where she had feared it would be. He lifted his dark eyes to hers.

That was all, merely one look into intensely black eyes. But Alyson did not react as if Damon's taut expression were ultimately condemning. Not at all. Her breasts seemed to swell, in fact, and of a sudden, a degree of heat she had never known suffused her, and she spun her back to him at once.

But Alyson did not forget that look: the heavier than usual droop of his eyelids, the almost velvety blackness of his eyes. At the Assembly, when they were announced, she recalled it the moment Miss Moresby came on her father's arm to speak to them.

Miss Moresby's décolletage was lower than Alyson's, and to her shame, Alyson could not control herself. She looked swiftly to gauge Damon's reaction to it. To her frustration she could not determine what he thought.

He smiled with apparent pleasure at the girl, who had, gratifyingly, frozen for just a moment as she took in Alyson's appearance. But he also inclined his head, preventing Alyson from seeing where his eyes lingered, or how dark they became.

He did, however, allow Miss Moresby and her father to draw him away to a circle of their friends, though Alyson marked, he did not allow the Moresbys to monopolize him. In truth they would have had to wrap themselves around Damon to keep him for Claudia. People pressed from all sides to speak to him, some meeting him for the first time, but others seeming to know him from town.

Of those previously met acquaintances, two or three were lushly figured women who seemed particularly familiar with Damon. Alyson saw him lead one, a bold redhead, onto the floor. He danced with the other two later, the redhead again, and Miss Moresby, too, twice. Alyson knew all that, yet she was not sitting dully with the dowagers while she noted Damon's partners.

Rather to her surprise, Alyson found she was as much a center of attention as Damon. She and Ned had attended the Assembly in Aylesbury with some regularity, and there were a good many people present that night who had not seen her since before Ned's death. They came to say how glad they were to see her out again, and it bolstered Alyson's spirits considerably that everyone seemed sincerely pleased.

Nor was all or even most of the interest Alyson excited that of old friends. From the moment she stepped over the threshold of the Assembly room, she found herself besieged by gentlemen. Their interest pleased her. How could it not? When Damon danced by with the redhead, she was on the arm of the Viscount Sudbury, a very attentive, attractive man of about Damon's age.

One gentleman did not attend her, though. Alyson spent a good many minutes worrying when Kit Moresby would pop out of the crowd to sadden her with a brave, gallant look, only to learn from his mother that Kit had left Buckinghamshire unexpectedly for a house party in Kent.

Mrs. Edwards laughingly said she thought he had run as fast as he could from her children, but the squire had a different opinion, which he voiced when he claimed Alyson for a turn at the refreshment tables during an interval in the music.

"It would seem young Moresby's hied off for other parts," he remarked, handing her a glass of the punch. "I'm not surprised, not at all. As everyone knows, there can be only one cock o' the walk."

Alyson met his twinkling gaze with some mystification. "Your fighting cocks have not gone to your head, have they, Squire? I cannot fathom what you mean."

"Can you not, Missy?" His face flushed with the warmth of the room and perhaps the punch he'd had. Squire Rundel wagged his eyebrows at Alyson. "Well, my dear, 'tis something you'll need to puzzle out for yourself. And you will. You will. I've no doubt of that at all!"

With a great laugh and a wave of his hand he dismissed the subject. Alyson did not press him, for she suspected the punch had more than a little to do with his humor, a suspicion his subsequent remarks did little to lessen.

"Ah, Missy!" He lifted his glass to her in elaborate salute. " 'Tis grand you look tonight. Those widow's weeds couldn't dim you entirely, of course, but what a change! It reminds me of my Betsy." Happily Alyson knew "his" Betsy to be one of his hounds. "She looked well enough when she was full of her pups. But after they were weaned! Lud, she was a beauty again. In her world she's your match, Missy, with her gleaming coat, her pure lines, and . . ."

"And what are you waxing so eloquent about, Squire?

We couldn't help but notice how you are holding forth to Alyson."

The squire looked around in surprise to see he had led Alyson, without realizing, up to a group composed of Sarah Davenport, who had been the speaker, Philip Davenport, and his own wife.

"Holding forth, am I? Well, I suppose I am. I was telling Missy how she's very like my bitch, Betsy—"

"Squire!" Mrs. Rundel looked as if she might faint. "Never say you are comparing Alyson to one of your hounds and . . . and in such terms!"

"Of course I am!" The squire looked in amazement at his dismayed wife. "She's not offended. She understands my Betsy's the best bitch I ever had."

"Oh, Squire!" Mrs. Rundel cried again in much the same stricken tone and began alternately to apologize to Alyson and to upbraid her husband.

Alyson could feel laughter welling in her and studiously avoided Sarah's eye. "Mrs. Rundel!" she exclaimed. "Please, do not distress yourself."

"Do you see?" the squire demanded, all offended dignity. "My Missy knows the value of a good bitch!"

At which Alyson's eye did meet Sarah's and a dam seemed to give way, for both young women and Philip, too, burst into gales of laughter.

Their hilarity attracted attention. Lady Edith came to ask what had them all so amused. She did not come alone, however. "Damon wished to procure me a glass of punch, but I told him that laughter is the best elixir in life. Now do tell us, Squire, for I know 'tis you have made the joke, what it is that has so convulsed everyone."

"Well, I was just saying that Missy reminds me of—"

"No, Squire!" His wife intervened with a wail. "Please, you must not repeat such a thing, though Alyson is the most forbearing lady I know."

Sarah's eye caught Alyson's eye again, and another wave of laughter brimmed up in them.

"Alyson! Sarah! You must not encourage him," Mrs. Rundel cried, so distressed that they would encourage her husband to offend the sensibilities of the Earl of St. Albans, that she spoke to Sarah and Alyson as if they were still young girls.

When she realized what she had done, Mrs. Rundel gave another cry, this the most despairing of all.

Seeing Mrs. Rundel's very real distress, Alyson instantly put her arm around the distraught woman. "Mrs. Rundel, you must know that nothing either you or the squire could say to me could ever offend me. Dear lady, whatever my title, I was once a girl sorely in need of the haven you both provided me."

" 'Twas the least we could do!" exclaimed the squire, off now on a new tack as Mrs. Rundel regarded Alyson with a mixture of relief and considerable affection. "Lud! What a man Haydon was. I'll never forget how he behaved in the months before you married St. Albans, Missy. Anyone would have thought he feared you intended to run off with a passing stranger the way he would not let you leave the house without either him or that hatchet-faced man of his by you. He even sent Simms with you when you came to the Manor!"

Alyson had to strain now to smile. "At least he permitted me to visit. That was the important thing. Ah! Here's the music started again," she finished on a note she could only hope did not sound as artificially bright to the others as it did to her.

Luckily the interval was, indeed, over. As the musicians tuned their instruments, Philip Davenport extended his hand to his wife. "Are you recovered sufficiently from your hilarity, my dear, to honor your promise to dance this dance with me? I shall be most disappointed if you do not."

"I would never disappoint you, Philip." Sarah laughed. "I know you've the Lord's ear."

The pair departed, Philip remonstrating with his exuberant wife in the mildest of tones, and Alyson watched them, half smiling until she realized a hush had fallen over the remainder of the group. Glancing about she found the squire, Mrs. Rundel, and Lady Bardstow all looking from her to Damon with an air of expectancy.

Humiliatingly aware of the heat creeping into her cheeks, Alyson stood helpless to master the situation. She knew he would not ask her to dance, and she could not think how to escape gracefully.

"Will you do me the honor, Alyson?"

She could not quite believe Damon had spoken until she glanced down and saw his hand, strong and commanding, reach out to her.

She almost bolted, afraid of a sudden for him to touch her. But already she could hear herself saying, "The pleasure is mine, my lord," as she was expected.

He took her arm, just at the elbow. It is only a dance, only a dance, she told herself repeatedly as they made their way to the floor, though she was so aware of his hand on her, of his body so close to her, that, though she stared straight ahead, Alyson could not have said what couple stood before them.

And then, as he turned to her, she nearly groaned aloud. It was to be a waltz.

At the feel of Damon's hand upon her waist, Alyson stiffened. And her eyes seemed to glue themselves to the diamond stick pin that was the only ornament he wore.

They began to move. He was too close. She could not think for the thudding of her heart. He surrounded her completely. His arms, his scent, his touch were the sum of her universe. She ached for him to pull her closer.

Damon was not less aware of Alyson. She was only inches from him, tantalizingly close. He looked out over her head, but he was really only aware of her: of her full breasts swelling toward him, of the lithe slenderness of her waist where he held her, and below his hand of the soft roundness of her hips.

She fit perfectly in his arms. Even stiff as he felt, they danced well together. Suddenly he spun about in a circle. It was a boy's trick he had not tried in years. As he'd known she must, she clung to him more tightly. He felt her breasts brush him.

Still she did not look at him. He studied the burnished curls arranged artlessly atop her head. Did she wish he were Kit Moresby?

"Tell me what the squire said that made you laugh so." Alyson looked up, but Damon was not surprised that she regarded him warily. He had spoken flatly, commanded her almost. He realized he was looking at her mouth. He met her eyes. "Please."

Damon knew he had not softened his tone and knew as well his expression was taut, but he could not help himself.

She studied him a moment. Then, suddenly, unexpectedly, a spark of humor lit her blue-green eyes. "The squire paid me the greatest compliment imaginable. He compared me to Betsy, his prize bitch."

For the merest half second Damon stared at her blankly. And then as she watched, his eyes lit, and his face split into that strong, white, so very appealing smile.

"I knew you would laugh," she said softly but a little grudgingly, too.

"You laughed," he pointed out, his black eyes still dancing.

"It's not the same. I think you are laughing at me."

Damon was silent for a moment, looking down into her eyes, brilliant blue-green eyes that were . . . vulnerable.

It was all he could do not to catch her to him there on the dance floor with half the county present. "If you believe that I am disparaging your looks, you have it quite, quite wrong. You are the most beautiful woman I have ever seen."

He had not meant to say it. The words had willed their way from his tongue. But Damon was not half so surprised by them as Alyson. She missed a step of the dance, staring, stunned at him.

Chapter 22

Damon did not sleep at all well that night, for thinking on Alyson's reaction when he had told her she was beautiful—nay, the most beautiful woman he'd ever seen. Drifting on the border between waking and dreams, he would hear himself say the words, then watch those crystal blue-green eyes of hers flare wide with amazement. For the hundredth time Damon jerked the covers he had dislodged back into place. Had she looked so startled, so uncertain, only to affect him?

And glad. He'd seen that, too, before she averted her face from him. Even before her shock had quite abated, pleasure had dawned in her eyes so suddenly and so unexpectedly he'd caught his breath. Nor had it been the coy, triumphant pleasure of an accomplished flirt. No, the moment she became aware of it, she averted her face, hiding the reaction, seeming as shy as a green girl.

And her hand had trembled in his.

Damon gave up thought of sleeping. The dawn had come. He would not continue to lie there helpless against recalling every flicker of her eye, every inadvertent movement of her hand. Perhaps she had been shaking with relief to be free of him. The last strains of the waltz had just died away.

Damon jerked the cord to summon his valet.

God's bones, but he did not want to think more about the evening! And why? Damon grimaced. He was weary with replaying it. Fatigued. Bored. Afraid.

Aye. Damon prowled to his window. He'd a view of Whitcombe's park, but it was his own grim visage he saw in the glass. He had led a charge at Corunna into a withering blast of French artillery fire. He had been afraid then, but exhilarated, too, and filled with a sense of invincibility.

He did not feel invincible now. Almost by the second he could feel his defenses against her crumbling. Jove, even her cat had crept into his good graces! He turned to eye Percy, a tight ball of white, sleeping undisturbed in a corner of his bed.

The cat had been in his room when he returned last evening. "Do you want your mistress?" he had asked, holding the door open, but Percy had stretched out lengthwise, presenting his chin and purring.

Damon had let him stay, though even at the time, he could not think why. Except, of course, that Percy reminded him of Alyson.

His valet appeared, and he growled a series of orders. The man, not unaccustomed to his master, merely nodded and proceeded to perform his duties as efficiently and silently as always. Sighing, Damon delivered himself into the man's hands only to find silence was not precisely what he required.

No sooner did the valet begin to shave him, than he was thinking of the Assembly again. Where had Moresby been? Damon had mulled upon the young man's absence from the moment he had realized Moresby was not present. He had not asked after him, though. He had not wanted to care where Kit Moresby was. Nor had he wanted to be told the prospective groom had gone posthaste to town to put an announcement of his betrothal in the papers.

The thought sent a surge of what Damon wanted to think was anger through him. But he was too honest. Oh, there was anger in him, but it was jealousy made him clench his fist.

There he had said it. Stupidity, unaccountably, he was jealous of a boy.

His defenses were not slipping. They were breached.

But heaven forbid, what an evening it had been for

stripping his defenses bare! Not only had he been obliged to dance with her, hold her in his arms again, smell her perfume, feel her curves beneath his hand, but there had been the squire's further and more disturbing revelations about Haydon.

The man had put a guard on Alyson until he saw her safely married to his choice. Damon had not expected that. He had not thought any man in that day and age could be so medieval. But something else had jarred him, too. Alyson had gone, for just the time it took to blink an eye, pale when Squire Rundel referred to Haydon's manner in the months before she married Ned. What could account for such a reaction so many years later—and for that hard note in the voice of a man as jovial as the squire?

His mouth tightened dangerously as his valet helped him into his coat. Was it possible Haydon had done her physical harm for falling in love with a man not of his choosing?

Dear God, he did not think he could bear that to be true. To learn that she had had to suffer physically, while he, in ignorance, had held her up to scorn . . .

Or was he only searching for excuses for her? Did he want her to be guiltless so much, he'd invent an ogre. The squire, though, was not a man given to fancies.

"My lord!" Hobbes hurried forward to greet his master in the breakfast room, his brow knit with worry, and Damon almost welcomed the possibility of a crisis. He wanted something with which to occupy his mind.

"My lord, I give you my gravest apologies! Through a confusion on the part of the new maid, the letters that came in the post yesterday were not delivered to you. I assure you, my lord, such an oversight will not occur again!"

The man looked as if his crime were the equivalent of mislaying the crown jewels. Damon knew better than to treat the matter lightly. "I am certain I can rely upon you to see it will not, Hobbes," he replied in tones as grave as the butler's had been.

There was a letter from his solicitor in Aylesbury. The old man had papers for him to sign and said he would come to Whitcombe whenever it was convenient for Damon.

Why should he not go to Aylesbury? The first answer, that he had returned from the county town only a few hours before, Damon dismissed. In the army he had become accustomed to an inordinate amount of exercise.

Coward. Another voice in his mind jeered at him, crying that a trip to Aylesbury appealed to him not because he desired to exercise, but because he desired to escape Alyson. She was out of mourning. She would wear colors that day, as she had last night. She was available.

A little distance from her could do no harm, he told the insidious voice curtly. Then his eye fell upon a letter addressed not to him at all, but to Alyson.

Under normal circumstances Damon would never even have seen it. Clearly the Hall's postal delivery had not been entirely restored to the routine in use before the new maid's arrival. Normally Alyson's letters were delivered directly to her. But there it was before him, and Damon could not help but see from the address that it came from a jeweler in Aylesbury.

The letter fell open easily. The jeweler said little, only informed her ladyship courteously that he had fulfilled her commission. In other words the bauble she had cajoled from Moresby was ready for her.

Damon rode Tristan hard on that trip into Aylesbury. Though he had told himself Moresby went to put an announcement of his betrothal to Alyson in the London papers, Damon had not in his heart of hearts accepted the fact of their union.

There had been that look, that one, melting look when she realized he complimented her. It had thrust Kit Moresby into some remote, unthreatening sphere.

How little it took to enthrall him! Just the one look and he forgot Moresby, thought only that she seemed again the girl with whom he'd fallen in love, the girl who had been so unbelievably unaware of herself, the ingenuous, uncalculating beauty in whose love he'd trusted.

But she was not that girl—never had been. He would take her the bauble. That would serve! He would make her aware that he knew she was affianced—or flirting outrageously. And he would have such proof in his hand, he could not resist it.

In Aylesbury Damon entered the shop with the jeweler's sign above it without further debate over the intrusion he made into Alyson's privacy.

At the abrupt jingling of the bell above the door, Mr. Luckett removed his eye piece and came hurrying forward. He'd long years' experience taking the measure of customers. Instinctively he knew the tall, dark man with the authoritative set to his shoulders to be a nobleman, and was not amazed to discover he was, to be precise, the Earl of St. Albans.

"You have come for Lady St. Albans, my lord?" Mr. Luckett queried, and at Damon's curt nod, hurried away to the back of his store. When he returned he held a leather pouch, a container quite unlike the velvet box Damon had expected. "I do hope Lady St. Albans will be pleased with what I managed to get for her," Mr. Luckett said, holding out the pouch.

Unease pricked Damon. It was obviously heavy, and the little jeweler made no move to open it, to display the contents within for inspection.

The unease grew to something far worse when Mr. Luckett added, "I shall confide to you, my lord, that I regretted carrying out this particular commission for her ladyship. She graced her jewels, not, as is usually the case, the other way around. But I know she cared little for them! It was her husband bought them all. Had he left the choice to her, I suspect she'd have selected something like that silver pin there."

It was a pretty thing, a delicate flower with small diamonds in the center. Oddly enough, it did look like something Alyson would wear.

Damon bought it.

He did not use any of the coins he accepted in the pouch he held. He directed the jeweler to send him a bill.

She had sold her jewels. Holding the pouch in his hand outside the shop, he stared at the street where he had lashed out at her for beguiling baubles from innocents. She had let him think what he pleased, encouraged him, even. That he could understand. She had too much pride to defend herself, particularly before a prejudiced judge.

He hefted the pouch. Mr. Luckett had done well for her. She could set up herself and Annie in a house, never mind the cottage. Was that what she had meant when she said, "I shall soon relieve you of the burden of supporting me"? Had she not referred to Moresby at all?

Damon declined his solicitor's invitation to luncheon. He could be at the Hall in only a little over an hour if he rode hard. Time enough to eat then, after he had seen Alyson.

Alyson awakened that morning in a far different frame of mind from Damon, though she awoke thinking of the very same moment from the night before that he had.

The first compliment Damon had paid her, the one Lady Bardstow had all but forced from him, Alyson had discounted. It had meant nothing more to her than the polite courtesy any gentleman might utter. But the second compliment, the one he had paid her while they danced. That one had been . . . different. So different. He had seemed to mean what he said.

She pulled the sheet over her face, to hide her sudden blush from the canopy overhead. It had such a way of telling tales. Alyson giggled. Beneath the covers she giggled at her nonsense. From sheer excess of good will she giggled. Damon thought her beautiful. Still. Even now. Despite everything.

He thought her more beautiful than any other woman. That must include Miss Moresby. She felt lighter than air and seemed to float from her bed, until it occurred to her to wonder if he found her more desirable than Miss Moresby.

He had said nothing of desire. No, but his eyes had. Her face burst into a smile. That moment she had been so taken aback she had stared witlessly. She had seen that hot light smoldering there at the back of his eyes. She blushed to recall that she had responded to it, too, for her blood had surged in her veins, and her hand, the one he held, had trembled.

But he admires Miss Moresby for her character, a small, still sane portion of her mind warned. He'll not entrust himself to you twice. He only flattered you because he had had too much punch. He will be cold today.

Perhaps. Perhaps not.

She bit her lip against a hope that might betray her. Damon was the one with the answers. She would breakfast with him. She would test the waters.

Hobbes gave Alyson the disappointing news. His lordship had left for Aylesbury only a little before. Alyson made a face. She would have to wait. Perhaps it was just as well she decided after a little. So long as she did not see him, she could still hope.

She desired some activity though and called for her trap to be brought around. She would go to visit the Sirls.

The squatters did take her mind from Damon, but not in the way Alyson had expected.

Even before she reached the clearing in the marsh, she knew something was wrong. She missed the scent of a fire, and she heard no children's cries.

The hut's door hung ajar, and the hut itself stood empty. Everything had been removed, from the rough bowls that had served as plates, to the thin, frayed pallets upon which the family slept. They had not been gone long, however. At the bottom of the fire, the ashes were still warm.

Where had they gone? Why had they abandoned their only shelter in midwinter?

She had no answer to the first question, but the second

gave her no difficulty. Damon had chased them off. There was no other conceivable reason Jim Sirls would take his family on the road in the middle of winter. Perhaps he had complimented her extravagantly, perhaps he had even meant what he said, but he did not respect her opinion or her wishes. Damon cared so little for them, in fact, that he had ignored everything she had said and had cast out the Sirls, though he knew she cared about them.

He would answer to her. Alyson swore it, standing there in the cold, damp, musty gloom of the abandoned hut. He might be the Earl of St. Albans, but by heaven, she would make it clear to him he could not play the cruel despot without fear of judgment.

Chapter 23

An angry light flashed in Alyson's eyes when she stormed into the Hall only to learn Damon still had not returned.

"Send to me the moment he does return, Hobbes," She instructed crisply. "I wish to speak with him."

"Will you be in Lady Bardstow's rooms, my lady? She and Lady Anne are taking tea together."

The news caused Alyson's expression to soften slightly. Annie adored taking tea with Lady Bardstow.

"Mama! Aunt Edie has allowed me to pour!" Annie exclaimed happily when her mother entered the sitting room in which a roaring fire burned.

Alyson smiled at the honor her daugher had been accorded. "My, my," she murmured approvingly as she exchanged a twinkling glance with Lady Bardstow. "You must have behaved very well, indeed, if Aunt Edie thought you might pour."

Annie demanded and received all Alyson's attention as she first poured then served her mother as if Alyson were the queen. Still, all the while she watched her daughter proudly, and all the while they chatted over tea, Alyson waited impatiently for some sign of Damon's return.

Percival, as usual, gave it. Ensconced contentedly upon an ottoman placed only a few feet from the fire, he lifted his head suddenly and looked to the door. He did not disturb himself further, however, only waited, his tail swishing, a certain sign he knew whoever approached very well.

It might be Hobbes. Percy tolerated the butler. But he no longer took flight when Damon appeared, either.

Alyson could feel her blood heating again. Damon Ashford would soon know what she thought of his actions in regard to people less fortunate than he. He was an earl! It was to him the other gentry would look. If he did not set a proper example, discharging the responsibilities as well as enjoying the privileges of his class, who would?

Damon entered the sitting room where Hobbes had said that Alyson awaited him, as aware of the pouch her jeweler had given him as if it still bulged heavily in his pocket. It did not because he had gone first to his study and divested himself of the weighty thing, dropping it in the top drawer of his desk. To discuss why she had felt it necessary to sell Ned's costliest gifts to her, Damon desired privacy. To make his apologies for opening her mail, he required it.

The pouch and his hasty, ill-judged actions weighing upon him, Damon found himself unsurprised when Alyson greeted him with frost in her eyes. He had thought it possible Hobbes might say something to her about her letter.

"We are glad to see you, Damon." Annie's studiously proper greeting, infused with all the delight of her mother's lack, forced Damon's attention from Alyson. "Would you care for some tea, my lord? I shall pour for you! Aunt Edie taught me how today, and I have not spilled a drop."

Annie's brown eyes shone with such pleasure Damon realized he could not disappoint her, though his first inclination had been to drag Alyson away and get his apologies to her done with. In his life he had rarely felt the need to excuse himself to another, but when he had, he had done so directly and efficiently. Forcing a smile for Annie, Damon settled himself in a chair beside the child's mother. It was enough that he knew he had erred; that he meant to apologize; and that he was humoring Alyson's child. He need not, he decided, go so far as to spend the next half hour looking across the tea table at a woman with daggers in her eyes.

Exact to the minute, Nanny Burgess arrived in half an hour to retrieve her charge. Annie, heady with her success over the tea tray, regarded her nurse mulishly until Alyson remarked softly, "We are very proud of you, Annie. Show us now how very well you deal with Nanny."

Thus appealed to, Annie made her farewells gracefully, kissing everyone, including Damon, upon the cheek before she sailed by Nanny with a regal lift to her chin.

Edie chuckled at the sight. "What a splendid duchess the child will make one day!"

Neither Alyson nor Damon appeared to see the least humor in the remark. Indeed, it seemed possible to Lady Bardstow that they had not heard it, they looked so grave. Then Damon was begging her pardon, asking if he and Alyson might be excused. Not certain whether to smile or frown, she said of course they could.

It seemed to Alyson to take a lifetime to reach Damon's study, though she kept a brisk pace. She wanted to have the interview over and done. She had begun to fear she would weaken. It was possible, though she felt strongly. He affected her. Even then she was acutely aware of him, of his looks, of his magnetism, although he walked a step behind her.

She would not let him overwhelm her. She would speak up quickly, she decided, and did so, preceeding Damon into the room and spinning about to speak almost before he closed the door.

Damon spoke at the same time, however.

"Damon, I demand to know . . . "

"Alyson, I . . . "

For just a moment Alyson thought Damon must have guessed what she meant to say, for he seemed oddly uncomfortable, but she waved the thought aside. He was too arrogant to be uncomfortable over any decision he'd made. In her impatience to take Damon to task she did not note how he had addressed her, nor, for the same reason, did she realize how easily his given name had slipped from her own tongue.

"I went to visit the Sirls today, Damon," she plunged on, taking full advantage of a lady's prerogative to go first. "Their place stood empty as you must know. I demand to know what you did, and where they have gone! It is unconscionable that you should turn them out in winter!" Alyson thought of Jeanie trudging down a frozen, rutted road, a child in her arms and another stumbling by her side. "They've a baby!" she spat, sparks heating her blue-green eyes, when she took in Damon's position. He had not moved from the door, but lounged with his broad shoulders propped against it and his arms folded over his chest in a casual stance that infuriated her. "How can you stand there lounging so comfortably in your warm home and fine clothes without any concern for those so much less fortunate than you? What if Jim Sirls does drink to excess? God knows in his position I might also! Where are they? I will know, I warn you!"

"I do believe you," Damon said. There was an odd gleam in his eye. Alyson could not read it and assumed in her anger that he was mocking her.

"I will not have you condescend to me!" she snapped, before Damon could continue. "You may be the Earl of St. Albans to everyone else, but to me you are merely Damon Ashford, a man like any other!"

The gleam in Damon's dark eyes seemed to intensify. "I shall keep that in mind, I assure you. But tell me, Alyson, what do you intend to do with the Sirls, when you find them?"

"I shall provide for them," she replied without hesitation.

"With whose funds?"

"With . . . " Alyson halted in midsentence. She had not yet heard from Mr. Luckett, the jeweler. What funds would she use? She had none of her own. Perhaps she could sell one of her dresses. She had heard there were shops that bought cast-off clothing.

Damon watched Alyson frown darkly as she considered the problem of the Sirls well-being. Had he called her both weak and shallow? He knew he was no inconsiderable opponent, yet she had taken him to task on the Sirls' account. And on behalf of that same, pitiful family, she looked prepared to sell whatever she had left of value.

"Alyson?"

"What?" Impatiently Alyson jerked her attention back to Damon.

"You have reached the wrong conclusion."

Alyson waited, saying nothing. It struck her suddenly that Damon did not seem the least angered by the sharp lecture she'd read him. He seemed, in fact, on the verge of smiling. The ground shifted suddenly and unsettlingly beneath her feet.

"The Sirls are nearby."

The ground moved completely out from under her. "Where?"

"I offered Jim a position as a gamekeeper here at Whitcombe. Old Michaels agreed he needs the assistance. They are living with him now, until some other arrangement can be made."

"Why did you not tell me?" Alyson demanded, trying not to wilt completely. Could she have judged him more unfairly? But how was she to have known?

"The arrangements were only completed yesterday," Damon said, keenly aware of the remorse altering Alyson's expression. "I did not think an Assembly the place to discuss the Sirls." That was not true. He had forgotten the Sirls entirely at the Assembly. The thought made him uncomfortable, and levering himself away from the door he began an aimless roaming of the room. The window behind his desk eventually drew him. Looking out it, he added, "I had thought to see you this morning and tell you then. But I, ah, had sudden business in Aylesbury." That was not true either.

Abruptly Damon swung about to face Alyson who was, by then, looking a little bewildered. He could not blame her. He had told two lies in the space of a few minutes, and if she did not realize that, precisely, she must realize from his manner he was evading something. It was time to confess at least one of his prevarications.

Confounded, Alyson watched as Damon raked his hand through his hair. He looked like a man who had a sin to confess, but she could not imagine what wrong he had done her. It was she who had been wrong in regard to him.

"Damon—" she began, but he cut her off with a sharp shake of his head.

"Nay, you needn't thank me on behalf of the Sirls." Damon's tone firmed, as if he found himself on surer ground. "I needed another gamekeeper. Who better to hire for the position than a poacher? This will be no charity position, however. Sirls must perform well, or he will be sent packing. There will be neither drinking when he is on duty nor turning a blind eye to an old friend come to take a rabbit or two. I won't set mantraps out. They are gruesome, medieval things, but I'll not allow open season on my woods either. No one near Whitcombe will starve to death. I will see to that, but it is I shall provide them their rabbits. This is my land, Alyson, and I'll not allow anyone to harbor the notion that they can appropriate what is mine as they please."

He might have been born to be earl, and it was not only the authority in his tone made her think so. "I think your decision eminently just," she spoke her thoughts aloud. "And as to the Sirls, I fully intend to commend you whether you wish me to or not. You may say you acted entirely for pragmatic reasons, and I don't doubt you did in great part, but I also believe you were touched by their desperate situation and reacted with all the nobility of a true nobleman."

Had he thought her eyes resembled green-blue crystal the night before when he had complimented her? They seemed to sparkle far more brightly now when she commended him for his generosity to a negligible family.

Noble. She thought him noble. Damon cursed. He had

not realized how much he wanted her good opinion, until now, when in his top drawer he'd the means to darken those lovely eyes.

"Let us see if you are as forgiving when I confess what I have done today." Even to his own ears, he sounded surly. Never mind, Damon nearly shouted at himself. Get on with it! "I read your mail this morning." The bald statement caused a reaction, but not what Damon had expected. No anger or contempt darkened her eyes. To the contrary she merely looked perplexed.

"But why?" she asked.

"The letter in question was brought to me by mistake. A new maid's fault somehow." He waved the responsibility for the initial error aside. "It was open, and I read the letter, knowing it was addressed to you." Damon had been playing with a letter opener on his desk, but now he threw it down and gave Alyson his full attention. "As I was going to Aylesbury anyway, I stopped by the jeweler's. He had said only that he had fulfilled your commission. I thought he'd a gift from Moresby for you, and I thought . . . I thought to have my worst suspicions concerning you confirmed." Damon opened the drawer of his desk and hefted the pouch in his hand. "Instead he gave me this."

She regarded the pouch a long moment, then looked back at Damon. He had not taken his eyes from her.

"Alyson . . . I never meant for you to sell Ned's gifts to you." She had never thought to see such chagrin in Damon Ashford's eyes. "I know they must have meant a great deal to you. I cannot replace them. . . . "

"Oh, no!" The cry burst from Alsyon. "I . . . they . . ." She faltered suddenly. How could she explain Ned's gifts had meant little of themselves to her? She made a futile gesture with her hand. "You must understand. Jewels mean little to me, actually. I do not dislike them, of course, but they do not fascinate me as they do many people."

Slowly, her eyes on the pouch now, Alyson extended a slender hand. Damon, for reasons he understood all too well, had to force himself to walk around his desk and relinquish her property to her. He did, of course.

Alyson had to hold it with both hands, it was so heavy. Peeking inside, she glimpsed a mound of gold sovereigns. "Oh!" she gasped. "There is so much. I can scarcely credit it is mine." She looked up at Damon, her beautiful eyes alight. "I have never had money of my own you see. I do not mean to say that Ned denied me," she added quickly, aware Damon's expression had darkened slightly. "But pin money is not quite the same as all this. I am a woman of independent means!"

She laughed. It was a joke, but it was at least a little true, too. She wanted him to share her amazement, her wonder even that she was independent. He had to fight a desire to scowl. "What do you intend to do with it?" he demanded more abruptly than he might have liked.

Alyson regarded Damon in surprise, more taken aback by his tone than the question. "Well, I don't know exactly. I don't know how much there is. I had thought Annie might enjoy a place by the sea—"

A knock at the door interrupted her.

"Yes, what is it?" Damon called out impatiently.

"Forgive me, my lord." Hobbes came into the room hesitantly. "Miss Moresby is here, sir. She, ah, says you'd an appointment to view a mare at the Bradys with her."

Damon cursed to himself. He had completely forgotten the appointment, he had, or rather Miss Moresby had made with him, the night before. She wanted his advice on a mare the Bradys wished to sell.

"Yes, thank you, Hobbes. Tell her I will be along, momentarily will you?"

The butler bowed himself out, and Damon turned back to Alyson, the heiress already forgotten. Alyson, however, had turned her back upon him and was almost to the door.

"Enjoy your outing with Miss Moresby, my lord," she murmured, addressing the door she fast approached. "And give my regards to the Bradys."

"Wait!"

Alyson looked back at Damon, her brow flying up in astonishment. He had not asked her to wait, but commanded her.

He had the grace to look apologetic. "I forget sometimes that I have left the army, and I did not want you to get away just yet."

"You needn't fear I'll move an inch now," she replied dryly. "I would fear a court-martial."

Alyson was unprepared for the effect of her humor. Damon laughed. The sun appearing after a dark, brooding rainstorm could not have produced any more dramatic effect. When her heart missed a beat, Alyson angrily reminded herself that Damon would soon ride off with Miss Moresby. Still, her heart beat erratically when she saw something in his hand.

"I wanted to give you this." He held out a small, square box wrapped in white paper. "It cannot replace the jewelry you sold, of course, but I did hope, just a little, to make amends."

Alyson stared at the box. It came from Mr. Luckett's. She recognized the packaging. Suddenly she could not swallow easily. A lump had lodged in her throat. "You needn't have." Her voice came out a whisper.

Damon stood very close. Alyson was as aware of him as she was of the square box she held. "It is not much," she heard him say softly.

It is from you. She took a deep breath to regain control of her breathing and began to undo the wrapping when suddenly there were footsteps in the hallway, and the door to Damon's study flew open without warning.

"St. Albans!" Claudia Moresby burst into the room, crying Damon's title with throaty possessiveness. "I simply could not wait any longer. You know how impatient I am when it comes to you. Ah! Lady St. Albans." Miss Moresby's eyes narrowed considerably as she glanced to the half-opened box Alyson held in her hand. "Have I interrupted something important?"

"No," Alyson declared immediately. "Of course, you

have not." She inclined her head in Damon's general direction. "Thank you, sir," she said without meeting his eyes. "Good day to you both."

And she was gone, the pouch and the package in her hand, but aware of nothing so much as that when Miss Moresby had crossed to entwine her arm about Damon's, he had not made a move to shake off the girl's claiming hold.

Chapter 24

Alyson closed the door of her room behind her, her gift and the pouch of sovereigns clenched tightly in her hand. It seemed hard to breathe. She forced herself to take in a great gulp of air, and when her chest trembled, she made herself take another.

Eventually, when she was breathing almost normally, she realized her hand hurt, and looking down, recalled the little box.

It held the first tangible gift Damon had ever given her. Her chest began to throb so, she held the little box to it. His gift meant nothing to him. He had felt bad about Ned's jewels, that was all. But she, when he had first given it to her, had felt an almost unbearable gladness.

Now she felt despair. She ought to be thankful he had changed his opinion of her enough to wish to give her a gift. She ought to be, but she was not. She'd have been grateful, had he sent Claudia on her way alone. He had not, and it was Alyson who stood alone, holding a gift he'd bought out of something akin to pity.

When a soft rapping came at her sitting room door, Alyson found it necessary to clear her throat before saying, "Yes?"

"It is I, Allie," Lady Bardstow called out. "May I come in?"

"Of course," Alyson bit her lip, trying to pull herself together. "What is it, Aunt Edie?"

"Nothing monstrously important, my dear. I was just consulting with Timms about my roses, and I wished to ask your opinion of our decisions. But what is that? Have you received an early birthday gift?"

Alyson again found herself regarding the small box she held. "It is a, ah, token, I suppose."

Lady Bardstow regarded the box a moment then asked softly, "Is it from Damon?"

Alyson's throat felt very thick. She nodded.

"Allie, was there something between you and Damon that one summer he was here at Whitcombe?"

A full moment went by before Alyson could bring herself to meet Lady Bardstow's eyes. She was a fool to be so slow. Lady Bardstow regarded her with the greatest gentleness. "Yes," Alyson admitted quietly. "There was. How did you guess?"

Lady Bardstow shrugged uncertainly. "Nothing in particular, but that I have sensed an odd tension between the two of you on occasion. At first I thought perhaps you resented him for replacing Ned, but you are not so childish. Indulge an old woman further?" she asked giving Alyson a close look.

"Perhaps," Alyson replied, but the wariness of her answer was offset by the affection in her slight smile.

"What happened to separate you?"

Alyson answered simply, "Mr. Haydon."

"He did not approve of Damon?"

"Ned had asked for me first."

"Ah. An earl."

Alyson nodded. "And his neighbor's son, as well. There was no question that I might follow my own heart, even though, when I met Lord St. Albans, I had no inkling that Ned had asked for me, and Mr. Haydon had agreed to the match."

"Lord St. Albans?" Lady Edith repeated ironically. "You must find it difficult to be so formal."

Alyson looked away to the box she yet held. "As perhaps you have guessed, we did not part on the best of terms. Mr. Haydon managed to convey the impression that I rejected Damon in favor of Ned and his title."

"I am so sorry such a ruthless man held sway over

you, Allie," Lady Bardstow said with such conviction, Alyson smiled again even as she shrugged off Mr. Haydon. "But you," the elderly lady went on, "what do you do? Merely shrug. You are a remarkable woman, lamb, and not merely because you do not hate your stepfather. Given the same circumstances, most women would have resented Ned so they'd have made a misery of his life and theirs, but you put your resentments behind you and made him a devoted wife."

Alyson found it impossible to meet the older woman's gaze. "I hope I did. I took an oath before God that I would."

"You are not harboring some question on the matter, are you?" Lady Bardstow studied Alyson's averted face. "There never was a better wife than you. Ned reveled in you from first to last. It is the truth!" she exclaimed when her overblown phrasing caused Alyson to smile just a little. Then she went unerringly to the heart of Alyson's distress. "You were what he wanted in his wife, my dear. He was not a man like Damon. Damon would demand of his wife every ounce of passion and interest she had to give, but Ned would have been appalled by too great a display of devotion. Why, had you run madly to him one night, he'd have lifted his brow and put up his quizzing glass just so."

Lady Bardstow mimicked Ned with such exactness that a watery chuckle escaped Alyson. "You are his image."

"I had the opportunity to observe him for several years, my dear. And therefore, you may take my word for it when I say that you were quite as devoted and loving as Ned desired you to be. But all that is in the past. What of now? What of you and Damon now?"

Alyson turned the box over in her hands a few times before answering, and when she did, she spoke so softly Lady Edith had to strain to hear her. "Damon fell out of love with me when I married Ned. He thought I ought to have stood full against Mr. Haydon, and, too, I think he finds it hard to forgive me for striving to be a good wife to Ned."

"Men!" Lady Bardstow exclaimed with surprising force. "How very unfair they are to make no stir at all when a woman hates two men at once but to fly into the highest bough imaginable, when she dares love two at the same time, never mind she loves them very differently."

Alyson felt a smile tug at her lips. "I am thinking of doing without men altogether," she confided suddenly, then chuckling at the surprise she had elicited, showed Lady Bardstow her "independence pouch." To her relief Lady Bardstow took her decision to sell Ned's jewels quite in stride. "He was the one loved them, Allie, not you. He bought them because he thought his countess ought to wear magnificent jewels. As they are yours, I think it quite right that you have put them to your own use. Will you leave Whitcombe?"

"Yes, I could not live with Miss Moresby." She made a wry face. "I'll not say another word on that subject, lest I disgrace with myself. But Aunt Edie, there is quite enough here to support you, too. I wish you to come with Annie and me, unless you prefer to remain at Whitcombe."

Lady Bardstow impulsively cupped Alyson's face in her hands. "You are the kindest girl! I should be devastated to live without you. But can you wait a little for my decision, Allie? There is much I should consider."

"Of course! I intend to go to Aylesbury tomorrow to ask Ned's solicitor to help me find a place near Portsmouth. I think Annie would like the sea."

"Undoubtedly," Lady Edith replied. "In the meantime, though, you might open Damon's gift. He learned what you did with Ned's jewels, I suppose?"

Alyson nodded, and Lady Bardstow kissed her forehead. "I suspected as much. Well, I shall leave you to look into it in privacy, lamb. No, don't object. You may show it to me later."

Studying the square box, Alyson did not watch Lady

Bardstow go. Had she, she might have seen the smile playing ever so slightly at the corners of the elder lady's mouth.

Alyson laid the box aside. She did not think she could bear to see the casual trinket Damon had selected with, she imagined, little thought. She flung herself down on the window seat and studying the late afternoon shadows, began to muse on Portsmouth. Or perhaps Annie would prefer Bath. Or what of some place in the country? They could live anywhere, really, so long as Alyson did not remain at Whitcombe. She had made light of her antipathy for Claudia Moresby. But there was nothing light at all about her feelings for the girl. She could not live with her.

She could not live with any woman who married Damon.

She pressed her fist hard to her mouth. She was going to lose him twice. She did not think she could bear it.

A sudden knock at the door startled her. Who would knock so, unless there were some emergency? Hurriedly she wiped tears from her cheeks and called out, "Yes?"

It was Damon. She stared, fearing the worst. He looked as if he came from some disaster, he strode in so forcefully, still dressed in his riding clothes. He'd given up his riding crop at the stables, of course, but had he held it still, she imagined he'd have been flicking it impatiently against his leg. His brow was drawn sharply down and his black eyes were fixed upon her. He regarded her intently, almost angrily.

She drew a sharp breath, trying to think what she had done. But as she did, as she stiffened before his forceful entrance, she also registered Damon's height, the breadth of his shoulders, the beauty of his strong, chiseled features. And it was into her bedroom he strode so boldly. Her heart raced, even as she lifted her chin to demand what he did in her own room.

She opened her mouth to speak, but his eyes had dropped to the low table before the window seat. Upon it lay the box he'd given her, its wrapping still clinging to it.

He lifted his dark eyes, pinning her. She thought him angry. Then she looked again and doubted that suddenly. He looked . . . surely not hurt.

"You have not opened it," he said, his tone accusing.

This was the emergency that had brought him charging into her bedroom and slamming the door behind him?

"Why?" he demanded in the next breath.

"I . . . I was waiting for you."

Why had she said that? It was not the truth at all. Or was it?

"It's nothing. Just a token," he said regarding her so fiercely she found it difficult to breathe, much less to think. And suddenly she thought she could not wait to see the present she had all but scorned minutes before.

"Won't you sit?" She gestured to the length of the window seat beside her. "It is a little uncomfortable looking up at you."

It was, for she had to arch her neck severely to meet his eyes. Also he seemed so large and filled with so much restless energy, he overwhelmed her, standing over her.

Damon did not appear to hear Alyson, though he looked directly at her. He stood still, frowning harshly at her. With suddenly shaky hands Alyson reached for the box and pulled off the last of the paper.

An unnerving silence reigned while she tossed the paper aside and lifted the top. She bit her lip then against a painful rush of emotion. She had expected nothing so very lovely as the pin Damon had chosen for her. It was quite perfect, a delicately and exquisitely wrought flower of the finest silver with a cluster of small diamonds at the center. She'd the impression she could sniff it for its scent.

"It is beautiful," she said, a wondering note in her voice.

He shrugged her pleasure off. "It was the least I could

do." He continued to regard her broodingly almost and then fairly barked abruptly, without preamble, "You are going to Aylesbury tomorrow to speak to the solicitor?"

Aunt Edie! Alyson could not quite credit that Lady Bardstow betrayed her plans. But it was no betrayal. She had meant to tell Damon herself. She thought he would be pleased. He did not look pleased, however.

Her heart began to beat hard against her chest. "Yes, I thought—"

But she did not get out what she thought. Before she realized what he did, Damon was before her, on her side of the table, reaching for her, lifting her by the arms and bringing her within inches of him.

"I don't want you to go, Allie."

Her heart had begun to beat so loudly, she thought she had misheard him. "But—"

"No buts, Allie," he growled as fiercely as a man might to his enemy. "Dear God, no buts and no nos, either!" He dragged her up to him, encircled her with his arms and buried his face in her thick hair. "I can't lose you twice. I won't," he added, growling again, into her hair.

When she began to cry, Alyson didn't know. She only realized as she wrapped her arms around his waist that she was crying.

He felt her shaking. "Don't cry, Allie." It was the hoarsest of pleas. "I cannot bear to see you cry."

Damon pulled back enough to look down into her shimmering eyes. He looked so right there close to her, more tears came, and with a groan he began to kiss her eyes and her cheeks, lightly at first and then more intently as he came closer to her lips.

Before he could take her mouth, Alyson made him stop, holding his dark, handsome face a little away, cupped in her hands. He went too fast for her.

"I thought you hated me," she said, thinking she might drown in the depths of his eyes.

He groaned again at her words and pulled her to him

again. She did not melt into him as she had done though. He sighed as he kissed the top of her burnished head.

"Shall we sit, then, as you wished," he whispered, and without waiting for her nod, though she gave it, he sat down upon the window seat, pulling her down with him, onto his lap.

He did not ask if he could do so, and the look in his dark eyes warned her against demanding to be released, as if she would be asking too much of him. Alyson made no objection, though. She'd have cried out in protest had he set her away from him.

Heady with the feel of him, Alyson almost forgot what they discussed. The dark self-doubt in his eyes reminded her.

"Can you forgive me, Allie? It is no wonder you thought I despised you. I thought so myself. At least I told myself I did. Can you understand? I was young then, myself. I had family and friends, but none meant as much to me as the wide world before me. In an earlier age I'd have taken ship with Sir Francis Drake and harried the Spanish, I suppose. I had no thought for the importance of family and roots. When Haydon objected to me, I expected you to snap your fingers at all you held dear and race away with me."

"But you did not know of Mr. Haydon's threat to keep me from my mother," Alyson defended Damon to himself.

He would have none of her defense, though. "I did not know how dire he'd made his threat, no, but any fool could see marrying me would cause a rift between you and your family. I simply did not appreciate in the least how difficult it would be for you to be taken from all you knew and loved. And you were only seventeen—"

Alyson interrupted Damon impetuously. She kissed him full on his sensuous mouth, tasting him, savoring him, until she pulled back breathless. "I have wanted to do that for so long," she whispered hoarsely, her blue-green eyes on his. Then she added, "And I'll not have you blame yourself for anything. It was a terrible time,

Damon. We were young and filled with such emotion. . . ."

"Aye. All that is true, but I carried my disappointment far beyond the bounds. Allie, I never meant to push you to the point of selling the jewels Ned gave you. I know how you loved him—"

"Oh, Damon!" she cried unevenly, interrupting him and burying her face against his shoulder. "I did love him, Damon, but so differently. You are thinking of the night you found me in the hallway crying, are you not? The anniversary of Ned's death?"

She felt him nod and struggled to regain her poise. Finally she flung up her head to look directly, unflinchingly into his black eyes. "I was sad that night, but not, God help me, because I missed Ned beyond bearing." Her voice was low and taut as she made her admission. "He was good to me, Damon, He doted upon, brought me presents, showed me off to his friends, was in all the right respects the very opposite of Mr. Haydon, but . . . but to me he never became more than the best of friends." Her eyes fell to Damon's white cravat. "I felt so guilty, you see, so very guilty that I could respond far more intensely to one glowering look from you than I ever had to all Ned's endearments."

The fiercest elation swept Damon. He wanted to shout it to the winds, but he did not. Alyson's head remained bowed.

He tipped up her chin with his knuckle. "Did Ned ever give you an indication he was disappointed?" he demanded levelly, though truth to tell it was hard for him, still, despite her confession, to think of Alyson with another man.

She shook her head, "Far from it."

"Well then, you'll not worry over that again," he pronounced decisively. "You gave Ned all you could, all he wanted, and that included a charming, quite dear daughter."

She held his dark, steady gaze a moment, then slowly, began to nod. "Aunt Edie said much the same, and I did honor my vows, though they were forced from me. If I continued to love you all that time, what woman would not?" she finished in a husky whisper that was Damon's undoing.

He caught her to him, taking her mouth. She arched into him, needing to feel his hard chest against her breasts, his hands on her back, her hips. Feverishly they tasted and touched, seeming intent upon making up for the six years they had lost as soon as possible.

But then Alyson pushed back, her hands on his chest, her eyes heavy with her passion. "What of Miss Moresby?" she demanded abruptly, no lightness at all softening her tone.

Perhaps that was why Damon grinned, for he did grin a very masculine, rakish, even cocky grin. "You needn't sound as if she were an insect, Allie. Nor should you be jealous of her. She was naught but a means to divert at least some of my attention from you. I might have gone mad without her. Or throttled you for the effect you have upon me. Do you know how hard it was to keep my eyes off you when you entered a room?" He groaned and began to kiss her neck, to lick the little hollow just behind her ear. "Dear God, all I wanted was to do this."

Alyson slanted her neck away, allowing Damon free access. Beneath her hands she could feel his heart beating as hard and fast as hers.

"I am so very glad to hear it," she whispered huskily in his ear. "For I desired you likewise, and still do. Oh, Damon, I do love you so very much."

"Not Kit Moresby?" he whispered thickly into her throat.

"Mr. Moresby?" she whimpered as Damon nipped the tip of her earlobe. "I never knew he'd the least interest in me!" she protested hastily. Damon kissed the place he'd bitten not so lightly. "And I am afraid I disappointed him," she added on a sigh.

"And a good thing it was that you did," Damon said half to himself as he kissed the length of Alyson's throat. "I wanted to kill him that night at the inn."

She knew he was teasing her. Or thought he was. But she lost the thread of their exchange when Damon cupped her breast and kissed it through the thin material of her dress. She cried out then and sank back as he urged her to lie full length upon the window seat.

It was a good while later that Alyson started up suddenly to look down at Damon. His half-lidded gaze remained upon her breasts, bare to him then and milky white in the moonlight.

"Dinner, Damon! The bell will ring at any minute."

It was a moment before he could focus on her concern. Her glorious hair streamed over her shoulder, teasing his lips. He twirled a long, silky strand around his finger.

"Dinner?" he said absently. "There won't be a bell. I told Hobbes not to expect us." He kissed the rosy crest of the breast nearest him. She cried out, forgetting dinner, until he desisted.

"You told Hobbes not to expect us for dinner?" she then whispered breathless.

He grinned, his smile a slash of white in his bronzed face. "Presumptuous of me?"

"Indeed." She grinned, too. "'And apt, it would seem. But what did Hobbes say? Was he shocked?"

Damon laughed. "Hobbes and all the staff adore you, Allie. I suspect they have been praying fervently that you might work your wiles upon me and remain at Whitcombe as my lady. And therefore Hobbes said in his inimitable way. 'Very good, my lord. I shall have Monsieur Fornet prepare a tray for you and my lady should you desire it.' By the by, you will be my lady, will you not, Allie, my love?"

"With all the joy and pleasure in the world, my lord."